Don't Break The Seal by A...vi. burrage

Alfred McLelland Burrage was born in Hillingdon, Middlesex on 1st July, 1889. His father and uncle were both writers, primarily of boy's fiction, and by age 16 AM Burrage had joined them. The young man had ambitions to write for the adult market too. The money was better and so was his writing.

From 1890 to 1914, prior to the mainstream appeal of cinema and radio the printed word, mainly in magazines, was the foremost mass entertainment. AM Burrage quickly became a master of the market publishing his stories regularly across a number of publications.

By the start of the Great War Burrage was well established but in 1916 he was conscripted to fight on the Western Front. He continued to write during these years documenting his experiences in the classic book War is War by Ex-Private X.

For the remainder of his life Burrage was rarely printed in book form but continued to write and be published on a prodigious scale in magazines and newspapers. In this volume we concentrate on his supernatural stories which are, by common consent, some of the best ever written. Succinct yet full of character each reveals a twist and a flavour that is unsettling.....sometimes menacing....always disturbing.

There are many other volumes available in this series together with a number of audiobooks. All are available from iTunes, Amazon and other fine digital stores.

Index Of Contents

Chapter I - Something to His Advantage
Chapter II - Lucky Meeting
Chapter III - Damsels in distress
Chapter IV - Mutual Advantage
Chapter V - The Forbidden Door
Chapter VI - A Talk with Perringer
Chapter VII – Another Small Mystery
Chapter VIII – Dr. Bligh Talks
Chapter IX– The Sommambulist
Chapter X – Important Visitor
Chapter XI – Strange Disappearance
Chapter XII – "It Suggests a Lot"
Chapter XIII – The Stars Looked Down
Chapter XIV – "Everything's Crazy"
Chapter XV – The Disappearing Corpse
Chapter XVI – Perringer Again
Chapter XVII – "A Great Deal to hide
Chapter XVIII – The Real Colonel Sandingford
Chapter XIX – A Little Surprise

Chapter XX – Message in Code
Chapter XXI – Message Decoded
Chapter XXII – "Something's Going to Happen"
Chapter XXIII – Enter Sir Anthony
Chapter XXIV – Sir Anthony Explains
Chapter XXV – "You Can Guess His Name"
A.M. Burrage – The Life and Times

CHAPTER I
SOMETHING TO HIS ADVANTAGE

For reasons connected with finance, and to ensure as fully as possible a whole Saturday's play, the Cricket Week at Arunford begins on a Saturday and ends on the following Friday.

For those brief June days the Town ground becomes the County ground, and the transformation is effected by roping off the boundaries, by setting up refreshment marquees and installing complicated score-boards, and by conjuring a number of hard chairs and benches from mysterious sources known only to the County Club Committee.

Fixtures between Arunshire and Stockshire date back to the early years of last century, but never before had a Stockshire eleven visited Arunford. Hitherto these visitors had been entertained on the County ground—the ground which was actually the club's headquarters—at Chalport.

Those who like cricket, and those not interested, must not be blandished nor deceived, for this is not a cricket tale—although it is mainly concerned with young Nick Rockwell, who was no mean cricketer. Also, through no fault of the chronicler, it must begin on the Arunford ground on the last day of the Arunford "week"—a Friday which promised fair, began to threaten in the forenoon, and fulfilled its threat of a steady and torrential downpour shortly before three o'clock. The tale contains little more of cricket than followed upon that dreary afternoon—and that was none at all.

The game was then in an interesting state with possibilities of a dramatic finish. Set to get 247 to win, the visitors had lost five of their best wickets for 151. The wicket had been a trifle fiery, and the rain—even if it should cease in time—seemed too heavy to promise any help to the bowlers. Given a fine night and hot sun on the morrow, the pitch would be a "glue-pot" by noon. But by that time the County match would have ended and the Arunford Town Club would be disporting itself once more on its own ground.

At a quarter to four the teams took early tea in the pavilion. Most of the "shilling" spectators who had been unable to crowd into the refreshment tents had sought cover outside the ground. The small pavilion was uncomfortably crowded by non-playing members and their lady friends. And still the rain drummed upon the roof.

At half-past four the two ancient umpires—known affectionately as Methuselah and Old Father Time—and alleged to have been stout cricketers in the days of top hats and one-piece bats—doddered out under the shelter of sacking and borrowed overcoats to inspect the wicket. Gravely they inspected it and with gestures they conferred. After which they parted, going solemnly one to either end. Then simultaneously, as if it were all a well-rehearsed drill movement, they pulled up the stumps. The match was over.

Nick Rockwell did not see the signal, but he had been expecting it, and he knew what had happened when certain amateurs suddenly abandoned their tea-cups and raided the bar. He was sorry yet slightly relieved. At twenty-four he was not blind to the dramatic side of things and he loved a tight finish. On the other hand, he had not fancied the prospect of continuing his innings—he was one of the Not Outs—playing against time on a dead ground which would yield runs only to forcing strokes. With him, hitting out generally meant getting out.

Nick was one of that band which has been described, rather unkindly, as Shamateurs. His father had died, and his income along with him, when Nick was nineteen and on the threshold of the University. He had not the means to qualify for a profession, but not for nothing had he been the best all-rounder of his school.

The young Nick Rockwells of this world need never despair if they have the ability and the residential qualifications to play cricket for a first-class county—and especially if half the com-mittee were personal friends of their fathers. Nor need they be tainted—if that be the word—with open professionalism. Nick's duties in the secretary's office occupied about four hours a week and his salary was three hundred a year. There was, however, a clause which demanded that he should play cricket for the County when required, and a sub-clause which guaranteed that reasonable expenses incurred by him would be met by the club.

These reasonable expenses often included first-class railway fares for journeys taken in somebody else's car. They assumed the most extortionate hotel charges, a strong thirst, and a knowing taste in liquor. They allowed for taxis, hospitalities and lavish tipping. Altogether these expenses would have shocked the conscience of a Victorian bagman.

Young Nick, essentially honest, had protested at first. He was told quietly, by the Voice of Authority itself, not to be a fool. If people subscribed vastly to keep cricket alive in the county, and if during the course of a three-days' match the turnstiles clicked twenty thousand times or more, he was surely entitled to a share of the spoils—and that without being compelled to carry his cricket-bag in and out of the professionals' dressing-room. Besides, he often addressed quite a lot of envelopes for the secretary and even—with two fingers—typed a few unimportant letters. Then, too, he was a Gentleman of the County and popular with the County's supporters—so that, it seemed, in all ways the labourer was worthy of his hire.

Now that the Arunshire match was over Nick was able to look forward to some days of leisure. Stockshire was without a match until a week from the following day. There was golf, of course, and lawn tennis, but to a cricketer these things are mere vanities. Besides—although he would have expressed it in terms less sermonish—he was not unaware of the dangers of drifting. . . . With the intention of letting the crowd in the dressing-room thin a little before he changed he helped himself to more tea, and over the cup he lapsed suddenly into brooding. That schoolboy ambition, the life of a County cricketer, was at the best a short and a blind alley, and in the alley itself there were ambushes and pitfalls.

What would become of him twenty years hence when he was past, or getting past, first-class cricket? They might make him secretary at a few hundreds a year—or they might not. His present patrons were old men who would probably be dead. The club might fail or another war might set a period upon its activities. Meanwhile, as he well knew, he enjoyed too facile a popularity. Men of his own class were glad to be seen about with him, and it led to too much time being spent in bars. It was not always easy to avoid drinking too heavily. And meanwhile the sisters of those young men—as he well knew—were being warned by worldly-wise Mammas that despite his meretricious popularity he was no more than a well-mannered young wastrel without a penny and without a future.

He knew that he should be doing something else with his life, especially during the long winter months. But what? But what? And then a charming lady—whose mission in life seemed to consist of waiting upon cricketers with the air of a conscientious and cheerful nurse—insisted on giving him another cup of stewed tea.

But the dismal reverie returned to him with a persistence which suggested a disordered liver. That, however, was not the cause, and he blamed the sudden change of weather. The murmur of rain on the roof was like the muffled voice of Doom, and for once in his life Nick had a presentiment that something was about to happen to him.

Cheerful voices outside the door made sudden and welcome intrusion upon his thoughts. Some of the players, it seemed, were already out of the dressing-room. There would be room now to change in comfort. One could have the undisputed use of a mirror and need not be jostled in the shower-bath. He rose and left the table.

The shower-bath and the subsequent rub-down did their work. Half an hour later Nick emerged into the centre of the pavilion, looking as if he had not a care in the world.

His face under a smooth thatch of dark brown hair was comely, almost classical. His shoulders, rather narrow, topped a long, lean body in which nearly every muscle was well developed. He looked tough, although in appearance he was no Hercules, and built of wire rather than of oak. And now, in all ways in a better humour, he smiled suddenly to see that the rain had ceased.

There was an exit from the ground close to the rear of the pavilion. He made his way through it, carrying his heavy bag, and saw some fifty yards in front of him a familiar figure also carrying a cricket-bag. It was the unmistakable back of Timmins, one of the pros.

Timmins was on the way to becoming one of the best slow bowlers in England. Five years before, one of the County "spotters" had halted his car beside a village green to see some youths practising at a net. A flash of supernormal intuition caused the good gentleman to leave his car and go to stand behind and watch. Timmins was one of the bowlers. And the spotter, spotting, saw that which brightened both his eyes.

He had heard it declared by authoritative voices that there is no such thing as swerve, and that so-called swerve from a bowler's hand is mere optical illusion. He did not know and he did not care. But he did know that any bowler who appeared to swerve half a yard from the leg—and especially if he could be taught to develop an off-break—would be an asset to any county. A chat with Timmins elicited the fact that he worked in a market-garden. How would another kind of gardening job—on the County ground staff—suit him? Oh, and there was extra money to be made, because of an evening he would be expected to bowl to the Gentlemen at the nets. Not a word was said to Timmins about the possibility of making a County cricketer of him.

Timmins scratched his head and "didn't quite know." But the wages tempted him, and two years later he made his first appearance for the County against Notts. In the second innings of that memorable match he took seven wickets for nineteen—and set all the experts and newspaper critics arguing once more as to the possibility or otherwise of actual swerve.

There must have been a touch of the psychic, besides cricket genius, in Timmins' composition, for he looked round suddenly, saw who was following and waited. Then, as Nick came up, he grinned and touched his hat in the approved manner of the loafer.

"Carry y'r bag, sir?"

"You go to hell," said Nick pleasantly.

"Well, I wouldn't call it that, although it's not much of a pub. Never mind the toffs, sir. You come along and have a drink along o' me and the boys."

"I was going to," said Nick.

The gap between amateurs and professionals had been closing of recent years, but much of it remained. The unpaid and the paid were quartered in different hotels. True, it made little difference, for later in the evening there would be amateurs in the bar of the *King and Keys* and professionals in the bar of the *Chequers*. Off the field they were as members of one family, except that the amateurs called the pros, by their baptismal or familiar names and the professionals occasionally let drop a Mr. or a Sir.

"Well," said Nick, as they fell in step, "you didn't get a second knock, and four not out in the first innings must have boosted your batting average a bit. What's it now? Point three re-curring?"

Timmins grinned. He knew that there were frequent arguments as to whether he was or was not quite the worst bat in first-class cricket. While very young he had been taught to handle a scythe, and early habits cling.

"Have a heart, sir. I got seventeen against Surrey, week before last."

"So you did. Almost a faultless knock. Only five chances and three appeals. You're coming along. And I dare say if this match hadn't fizzled out"

"Bit of luck for you, Mr. Rockwell."

Nick eyed the professional with mock severity.

"What d'you mean? I'd scratched a few, hadn't I? Think I can't bat on a wet wicket?"

"I didn't mean that, sir. I meant that advertisement in the *Telegraph*. Must ha' been a coincidence. You being in the very town, I mean."

"Look here," said Nick, "what are you talking about?"

"Mean to say you haven't seen it, sir? None of us chaps didn't like to say nothing. Thought you'd have seen it, or maybe one of the other gents would have pointed it out to you. Your name all right, sir. Yours in full. Asked to get in touch with a firm in the town. Looked like lawyers. Something to your advantage, it said."

Nick halted suddenly at the end of a stride. He was not of a phlegmatic type. When Hope threw him a life-line he leaped to catch it.

"Well! First I've heard of it. Are you sure? Wait a bit. My people—or some of them—came from this part of the world.

I wonder If you're pulling my leg, Master Timmins, I'll pull your neck."

"All right," said Timmins. "I'll show it you in a minute—if they've still got the paper. They take in the *Telegraph* at our pub, and that was where—Simmonds it was—spotted it at breakfast time. There was an argument like, whether it was you or not, but I knew it was you because I'd seen your name written out in full on a document in the office."

Five minutes later they were in the hotel bar. The morning paper had been preserved and, after Nick had ordered two pints of bitter, it was handed over to him. Timmins obligingly pointed out the advertisement.

Well, there it was! And the landlord supplied the information that Blore and Matthews were local solicitors, so that—unless the advertisement were a mean kind of lure—it smacked of an unexpected legacy.

Nick finished his beer with an air of nonchalance, but noticed, as the tankard grew lighter, that it shook a little in his hand. Then feeling somewhat as if he were going out to bat in a test match, he strolled to the telephone.

Already he was thankful for many things. The early ending of the match seemed now a blessing in disguise. Otherwise he would have missed the chance of catching the lawyers in their office. Nor might he have seen the paper in time if the local bench had not granted an extension of hours during the Cricket Week. Less than an hour ago he had felt wretchedly depressed: now he had shaken the mire from his feet and trod on air.

Mr. Blore, it seemed, was not in his office, and very rarely was—but Mr. Matthews was summoned to speak on the telephone. Nick announced his name.

"Quite by chance," he said, "I happen to be here in the town. What's it all about, please?"

"I'm sorry, Mr. Rockwell," said the Voice. "First I must ask for some proof of your identity."

"Well, I've letters addressed to me. You'll see my name in the papers. I'm a County cricketer. That's why I happen to be here. If you care to walk down to the hotel there are at least two cricket teams, two umpires and two scorers to swear to me."

"Oh, cricketer, are you?" said the Voice, obviously unimpressed. "But I'm afraid all those people are strangers to me. Will you tell me where you were born and what was your father's name in full?"

Nick supplied the information.

"Um," said the Voice.

"And I'll tell you what," Nick continued. "If you're not convinced, ring up Lord Ethingstone. It's rather a long trunk call, but I'll give you the number and I dare say you'll catch him. He's on our committee, and he knew my father, and of course he knows I'm playing cricket here. I'm leaving here early to-morrow, and it would be rather a nuisance to have to come crashing back with a crowd of witnesses when I'm already on the spot."

There was a pause.

"That will do to go on with," said the Voice. "I suppose you carry some letters addressed to you? I shall have to trouble you for complete proof a little later. Meanwhile, where can I find you on the telephone this evening?"

"*Chequers,*" Nick answered.

"All right, thank you. Then I'll give you a call. Good-bye for the present."

At that stage Nick had not liked to ask what it was all about. He returned to the bar still outwardly calm but fermenting inwardly. It now contained more cricketers of both clubs and not a few townsmen, some of them with autograph books. Brooks, the wicket-keeper, who had just come in, scowled at Nick over a fizzing glass of tonic-water. There was a rumour that Brooks had once committed some major crime and drank tonic-water thereafter by way of penance.

"What's the matter with you, Happy Face?" Nick inquired.

"Bitter for you, sir, I s'pose?" said Brooks, feeling in a pocket with a right hand which looked as if it had been hammered on a blacksmith's anvil.

"Thanks. Clever of you to guess. But why the happy smile?"

Brooks explained, after his order had been executed.

"What I want to know." he said, "is why they run County matches in a one-eyed, out-of-the-way hole like this. No chance of gettin' home to-night. Nothin' to do but sit about in pubs and gettin' told by strangers 'ow you missed that chance of stumpin' Edrich at Lords four years ago."

"There's a show on at the gatf," said Nick. "*The Valparaiso Maiden*. Number ten musical comedy company, I should think. Why don't you go? You might spot something nice in the chorus. Time you got off."

"There *was* a show, you mean," Brooks returned gloomily. "Haven't you heard? It's all over the town."

"What?"

"Dud company run by a dud man. Been losin' money for weeks, I s'pose. Anyhow, some chaps with a writ have turned up and pinched all the props. So if they go on to-night they'll have to manage without scenery, dresses and music."

Nick frowned while Brooks laughed.

"Pretty foul luck, though. I wonder what's going to happen to the company. I suppose they're stranded?"

"Serve 'em right. I've no time for those people. I lent half a crown to an actor once. He promised to turn up and pay me on the Sunday."

"And didn't he?"

"Oh, he turned up all right—just as we were sittin' down to our dinner—so we had to ask him. And afterwards he wanted me to make it five bob."

Brooks had many such reminiscences and no profession seemed to be untainted. Nick left him after another minute or two and, quitting the bar, strolled in the direction of the other hostelry.

On the way he paused to look into the window of a tobacconist, and was gazing idly at some meerschaum pipes—the like of which he had never dreamed of smoking—when a hand fell on his shoulder and a voice charged with excitement and relief gasped in his ear:

"Nick! Nick, old lad! Thank God I've found you!"

CHAPTER II
LUCKY MEETING

Nick turned and stared, and then grinned broadly, eyes suddenly alight. Those eyes beheld a man of his own age and of a like build, a pale, fair young man with pinched cheeks and tired grey eyes.

"Basil!" he cried. "Great Scot!"

"Knew you were in the town," said Basil Hailsham, gabbling under the stress of emotion. "Saw your name in the paper. Cricket, I mean. Been looking for you everywhere."

Nick laughed.

"Why didn't you try the cricket ground? Or I suppose you guessed I'd be staying at one of the local pubs?"

"Same bar applied to both. Price of admission. Can't lurk on licensed premises and spend nothing. Better own up at once. I want to touch you."

Nick laughed again.

"Well, you'll be lucky! Time I've paid my bill I shan't have. Still, I dare say they'll take my cheque or I can get something off one of the players. What's wrong?"

Basil Hailsham was still inclined to gasp.

"Long story. You know I went on the stage? And Milly?"

"Milly?"

"You know my sister Milly? You met her one Speech Day. Long story. Tell you. Few words. You knew we were orphans? Brought up by aunt. Well, Aunt Kate's money went. Aunt Kate, instead of being hard up on three thousand a year, now tolerably well off on two-fifty. Living in a barracks—which calls itself a private residential hotel—in West Kensington. Got that?

"So little Milly and little Basil had to do something for themselves in a hurry. We could both dance a bit and act a bit and sing a bit. So the stage rather naturally suggested itself. And that brings us to this foul town."

"Your sister with you? Where is she?"

"Interned."

"What?"

"In our rooms. With our props. You see, old lad, the ghost isn't going to walk this week. Ought never to have booked up for this tour. Never quite liked the smell of it. We've been playing all the week at the local blood-tub. Been doing bad business everywhere. This afternoon, as ever was, rude men descended upon the gaff, waved writs about and pinched everything. Our charming chief has greased off. And here we are. Milly and I have got about fourpence between us."

"Good Lord!"

"Trifle thick. I was wondering what the hell to do. Don't know a soul in these parts. And then I happened to look at the cricket in one of the papers and saw you were down here. And I thought"

He went rambling on. and Nick listened in silent sympathy. At school he had not been a close friend of Basil Hailsham, but they had been thrown much together and had liked each other very well. Old associations drew them together now. The most faithful sons of Alma Mater are generally those who have seen the seamy side of life beyond her environments.

"Come along to my pub," said Nick, "and meet some of the chaps and have a drink. Here's ten bob to be getting on with—and then we'll see what can be done. I shall have to stand by for a 'phone call and I may have to buzz off for a bit at any moment. Looks as if I've had a spot of luck. I'd like to ask your sister and you to dinner, but I don't know how I'm going to be fixed. But I'll tell you all that presently. How much do you owe your jolly old landlady?"

Basil, who had suddenly cheered up, began to grin.

"Only about three quid. Theatrical digs are cheap. Oh, and there's Melisande, too. Better say four pound ten."

"H'm. Fares to Town for three about another thirty bob. All right when you get to London?"

"Well," said Basil, "there's digs in Redburn Street. Chelsea, where the old Ma won't begin to panic for a fortnight or so."

"Good! Who's Melisande? I've never been able to read Maeterlinck."

"Melisande," said Basil simply, "is the best little comedy actress whose talent hasn't yet been properly recognized. Incidentally she's the girl I'm going to marry."

"Congrats to both of you." Nick, humming, began to consider. "First move is to stab somebody for about seven pounds ten. Then I suppose you can all stay on at your rooms for another night?"

Basil said that it was frightfully decent of him, and before he had ceased enlarging on the subject they reached the *Chequers*. Here Nick left his friend for a moment and went to interview the manageress in her office.

The manageress was an agreeable person who knew Nick's status in the Stockshire C.C. Nick wrote out a cheque while she unlocked and explored a cash-box. Then he rejoined his friend and slipped a wad of paper into his hand.

"Come and have just one drink," he said, "while I tell you something. Then you can fade out for a bit and set the ladies' minds at rest. As I told you, I've got to hang around."

"You're staying in the town to-night?" Basil asked.

"Well, I wasn't going to, but looks as if I shall have to now. We're not playing to-morrow so it doesn't much matter."

"Then why not come round to our digs? I know there's another room, and the old girl won't charge you more than three or four bob. Two quart bottles of light dinner ale and fifty gaspers, and we'll make a Bacchanalian orgy of it. Now what's your news?"

In the smoke-room bar Nick ordered drinks and then proceeded to tell him as much as he knew.

"Looks like money," he said in conclusion.

"It does! Were you expecting any?"

"Not exactly. But I had an uncle, my mother's brother, who lived not far from here. He was a bachelor and supposed to be pretty well off. Sir Anthony Cromer—if you've ever heard of him. When I read of his death I kind of had some distant 'opes, but he hadn't seen me since I was a kid. Well, even a hundred 'ud be better than nothing."

Basil, remarking that he didn't know there was so much money in the world, began to scribble on the back of an envelope.

"Here's the address of the digs," he said, passing it over. "Can you read my fist? This is Ormville '—this is. And that's ' Teresa Road '—that is. Better tell the Boots to shoot your traps round. Dare say the jolly old lawyer will invite you to stick a fork into his cold mutton, but we'll scratch up some sort of a meal for you in case he doesn't, and expect you when we see you. Don't forget the smokes and drinks."

Nick felt in one of his pockets for silver.

"Better take those round yourself," he said, "because I don't quite know when I shall be along."

"Now that," said Basil. "*is* an idea. Come as soon as you can and any time you like. You'll find Welcome on the mat. And now as soon as I've got hold of a fish-basket or anything that will carry the beer, I'll dash off and comfort the Weeping Women. So long for the present and good luck with the lawyer, dear old lad. And thanks awfully."

Five minutes later he was gone. Shortly before eight o'clock a waiter informed Nick that he was wanted on the telephone.

Two young girls with wan and troubled faces sat in the bow windows of a hideous villa where they were presented with a view of similar villas on the farther side of a sandy road. The fair and taller girl was known on the stage as Milly Frobisher and privately as Milly Hailsham. The smaller and dark girl—a Cockney beauty who reminded one of a drawing by Phil May of ancient memory—was known on provincial play-bills as Miss Melisande d'Havrincourt. Among her close friends she answered to the name Betty. Few knew her patronymic—which was Higson. Milly was sitting on the arm of Betty's chair when the brunette suddenly raised her voice.

"Oh, fwhy, fwhy did we book for this fwightful touah—fwhen we maight have been dooing concert pairty work? I knew that that fellah was no gentleman. Something toald me fwhen I first set eyes on him that he was going to shop us. And these fwightful digs"

Melisande, while speaking, glanced back into the room. Then with a start she uttered a sharp scream and spoke in her natural voice.

"Blimey!" she cried. "There's a bleeding mouse!"

Milly gave her hand a sharp slap.

"But go on," she said. "That's better."

"Fwhat's better, dahlceng?"

"Talk in your natural voice or I shall scream, dear. And don't pretend you're afraid of mice. You may be glad to eat some before very long."

Betty, no longer Melisande, sighed and responded with a change of tone in which there was not the least note suggestive of ruffled humour.

"O.K., dear, I'll be common. On'y let's talk about something or other. Wonder if Basilco's 'ad any luck. He's been gone long enough."

"I know he'll hate it," said Milly, frowning. "After all, he wasn't an intimate friend of Nick Rockwell and he's got no claim on him. And just because N.R. plays County cricket as an amateur it doesn't mean that he's got any spare cash. In fact, Basil thinks that he hit the road pretty hard—same as we did."

"What was he like when you met him—this Nick?"

"My dear! He was the most important boy in a big school and I was a little mouse of thirteen. He was very polite to me for about fifteen seconds, and then he didn't seem to take any more notice of me. I goggled at his back and worshipped him from afar. Next time we had cherry tart I asked the stones when I was going to marry him. They said Sometime—which wasn't so bad."

"Well, when he sees you *this* time," said Betty, "if Basilco manages to rope him along, I guess it will be somebody else who'll do the distant worship act. After all, why shouldn't he put his hand in his pocket—if he's got a pocket? What's all this guff for about the Old School Tie. I know among our own crowd"

"Pros, are different," Milly answered. "*You* ought to know that, my dear. That's where we make our mistakes—thinking that all the rest of the world is, or ought to be, just like ourselves. Our outlook on life's all different. We're too frank. And because we leave most of our petty pretensions in the green-room we get laughed at and sneered at and have silly stories invented about us. Did you ever meet a man—who knew no more about you except that you were on the stage and not a leading lady— who didn't immediately jump to the conclusion that you were fair game?"

Betty frowned.

"I dunno," she said. "Real gentlemen like Basilco"

"Leave him out. Basil's on our side of the curtain. Besides which he respects you because he's genuinely in love with you. But neither you nor I have seen our little Basil with other girls. And if our little Basil were a young blood about town I don't suppose he'd be a great deal different from most other little Basils."

"You needn't go runnin' him down," said Betty with a sniff.

"My dear, I wasn't. But I've learned a great deal about the world I live in—which is just as well for me. And talk of the devil   Run and let him in, dear."

Basil, grinning all over his face, was thrusting his way through the garden gate.

"Blimey, he's clicked!" exclaimed Betty. "Sorry for saying Blimey, darling, but he's got beer with him, and the vile word escaped ma lips before

'S'all right, dear. Mrs. Moaning's going to let him in."

Subsequently they heard voices in the hall-passage.

"All right, Mrs. Smith. If you'll fetch the bill, made out until to-morrow, I'll settle it at once. . . . What? Yes, we shall be here for one more night. And wait a moment. How much do you want for that back room just for to-night? Got a friend coming. . . . What? Have a heart! . . . Well, make it three and six then. . . . That a do? . . . Right."

"Hell!" said Betty. "I bet he's picked up that Addison boy. Can't stand him at any price. Still, I suppose the poor devil's been kicked out and got nowhere to go."

Both girls sprang up and rushed across the room to embrace Basil as he entered it, so that he disturbed the beer by dropping the great bottles.

"Honey-pie, you've got *beer*" cried Betty, bussing him violently on the cheek.

"And he's managed to bite the ear of his old school chum, bless him!" Milly pecked the ear of her brother as she spoke. "So, after all, my girlish heart made no mistake with that lad."

"Shut up, you two," said Basil, grinning, "and listen. I've got enough to square things here and carry us over for a bit. Damn nice fellow, Nick Rockwell. Save some beer and a bit of grub for him in case he wants it. He'll be along"

"What!" cried Milly. "Be still, my girlish heart!"

Basil extricated himself from female clutches and sat down.

"Listen, you pair of lunatics. He's got to stay in the town tonight. Got to see a lawyer. And since he's not well off—I dare say I pretty well skinned him—he's coming here."

"Bon," said Betty, and there was a moment's silence before she spoke again. "What's he want to see a local lawyer for? Doesn't live around here, does he?"

"No, but some of his people did. He's been advertised for. Looks as if he's clicked for some money—and I hope for his sake he has. But in any case you needn't think that I'm going to try to sponge on him for more."

"I should say not!" This was Milly in a firm voice. "As it is I'm wondering how we're going to pay him."

Her brother offered cigarettes and lit one himself.

"I'm not exactly wondering how," he said. "But I'm rather wondering when. Not that he'll worry. I tell you he's a good scout, and he'll think no more of it until he hears from us. Just one word of warning, though—if I may say it without having any bricks chucked at me."

Betty, who had crossed to the fireplace, picked up a cheap vase and stood poising it.

"Yes, darling?" she said sweetly and dangerously. "Well, darling?"

"Talking to Milly now." Basil was hardly smiling. "Don't drop that damn' thing or it'll cost about fifteen bob. Seriously, though, don't shock the poor lad when he comes. He mayn't understand all our free and happy little ways. Dare say in his job—off the cricket field, I mean—he mixes in a pretty sticky and crusted set. Be as you used to was before you went on the stage."

"And got mixed up with common little cats like me," said Betty, showing him the tip of her tongue. "All right, sweetie. I'll go to bed as soon as I hear him knock."

"You go to hell," retorted Basil, grinning. "If you go to bed I'll get him to come and help me lug you out."

"Which," said Milly without a smile, "would give the lad an immediate glimpse of our carefree Bohemian ways. But I know what Basil means."

Betty turned up her nose.

"Raight *ho*! Ai'll be most karful to talk laike a laidy."

Basil, standing beside her, passed an arm around her shoulders and drew her to rest against him.

"No, you don't, angel. None of the Melisande stuff. Just be your sweet natural self without frills. I don't think he's got an ounce of side, but he won't expect to be treated as you'd treat Archie Baines or Sam Stakker. 'Member the shocks we had, Milly, when we first joined the happy Thespians? Just be as you would have been if"

Betty showed signs of becoming restive.

"Aw, hell," she said. "Is it the King of the Canary Islands or the Pope of Rome that's goin' to honour us?"

"It's neither," Basil answered promptly, a sudden edge to his tone. "It's just a damned decent bloke who happens to be a gentleman and has just got us out of a hell of a jam. He'll be all right as soon as he understands us. And if he joined the mob he'd be one of us inside a week."

They sat on, talking intermittently and smoking, over a period of waiting which soon became wearisome. Night began to fall, and it was not until a little after ten that a car, having previously slackened speed to a tentative crawl, drew up outside the gate.

"Oho," said Betty, "he's clicked already. Prince Charming arrives, rolling in bullion, in his fairy coach."

Basil was at the window.

"I expect," he said, without looking round, "his fairy godfather's driven him down or sent him along in the family barouche."

Suddenly he waved and turned abruptly from the window. Betty, finger on lips in burlesque of theatrical espionage, crept towards the glass as he hurried out of the room in the direction of the front door. They heard him greet Nick, and half a minute later Nick, grinning shyly, was in the room.

"Do you remember Milly? Don't suppose you'd know her if you do. She was all legs and coy smile last time you saw her."

"I'm afraid the smile isn't quite so coy nowadays," said Milly. "So glad to see you again. And thanks awfully for getting us out of this jam. Well, *you* haven't changed much. But then you were almost a man, weren't you? Oh, let me introduce you to Miss Melisande d'Havrincourt. It's rather a lot to say at once so you may call her Betty."

"He may if I say so," said Betty, coming forward and offering her hand. "Anyhow, I'm going to call him Nick. Howdy, Nick? Oh, there I go, you see—and I promised 'em I wouldn't be common."

Basil advanced upon her, flung an arm around her shoulders, shook her and audibly breathed the word *Cat* into one of her ears.

"Take a pew, old boy," he said, turning to Nick. "Make him feel at home, Milly, and then what about some food for him?"

"Sorry, but I've fed, thanks. Mr. Matthews said most of his piece to me over the board."

"Well, what about some coffee? Kettle boiling?"

Their earliest experience of theatrical lodgings had taught them to carry everywhere an oil-stove and a kettle. The big, broad-bottomed tin kettle had in fact been steaming gently for nearly an hour. Milly made coffee while her brother set glasses and bottles on the table.

Conversation was forced for a while after they were all seated. Three of that party were waiting for the fourth to become communicative, and Nick, slightly preoccupied behind a mask of geniality, was shy of talking about himself and needed at least a broad hint.

"Well, old boy," said Basil at last, with a preoccupied glance at the glowing end of his cigarette, "I told the girls as much as you told me. Hope you don't mind, but I imagined that it was what you'd expect me to do. And if you hear any tapes and laces going pop it's simply because they're bursting with curiosity. How did you get on?"

"Sorry! Hut it's all like a dream. As soon as I've established my identity"

"Haven't you done that yet?"

"Well, practically. All bar a formality. Matthews has been on the 'phone about me, and I showed him letters addressed to me and my photograph in a newspaper cutting. *He's* satisfied all right. At least he told me something I wanted to know and something else I didn't want to know, and—I feel in my bones— he left a lot unsaid."

"Making difficulties, I dare say. Some of 'em like doing that."

"Not his fault, though. They're in the will. He showed me a copy. If I'm willing to accept certain conditions I've been left a pretty big house—Mardstone Manor it's called—and certain invested moneys which are bringing in about eight thousand a year."

"*Wah!*" yelled Betty, and she pretended to faint.

Nick had been speaking in low and level tones which sounded almost bored. This was because he was still slightly dazed by his sudden change of fortune and worried and bemused by the conditions imposed on him.

"Yes," he said with sudden slight animation, "but there's a snag. Two or three snags, in fact. I'd better tell you everything in some sort of order, otherwise you'll never get the hang of it.

"My uncle was a pretty extensive traveller and fancied himself as a social reformer. He was the last of his direct line, by the way, and the title died with him. I was the son of his sister, and his only other surviving relatives are on his mother's side. He was a bachelor, and he seems to have been a pretty queer fish. That's what Matthews said, but not in so many words.

"A few years ago he came home from South America, where he'd been messing about for some years, bringing with him his valet—a bloke named Perringer who'd been all over the world with him. He was still a long way off being an old man, and when he bought Mardstone Manor everybody thought that he intended to marry and settle down.

"Well, he settled down all right, but he never married. And it seems as if he bought Mardstone Manor because he didn't believe in ghosts and wanted to see one. There is a room there supposed to be haunted by a seventeenth-century gentleman who dislikes intruders."

Nick paused. He paused for so long that Milly applied a verbal nudge.

"Of course he didn't see the ghost," she said.

"But he did. Or he thought he did. He was a pretty hard bitten sort of man, but he had an experience in that room which, real or imaginary, shook him up above a bit. He never said what it was, but he had the room locked up and the windows shuttered and a seal put on the lock. That's how things are today, and I get the income from my uncle's money only for so long as that seal remains intact. If that's bust, I'm bust."

"Lordy!" said Betty, unable to repress an exclamation.

"Oh, that's not all. Not by a damned long chalk. I've got to live in the house. That's to say I've got to guarantee not to spend a night away from it. Be a kind of prisoner, in fact. That, I suppose, is to prevent anybody from breaking in and interfering with that sealed room."

"But it's mad!" exclaimed Basil. "Who'd want to? Besides, who's looking after it now?"

"Perringer."

"What? The valet?"

"Yes. He's the next snag. Or he may be. He's a fixture. I can't sack him. He can be as insolent and lazy as he pleases, but I can't get rid of him. At least, not without special leave of the trustees, who have the right—the *right*, mark you—to appoint his successor."

He paused again and a heavy silence lingered on the air. Basil spoke next in a quiet and measured tone.

"Of course," he said, "the whole thing is madness. Sorry, old boy, but your uncle couldn't have been *compos* when he made that will, and I wonder his lawyers allowed it. Seems to me you could make an appeal in Chancery or the High Court or somewhere and get those conditions set aside."

"Yes. That's just what old man Matthews warned me about. He said that it mightn't be so hard to get the whole will set aside once the legal machinery got in motion. And where should I be then?"

That aspect of the case appealed to his hearers, who exchanged glances and nods.

"So," said Basil, "what are you going to do? Bury yourself alive for the rest of your life?"

"Not if I know it." Nick roused himself suddenly to utter an energetic laugh. "I've been thinking it out. I'll put in a year or two there and save money. Then when I've got a few thousand behind me I'll write to the trustees and tell them they can find some other mug on the other side of the family to stick the lunatic conditions and pouch the money. There's nothing to stop me from doing that. Nothing at all."

Basil's face suddenly lit up.

"Now you're talking! Isn't he talking, you dames? Gad! He can live like a fighting cock and walk out in about five years' time with his tongue in one cheek and thirty thousand quid rolled up in the other. Nick, old lad, you've got brains. Why, many a lag has done five years in Portland—where it can't be as comfortable as where you're going—for damn' sight less."

"Yes," said Milly, watching Nick's face, "but what is the poor lad going to do with himself? In Portland they'd give him some oakum to play with, or a pick and shovel, or something. I don't suppose he'll have many friendly neighbours. There must be some dusky rumours floating around about a house like that. How's he going to manage for company?"

Nick grinned and cleared his throat a little awkwardly.

"I've been thinking about that, too," he said. "Didn't do much talking at first, did I? That's because my brain was working like a hive. I couldn't stick it alone with that fellow Perringer, whatever he may be like. At the least I'd have to get a companion-secretary or something, and it would take a rather unusual bloke to stick it out with me. But I thought three companion-secretaries might make life a bit brighter. There'd at least be four for bridge. So what about it?"

He eyed them each in turn and rather slowly his meaning dawned on them. He heard muffled exclamations.

"Look here," he resumed, "let's put it on a common-sense and business footing. You three are in a jam because you've nothing before you in the immediate future. I shall soon be in a jam for want of company—*your* company. Please don't think I'm making the offer only to help you. I shall be jolly glad if it does, of course, but that's neither here nor there. Point is you'll be doing me no end of a good turn—if you can stick living in a house which, I should say, is more than a trifle spooky."

Nick saw his hearers look at one another, and each seemed to wait for one of the others to speak.

"Well, leave me out, thanks all the same," said Betty. "Can't somehow see myself in that setting. Besides, what good would I be?"

"Nonsense!" Nick laughed. "Four's the only possible number. I don't think Basil would stick it long without you. Milly would be pretty lost without a girlfriend. And there's another point occurs to me. I hardly like to mention it."

Betty answered, having first permitted herself a wry smile.

"Well, blurt it out, dear—an' feel light 'earted."

"It's just this. No servants there except an ex-valet who seems to be an immovable fixture. Might be a bit of a job to get servants, even if approved by trustees. Anyway, they might be curious. Did I mention that one or more of the trustees are apt to descend at any time and examine that seal? Anyhow, that's the state of things. But if we made a picnic of it, and split up the work between us, and did our own cooking"

Betty jumped and clapped her hands.

"Fine!" she cried. "I'll be the skivvy. I've had that part four times. Feather duster, saucy French apron, and flirtin' with the page."

"Thanks," laughed Nick, "but I'm afraid you can't be the only one. Big house. Plenty of work for all four of us—with the cleaning, catering, cooking and one thing and another. If you like the idea there'll be no difficulty about fixing terms. My friends aren't barred. If you get sick of it later, when you've got a bit put by, you can look up the theatrical agents again."

He saw at once that the idea had made a hit with Miss Melisande d'Havrincourt, familiarly known as Betty. There was a gleam in her eyes as she turned them upon the other two. Basil was looking straight at Milly. Betty and he seemed to be waiting upon her word. But Milly was looking past her brother at Nick. There was a heightened colour in her cheeks.

"It's terribly sweet of you," she said. "There's a kind of magic in that word Picnic. But there's just one thing I'd like to know. Are you making this offer for our sakes—or your own?"

Obviously she was at a loss for words and hesitated over a speech which otherwise would have sounded blunt. Nick answered her frankly and on the whole sincerely.

"Mutual advantage," he said. "It sticks out a mile. Anybody who wasn't directly concerned would see it in a flash. You three are in a jam. I'm in another sort of jam. If you let me help you out of yours in the way I've suggested you'll be helping me out of mine. Don't you see?"

Milly glanced at her brother.

"Well?" she prompted him. "Say something."

It was Betty, however, who made the next contribution. She pirouetted up to Nick, stood on tiptoe, and solemnly kissed him on the cheek. Then linking an arm in one of his, she postured and faced the other two.

"He's a love," she announced. "I'm goin' with him, anyhow. Then, Basilco, you'll be jealous and have to come too—for the sake of the Properties, or whatever they call them. He might rewin a pore innocent gairl like me—the dirty dog. So, Milly, if you don't come along of us you'll be left out all alone in the great big cold draughty world. Won't you, darling?"

Basil grinned at his sister.

"Come on," he said. "No use voting the other way when you're outvoted already. It's damned decent of old Nick. I won't pretend we shan't be under an obligation, but I don't care about that when it's a fellow like him. Besides, what he's said isn't all boloney. Of course he'll need people in the house. You girls can do your domestic stuff—if you haven't forgotten how. I can hew water and draw wood and help Nick chain up the family ghost when it breaks out. We'll all be pulling our weight." Nick spoke across to her, calling her by her Christian name.

"Be a sport, Milly. We can have lots of fun. Don't go and muck up everything by putting a spoke in the wheel."

For a moment he thought he saw a light in her eyes—like the light he had once seen in the eyes of a child offering frank worship to a lanky boy.

"I think" She spoke at last a little huskily. "I think it's perfectly sweet of you, Nick. I didn't want to say no. And now I can't say no."

It was as if the atmosphere breathed by the little party of four were subject to some swift and mysterious chemical change. One of the better sort of fairies, perhaps, fluttered through the room above their heads and flickered good wishes at them from a wand's end. They toasted one another in the contents of the large bottles, and Milly began suddenly to shake with unreasonable laughter, as if the light dinner-ale were heady stuff.

"It's all so hopelessly looney," she said when questioned. "Well, isn't it now?"

Basil broke suddenly into song—and remained so until reminded of the existence of next-door neighbours, and of the fact that the landlady was an early riser who probably cherished early sleep. Nick called them suddenly to order.

"Half a moment, you light-hearted mummers. There's one or two things to be considered. To-morrow."

"Yes?" Basil suddenly squatted almost upright on the edge of the table. "What happens to-morrow?"

Nick considered, frowning.

"Well, first thing I'll have to do is ring up the club. Another trunk-call, and I don't know how long it will take. Explain matters. The secretary won't really miss me. I did next to no work, and it was only a blind so as I could play cricket as an amateur. Puts a stopper on cricket, I'm afraid. I don't know, though. There's matches at Lord's, Leyton and the Oval, and if I'm wanted I could manage those and get back every night.

"After that I think I'd better hire a car and run over by myself to see the house and make the acquaintance of the Immovable Object. I mean this Perringer chap, of course. Tell him that I've come to stay and break the news that you'll be coming along later. Otherwise there'll be damp beds and nothing to eat. Then I'll swoop back as soon as I can and collect you."
Basil nodded cheerfully.

"Good enough, squire. Anything you say. About how far is it to the House of Usher?"

"'Bout seven miles. There's a village of sorts close handy— one church, two shops, three pubs— and a railway station with trains now and then, so it's not worth training. If you three wouldn't mind standing by until I come back Oh, and you'd

I better do some packing, Basil, and I'll take your traps over along with mine. Won't be room for all your stuff and all the girls' in one taxi."

Basil grinned at the girls.

"Thoughtful chap, isn't he? Comes of being a secretary."

"Better trainin' than yours," Nick retorted, with several nods. "You fellows never seem to remember anything at all. Dunno how you manage to learn your parts and get on the stage in time and get from one place to another without losing yourselves." Basil uttered a grim chuckle.

"Well," he said, "I don't know what you think: but it looks to me as if the three of us have had a damn narrow shave of *not* getting from one place to another."

CHAPTER V
THE FORBIDDEN DOOR

The lodge gates of Mardstone Manor, flanked on one side by an empty hovel with broken windows, stood on the main road from London about a quarter of a mile short of the outskirts of Mardstone village. The "drive" had the appearance of an ill-kept country lane. Only the lodge suggested the presence of a large house somewhere out of view.

Like many country houses of its period it was fugitive—as if the builders had wished to hide it from strangers passing along the high road. One came upon it suddenly and almost surprisingly, and an amateur of architecture would have been prompt in calling it Jacobean.

He would have been partly right. 1617 was the year of its rebuilding. But it had been built on to and around the ruins of a mediaeval grange which had been partly destroyed—presumably by fire—at some period unknown. The great nail-studded door and entrance-hall were centuries older than the rooms to right and left and the broad, squat staircase which rose to the low floor above.

Some five feet above the level of the top step there was a shuttered grille in the massive door, the ironwork of the frame now rusty and thin as paper. To the left a long iron ball-handle depended from a massive chain. Some muscular strength was needed to obtain any response from the bell within, and a child could have swung on the chain without evoking a sound. Nick set the clapper of the bell in motion and looked around at the driver of the hired car who was lifting out his luggage. Two minutes passed and the man, having fulfilled his task, looked inquiringly at Nick, who turned once more to the bell. He was about to tug at it again when he heard a metallic sound on a level with his shoulder, and turned sharply to see that the shutter behind the grille had been pushed back. He was aware of the gleam of eyes and the pallor of a face.

"Yes?" said a male voice abruptly. "Who is it, please?" Nick announced himself abruptly and felt himself frowning.

"You're Perringer, I suppose," he added. "No doubt you were expecting me sooner or later. I don't know if you heard from Mr. Matthews this morning. Anyhow, I have a note to you from him."

Some of the speech was probably wasted because of a noise suggestive of the drawing of a heavy bolt. The great door moved slowly and Nick found himself confronted by a tall, lean, sallow man in the middle forties, whose spare but sinuous form was covered by an exceedingly well-cut suit of blue serge. A somewhat casually dressed master thus became acquainted with his own beautifully groomed servant.

"If you would be good enough to step inside, sir?" said Perringer. "And also if you would be good enough to show me the note from Mr. Matthews?"

"Oh, yes. Here you are."

The envelope was unsealed. Perringer extracted its contents slowly with a deprecatory air. Then he drew aside with a slight inclination of head and shoulders.

"Welcome home, sir," he said, "if you will permit me to say it. I had intended to prepare a little speech more worthy of the occasion, but I had hardly expected you, sir, quite so soon."

"That's all right," said Nick, wondering how much or how little he was going to like the man. "I'm afraid I've taken you almost by surprise. I happened to be in Arunford yesterday when the advertisement appeared. Playing cricket, you know."

"Cricket? Indeed, sir? Yes, sir!"

It was evident from Perringer's manner that he took no interest in the County Championship. Nick was vaguely sorry to lose a possible bond of sympathy.

"Will you come into the breakfast-room, sir, and take some refreshment? My late master used it as a general living-room. Before I show you over the house, sir, I must apologize for its condition. It would take more than one pair of hands, sir, to keep it as it should be kept."

"Rather! Why didn't you get some help? Mr. Matthews, I suppose, would have found the money and charged it to the estate."

Perringer drew thin lips together.

"We had servants, of course, in your late uncle's day, sir. But I had very implicit instructions from him what to do—if or when he should—er—depart this life. I trust that I am conscientious. As far as possible I have obeyed his wishes to the letter."

They walked as they talked and were now in the morning room. Like most of the other rooms— as Nick was soon to discover—it was panelled in dark oak and gloomy, ill-lit and sparsely furnished.

"May I get you some refreshments, sir? There is, if I may say it, an excellent cellar. Mr. Matthews has an inventory of the wines and spirits found after your late uncle's decease. I shall be happy to check it with you when it comes. Perhaps I may take this opportunity to tell you, sir, that I personally am a teetotaller."

"Well, at this hour I'd as soon have a cup of tea as anything," said Nick.

"I have water on the boil, sir."

"Then if you feel like tea yourself bring two cups."

Perringer did not leave him for long, and Nick made use of his short absence by framing a number of questions. When the man returned with a laden tray he was invited to sit—which he did with an air of facile compliance which was almost courtly.

"Now, Perringer, let's have a little talk. You are aware, no doubt, of the peculiar circumstances under which—er—I've found myself here. You must have expected that there'd be a great deal I should be wanting you to tell me. And first of all I want to know why the jiggery-pokery? That spy-hole in the front door, I mean. It's like trying to get into the lodge of a secret society."

Perringer smiled quite frankly and naturally.

"The door, sir, is as it was some hundreds of years ago. Since the peep-hole was already there my late master instructed me to use it. He did not, if I may say so, encourage visitors. So I got into the way of looking out before unbarring the door, and I suppose the old habit remains."

"He must have been a very peculiar man—Sir Anthony," said Nick bluntly.

"Possibly, sir, he had reason to be. But—he was a very good man, if I may be permitted to say it."

"Ah!" Nick suddenly followed another train of thought. "Let me see—he died of an accident, didn't he?"

"Yes, sir. It was a terrible shock. He was knocked down by a car at night outside the lodge gates. I almost saw it happen. I was coming down the drive at the time to look for him, for I wanted urgently to see him about something. He was already dead and terribly disfigured when I carried him into the empty lodge."

"Didn't the driver stop?"

"No, sir, but I do not think it was his fault. He was exonerated. He owned to feeling a jar, and when he got into Arunford and found one of his wings slightly bent he went straight to the police-station and left his name and address." Nick nodded thoughtfully several times.

"Well," he said, unwarily speaking his thought aloud, "there seems to have been no mystery about his death, but there was plenty of mystery about his life."

"Indeed, sir?"

"Oh, no doubt I oughtn't to say it to you." Nick showed sudden irritation at the implied reproof. "But what is the use of trying to pretend that he was a normal man? You knew him perhaps better than anybody. Apparently he never married. He spent a life of travel and adventure, about which his own family knows nothing, or next to nothing. Then he settles down in this lonely house, locks up a room and tries to make provision that nobody shall ever enter it again. Further, he makes his heir a kind of prisoner."

"The late Sir Anthony, sir, was a very good man. A noble man."

"I'm very glad to hear you say it. I've never heard nor supposed anything to the contrary."

"And it's the good men, sir, who have the bad enemies."

"I'm afraid I don't quite get you."

"Reverting to the matter of the sealed room, sir," said Perringer, somewhat hastily, "I think I can enlighten you. Your late uncle was a sceptic concerning ghosts. So, in fact, was I. I think that one of the main reasons which induced him to buy this property—for there were many others equally suitable—was because it was alleged to have a haunted room. We had been warned against that room. He slept in it on the night of our arrival here. That was the only occasion. Afterwards he kept it shuttered and locked and set a seal upon the door."

Nick whistled softly.

"Did he tell you what he saw or thought he saw?"

"He did not tell me much, sir, for he was a badly shaken man. But there was no need. Afterwards I saw it for myself."

Nick stared hard at the man, his lips pursed for the moment in silence.

"*You've* been in that room, then?"

"No, sir. Not since the morning that followed. But I've seen it. *It comes out sometimes.*"

Perringer put no dramatic effort beyond slight emphasis into his words. They fell upon Nick's ears cold and infinitely sinister.

"What have you seen?"

"Will you forgive me, sir," said Perringer, almost tonelessly, "if I do not talk of it? I trust, sir, that you will never be brought to realize why I make the request. Your late uncle, sir, was no coward and a much-travelled man. I too am fairly hard-bitten. Will you leave it at that, sir?"

Nick, smiling now for sheer bewilderment, expelled a great gust of breath.

"But damn it, man, tell me *something*! I suppose there's some kind of yarn attached to the room?"

"Yes, sir. I can tell you about that. It is commonly known. In the latter days of the seventeenth century, it seems, the Lord of the Manor was a certain Colonel Harboys. He was a Jacobite. After the accession of William of Orange he was privy to one of the many plots to restore James the Second to the throne. Unfortunately for him his wife had other sympathies. Finding himself betrayed and about to be arrested he killed his lady in that room and then fell upon his sword. That, sir, is the tale in brief." Nick took out a cigarette, and as Perringer hastily struck a match for him remarked:

"Well, it's not so ghastly as legends go. One can imagine the poor old Jacobite getting a bit irritated with his better half—who probably had some other gentleman in her mind's eye. Considering the age he lived in he may not have been such a very bad sort."

Once more Perringer showed signs of animation.

"I beg your pardon, sir. He was in all ways vile."

"I don't see how you can possibly know that."

Perringer shut his eyes tightly for a moment.

"If you had seen him, sir, you would understand."

Nick felt—and owned to it afterwards—a sudden slight squeamishness. Perringer's manner was not unproductive of effect.

"Let's have a look at this room, or rather the outside of it," he said suddenly.

The valet-cum-major-domo inclined his head.

"I can take you over the house the moment you are ready, sir. Do you wish to see the Sealed Door first, or shall we take it on our way around the house?"

"Oh," said Nick, rising, "we'll take it in our stride, I think." Within, the house seemed larger than had been suggested by the view of its facade. It was rather barely and even Spartanly furnished, but there were some old pictures which looked valuable and a deal of massive silver. The rooms were not swept and garnished to suit a neat and matronly taste, but, Nick reflected, one pair of hands must have worked hard to keep them even reasonably clean. Most of the rooms contained their original dark oak panels and, with the exception of those on the ground floor, they were ill-lit and gloomy.

It was like the traditional haunted house described in so many tales in Christmas supplements, Nick reflected, and went on to try to make up his mind about Perringer. The quiet, well-mannered man, striding along beside him over the echoing floors, and addressing him from time to time with faultless civility, constituted a problem. He was aware—and grew angry at the thought—that Perringer knew a great deal more about something than he had cared to disclose. But his silence was secure from challenge, for Nick was at a loss to know what that something was. Meanwhile the stillness of the house was oppressive, their footfalls and the occasional responsive echoes did nothing to lift the veil of gloom. All sounds seemed like intrusions upon the brooding Past—and intrusions which caused resentment in some living Consciousness.

On the first floor Perringer pointed to a corridor.

"That is the west wing," he said. "The sealed room is at the end. You cannot mistake its windows from the outside, sir, for they are shuttered and they stand on two sides of the angle of the house."

As they approached the door of the sealed room Nick's vague sense of discomfort increased considerably. It was all so eerie and, he thought, so unhealthy. He would have given quite a respectable sum to hear commonplace voices, and laughter, and the crack of bat on leather, and tried to cheer himself with the thought that these comfortable sounds were still to be heard at no great distance in the world outside.

Yes, but the outside world *was* a great distance away. It was as if he had crossed some dream-threshold into another life, another age. He had experienced something like this before in incipient nightmare. . . .

"This is the door, sir." Perringer's voice was speaking in its customary monotone. "There, sir, is the seal. May I recommend you, sir, if you must touch it, to handle it very gently?"

To be sure the blotch of deep-red wax looked far from fragile, but Nick did not touch it with his fingers. Instead, he bent low over it and tried to make something of the device. Two male figures, it seemed, one in armour, each holding something—was it sword or keys?—which crossed in the centre. Below there was a scroll and an undecipherable motto.

"Somebody's crest," Nick said aloud.

"Yes, sir, but I do not think your late uncle's. He never used armorial bearings."

"No?" said Nick indifferently. "I saw his arms once in Burke. I've forgotten the crest, but I don't think it was like this." Perringer seemed to become slightly restless.

"I am afraid, sir," he said, "that there is nothing more here to see. But there is the other wing of the house, sir, and the attics, servants' quarters and cellars—if you wish to see everything."

Nick stood upright and let his gaze run over the full, forbidding face of the great door. Suddenly he forced himself to grin, and spoke without looking around at Perringer.

"I wonder what's behind that," he said.

"Probably nothing and nobody, sir. And to-night possibly nothing and nobody. But some nights, sir, there is somebody—or *something.*"

Nick did not like the sound of his own laughter just then, but he forced himself to utter a laugh as he turned away.

"D'you know, Perringer," he said, "I believe you're rather good at giving people the creeps." The ghost of a smile lengthened Perringer's thin lips.

"Am I, sir? I beg your pardon. Perhaps I have become a trifle morbid, living here alone, with my late master's death for ever weighing upon my thoughts."

"Yes. I wonder you haven't gone out of your mind. I'm not seeing the house at its best, of course. It will seem another place with a few cheery people larking about in it."

Perringer drew in his lips.

"It would make the house much brighter, sir, no doubt. I can only share with you, sir, the regret that such a state of affairs is quite impossible."

Nick thought that the time had arrived to explode his bomb.

"There you are wrong, Perringer," he said. "Three of my friends will be arriving later in the day and they will be staying indefinitely."

The sight of Perringer's face rewarded Nick, and the man halted as if the floor had opened before his feet.

"But that—that is impossible, sir. It is not permitted."

Nick was not often hasty-tempered, but his nerves were on edge and his ire rose suddenly without warning.

"And who the devil's to forbid it? *You?*"

Perringer's lost composure did not return at once, but he changed his tone.

"No, sir, no, sir. Please do not misunderstand me if I spoke hastily. You—what you said, sir—gave me a shock. I supposed—I imagined—Mr. Matthews would have told you. To a very great extent I enjoyed the confidence of your late uncle. What you intend would not be in accordance with his wishes. I assure you, sir."

Nick halted and brought the other to a sudden standstill.

"Now look here, Perringer. Time, I think, that we began an understanding. My late uncle seems to have been, to say the least, a trifle eccentric. His will was already burdened with enough peculiar conditions, but I have seen a copy, and there was nothing in it that will prevent me from entertaining my friends when I please and for so long as I please. Naturally I should like to fall in with any known wish of his if it were at all reasonable. But this isn't reasonable, and I've only your word that he ever expressed such a wish."

"I'm sorry, sir. I spoke perhaps a little indiscreetly. I don't know how I could have got it in my head. I must have assumed it from something he said to me, and I thought it was down in his will. If it wasn't it can't be helped. I don't know, sir, if he expressed any wishes to anybody else, sir—in writing or otherwise—outside the will. But if so the trustees or Mr. Matthews would know, sir."

"Trustees?" Nick seized upon the word. "Colonel Sandingford and Dr. Whitemill, aren't they? Got the right to walk in here and examine that seal whenever they like. Has either of them been down, by the way, since my uncle's death?"

"Yes, sir. Dr. Whitemill has been down twice. A very nice gentleman indeed. But Colonel Sandingford has not been here since—since the tragedy."

Nick nodded indifferently. Old friends of his late uncle, he supposed. Their names had conveyed nothing to him when Matthews mentioned them. But he supposed that Matthews had already communicated with them and that he would hear from one or the other within two or three days.

"Let's resume our talk downstairs," said Nick. "There's a great deal more that I want to know. And I may as well tell you straight out, Perringer, that you won't improve our relations if you are otherwise than frank with me."

CHAPTER VI
A TALK WITH PERRINGER

Two or three minutes later Nick was seated and staring straight at Perringer. Perringer met his eyes for a moment, then looked downwards. Whether he deflected his gaze because of discomfort, or because he thought it was not his place to stare, it was almost impossible to determine. "About the gentlemen appointed by my late uncle as trustees. They were old friends of his, I believe, but they were not local men?"

"Oh, no, sir. The Colonel lives up in Warwickshire and the other gentleman in London."

"What about his local friends? Whom am I likely to meet?" Perringer frowned thoughtfully. "I'm afraid, sir, that he hadn't any local friends, as you might say. A few gentlemen called on him, and I will bring you the bowl containing their cards. But there not being a lady in the house, sir, made things awkward in that way—for it's ladies who generally like paying calls. Sir Anthony didn't return the calls—or at least not many. He was a gentleman who liked keeping himself to himself."

"He didn't entertain at all, then?"

"Not beyond a cup of tea, or sometimes a glass of sherry, according to the time of day. I don't know that he ever invited anybody here. But he was on quite friendly terms with Mr. Crossley— the Rev. Mr. Crossley, the Vicar, sir—and with Dr. Bligh."

"Yes? What are they like?"

Perringer hesitated before speaking slowly and deliberately.

"Well, sir, I expect you will be seeing them before long. They are both nice gentlemen. Mr. Crossley is rather old—I believe he has grandchildren—and most people, I believe, do not consider him to be particularly interesting. Though, mind you, sir, he is quite well liked. Dr. Bligh, though, is quite different. If I may say so, he's not much older than you, sir, and this, I believe, is his first practice."

Perringer paused and seemed to look into the distance.

"What else can I tell you about him, sir? Well, I should say he is a jolly, hearty sort of gentleman. He's married and had a baby—or rather his lady had one—not many months ago." "And those are the only local people he knew?"

"The only ones with whom you could say he was friendly. Not that he made himself unpleasant to others. He just didn't want to be bothered with them."

There was a pause, and it was Perringer who ended it by speaking again.

"Excuse me, sir, if I ask you a question."

"Well?"

"It will sound queer, sir, unless I explain. We're in a lonely part here, and the house contains many articles of value. My late master was always conscious of the possibility of being burgled, and I wanted to ask you, sir, if you can use a gun—a revolver, I mean."

"Yes," said Nick, wondering. "Well, I've fired a revolver at a range. I'm not a good shot, though, by any means."

"Well, sir, I can provide you with a weapon and I will show you where you can get a little target practice. May I mention, sir, my late master's instructions to me? I am sure he would wish me to pass them on to you."

Nick suddenly began to laugh.

"This is getting madder and madder," he said, choking. "Revolvers now! Go on, go on." Perringer ignored the unseemly merriment.

"Sir Anthony, sir, urged me never to fire unless it was necessary. Indeed, that is against the law. So I know, sir, he would have wished me to mention this to you."

Nick laughed again at this artless admonition and brought himself a glance of pained but respectful reproach.

"All right, Perringer," he said. "Don't mind me. I'll take your words to heart. Will it relieve you to be told that I have killed very few men as yet—even in the way of justifiable homicide."

Perringer smiled dutifully, as one who had learned to suffer weak pleasantries gladly from the lips of his superiors.

"And now, sir," he said, "if you will permit me I will get some bedding aired. I have prepared a room which I trust you will find suitable—my late master's own room. But I was unprepared to receive others, although fortunately there is food and to spare. Er—how many guests did you say, sir?"

"Two young ladies and one gentleman."

Nick hid a smile with difficulty as he watched Perringer's expressionless face.

"The gentleman," he continued, "is the brother of one of the young ladies. I hope that will satisfy the local conventions. Er —particularly as this house has a cheerless air and a sinister reputation it is possible that the two ladies may care to share a room—but we can find out later."

Perringer bowed.

"Meanwhile, sir," he said, "I will get some bedding aired. Fortunately the house is beautifully dry, but no doubt the mattresses will be none the worse for a turn by the kitchen fire. As for the blankets and bed-linen, this is an old-fashioned house, sir, and the hot cupboard is in the kitchen close to the range. I can guarantee all the sheets and blankets and pillow-cases."

"Good," said Nick.

He listened to further domestic details, which he tried to bear in mind in order that he might pass them on to Milly and Betty and actually he contrived to remember a few of them when the time came. Domesticity was a burden which he had never been called upon to bear. He felt rather unnecessarily grateful to the two girls for being about to take the load on to their own shoulders, little guessing that throughout their latter and nomadic lives they had been dreaming wistfully and rather hopelessly of a place that they could call Home.

The kitchen did not greatly interest him, nor for that matter did the cellars, well stocked as they were, but he was disposed to humour Perringer, who seemed anxious to display everything. Having heard what food Perringer had in the house, and what other food Perringer thought he could obtain at short notice, he gave an order for dinner and went back to the car.

Basil was sitting on a bag in the little hall-passage, smoking a cigarette and waiting, when Nick returned.

"Hullo!" he said. "Girls were all packed up and ready to move off an hour ago. Now they've gone up again to pack the other things which they'd forgotten. Always the same—especially when there's a train which simply has to be caught. Putting grey hairs on me before my time. Silver threads amid the gold. Well, what's the news?"

"Fine old house," said Nick, "but damned eerie. Furnished to suit the same taste. Sort of place where you expect to be told to take no notice of Screams in the Night, because it's only the Grey Lady doing her stuff—and she always carries on like that when somebody's going to die."

"And the man there? What's his name?"

"Oh, Perringer's an animated statue with a strong sense of duty. Didn't approve your coming— or the girls'. Late Master wouldn't have liked it. As if my poor old uncle, who I trust is now amusing himself with a harp, would care two straws about what happens down here. But the sealed room is another matter. It's part of a binding contract."

"Might get in from the outside," Basil suggested. "Seen the windows?"

"No. Hadn't time to potter about outside. But I know they're shuttered and barred. Ah, I hear female voices. Looks as if we might be going to make a start sooner or later." He lifted his head to call: "Come along!"

"Half a moment." Basil glanced up the stairs and lowered his voice. "Between ourselves— before they come down—what do you make of it all so far? The Room—this Perringer— everything?"

Nick laughed.

"Well," he said, "putting all I've heard into one lump, and looking at it like that, I've no doubt at all that my late uncle was bats. And Perringer? Perringer knew it all the time, of course, and, knowing where his bread was buttered, he played up. No doubt he thought he was going to get more out of the will than he's going to get. But I'll give him marks for being a conscientious brute according to his lights. He seems most anxious that his late guv'nor's smallest wishes should be carried out to the letter."

Betty's voice rang out from the middle of the short flight of stairs.

"Hullo! Hullo! I've been screaming hullo for the last hour. Catch me, Basilco, I'm goin' to jump." Basil caught her, but not her heavy bag, which made its own contribution in a sudden series of bumps and crashes. The young man went down under weight and cracked his head against the wall. The car-driver, standing in the open doorway, crowed with joy like an enormous babe. The kitchen door at the farther end of the passage sprang ajar, and the landlady—as represented by one baleful eye—became partly visible. And Betty, who had landed lightly, remained gracefully poised.

"Not so bad, duck," she said. "But looks as if we'll have to practise this act a bit before we put it on."

CHAPTER VII
ANOTHER SMALL MYSTERY

"Curse the man Perringer," said Betty, gnashing her teeth. "Curse him, I say!"

"What's the matter with him?" demanded Milly, sipping the Chateau-Laffitte with which Perringer had lately replenished her glass. The man was gone from the room, having just removed the wreck of a large fowl. "At least," she conceded, "he can cook."

"That's just the trouble," Betty complained. "He can cook better than I can. And I was going to be cook."

"Don't you worry, old girl," said Basil. "You'll find plenty to do. I've seen enough work already in this barracks of a place to keep fifty charwomen happy for a month."

"All the same," Betty insisted, "I don't like him. He's not yuman. I've been tryin' to vamp him. And did he respond? Not a sossidge!"

Basil, not quite so amused as he wished it to appear, looked across the table at Nick.

"What are we to do with her?" he asked. "Trying to flirt with the servant now."

"Every woman," declaimed Betty in her best theatrical manner, "likes to demonstrate her power over men. But," she added in another tone, "I've known a piece of cheese to be more responsive. Well, I meanter say, some sorts of cheese *do* seem to meet you half-way, don't they?"

Having raised a smile, she rolled her eyes inimitably and laughed.

"Oo!" she continued, at a tangent, "when are we goin' to see the haunted room?"

"The inside—probably never," said Milly. "But what about the Mysterious Door, Nick?"

Nick considered.

"Well, there'll be plenty of light for some time. After dinner, if you like. As soon as Perringer's gone to ground."

Milly caught Nick's gaze and laughed.

"My dear," she said, "I believe you're half afraid of that man."

"No-o." Nick pretended to take the jibe seriously and he answered it as truthfully as he knew how. "He knows, of course, that I'm going to show you that door. He knows I'd have to explain—even if I hadn't already—that you mustn't touch the seal. All the same—it's a funny thing, but all the same I shouldn't like him to see me exhibiting it to you."

"He's a disapproving brute," remarked Basil. "Still, he's civil enough, and you've got to put up with him, so it isn't for us to complain. In the queer position he holds he might be a great deal worse."

"I'll tell you what." Nick glanced around at his three guests. "I've told him we'll be taking coffee in the drawing-room. When he's gone to ground he'll wait until we ring. After he's put the monkey-nuts—or whatever he's got by way of dessert—on the table we'll give you girls five minutes' grace in the drawing-room. Be ready to slip out when you hear us coming and we'll go straight on upstairs."

Thereafter they were a rather silent but by no means depressed little company of four. There were certain elements in the situation which lent themselves to childish—and quite delightful—make-believe. Each in his or her own way was conscious of living in a changed world of romance, of having crossed an undefinable frontier into a realm of mystery and even peril. They found themselves actually living in the kind of romance which hitherto had been accessible only at second-hand and to be found only between the covers of a book.

Perringer at last removed the cheese plates and laid the finger-bowls and the modest dessert.

"Coffee in about a quarter of an hour, sir?" he asked.

"Thank you, Perringer—yes. In the drawing-room. But wait until we ring."

"Yes, sir. Thank you, sir."

"Now, you young women." Basil's glance shifted from the door as it closed behind Perringer, and visited in turn his sister and his fiancee. "Have a banana each and buzz off. Perringer's all right now. He's gone to ground and he'll wait for the bell. Is that port he's decanted, Nick? I'll just investigate and tell you in a minute."

He investigated while Nick opened and held the door for the two girls.

"Port it is," he said a few moments later, "and if Providence had only allotted me a gentleman's palate—instead of a beer palate—I should be able to tell you how good it is. But I'm sure it's pretty good."

Nick took a sip and thought so too.

"Shouldn't be surprised," he said, "if we're necking the stuff of the gods and don't know it. Comes of having been poor at a critical period of one's education. Don't suppose I shall ever have a mind much above a pint of wallop."

They gave the girls five minutes' grace and then stepped out into the hall, talking noisily. Almost instantly the drawing-room door opened wide and the two girls slipped out. Nick turned immediately to the broad staircase and, with a word of apology, led the way.

"Here you are," he said presently, coming to a halt. "Behold mysterious door. Observe seal."

They all gazed with an air of half-humorous expectancy. Then the two girls bent in turn to examine the seal, Betty taking the place of Milly.

"Notice anything?" Milly asked in a whisper, as Betty withdrew.

"Such as?" said Betty, looking around her.

Milly stood away from the door and looked at her brother and Nick.

"You notice anything?" she inquired.

"Nothing much," her brother answered lightly. "Only a muffled groan or two and the rattling of a chain. But it's a bit early in the evening for the haunting to begin in earnest."

Milly touched his arm and laid her other hand on the arm of Nick.

"Come on," she said in a small voice, "let's go."

They had left the door half a dozen yards behind them when Basil addressed his sister in an undertone.

"What's wrong? Don't start getting jumpy. You didn't hear anything?"

"No."

"Then what's up?"

Milly was silent, and remained so until they had reached the drawing-room—where she began to laugh rather unnaturally and forestalled a question.

"Didn't hear anything," she said, "and of course didn't see anything. But—the ghost smokes very nice cigars."

Nick stared at her and laughed.

"What on earth do you mean?"

"Just what I said. Basil, you've often called me the Human Bloodhound. Directly you put your head inside a room your little sister knows whether you've had a glass of beer. Well, somebody inside that room—or just outside it—had been smoking a cigar. Recently too. And I should say a very nice cigar."

Nick laughed again.

"Never heard of ghosts smoking cigars," he remarked. "But if they do it explains why it's mostly the big houses that are haunted. Only the well-to-do can afford to keep a ghost in the way it's been accustomed."

Betty glanced at him unhappily.

"Now don't you get makin' fun of ghosts," she said. "If you do I shouldn't be surprised if you get a nasty jar before long."

She brought the gaze of three pairs of eyes upon herself. Milly's stare was almost incredulous.

"Why, *you* don't believe—"

"Oh, yes, I do." Suddenly and most unexpectedly they saw her struggling with emotion. "Seeing and hearing's believing, I reckon—'specially when there's two of you.

"I'll tell you now what happened. Four years ago it was, a few months after Dad died. Mum had sold up, and we went to live in a combined room in Brixton. It was before I joined the profession, and I wasn't hardly old enough to earn my own keep. Terribly poor we were.

"One night Mum was cryin' and nearly makin' me cry, when I looked up, and there was Dad standin' in the middle of the room. I don't know as I was frightened—not at the time. I was just surprised, and I heard myself call out, '*Look. Mum!*'

"And I heard Mum let out a squeal, and he smiled at her and spoke to both of us.

"I don't think we heard his words. It was a different kind of hearing to that. But we both agreed afterwards about what he said. He said he was happy and often nearer to us than we thought. And he told us to buck up and everything would come right. Then Mum started to say something and he was gone— like *that*. Might have been a candle she'd puffed out.

"But he was there all right. We *both* saw him. We *both* understood what he said to us. Mum and me couldn't talk about anything else for a long time after. We still talk about it when I see her. And it's as clear in the memories of both of us as it was the day after it happened."

Betty concluded in a tone of suppressed defiance, and for the moment her gaze, directed impartially on the others, was challenging and almost hostile. It was as if she were daring her hearers to utter a word of doubt, and she was so obviously sincere that there was nothing to be said. In the ensuing and uncomfortable silence each of her three hearers was thinking that she was about the last person in the world of whom they would have expected such a story.

"Well," said Milly at last, "we've all got souls—or so we're told—that go on living somewhere. I can imagine a ghost returning to comfort somebody in trouble. But rooms that are supposed to have been haunted for hundreds of years, and ghosts who scare people who've never been in any way connected with them—well, that's another story."

"What about that coffee?" Betty suggested.

Nick moved to an old-fashioned bell-pull beside the fireplace, and rang. After a short wait there was a tap on the door, and Perringer entered, bearing a tray.

"Thank you, Perringer," said Nick. "Mr. Hailsham was just remarking that a cigar would be rather nice. I'm inclined to agree. Are there any in the house?"

Perringer's face was all innocence.

"Yes, sir. I believe I could find you a few. My late master's supply, however, was getting rather low. I believe he had been about to write for a further consignment."

"Thank you. We shan't be robbing you?"

"Certainly not, sir. They are not my property. Besides, sir, I do not care for cigars. I have smoked them only in foreign countries where Virginian cigarettes are not easily obtainable. I will go and look in the library, sir."

Nick thanked him and lowered an eyelid as the door closed.

"What do we learn from that, dear brethren?" he said. "Would he have smoked a cigar while he was cooking and serving dinner?" said Milly. "We might have had the ash in our food."

"No." Nick was smiling quietly at his own thought "Smell of cigars hangs about a bit, you know. He probably popped up there earlier in the evening to see if we were snooping around and to make sure the seal was still all right."

Perringer returned shortly with a cigar-box on a salver.

"I am afraid, sir, that there are only eleven. I knew the supply was low."

He offered the box to Basil and then to Nick. Nick felt and selected one, and looked up to smile at the man.

"Sure we're not robbing you? I think you might have regarded a broken box of cigars as a perquisite."

"Oh, no, sir. I should not have touched them. It's hardly once in a year that I have the fancy for one."

He left them once more, and Nick looked around out of amused and knowing eyes.

"General verdict?" he suggested.

Basil laughed.

"Not so difficult. The excellent Perringer's been helping himself, but doesn't like to own up. Still less would he like to own that he'd been hanging about outside the sealed door long enough to leave the flavour of a Corona on the atmosphere. But what else strikes you as a trifle queer, my lad?"

"Well, what?" asked Nick.

"Cigars come out of box presumably opened in your uncle's lifetime. How long's he been dead? These cigars haven't been kept in silver-foil. Yet they're in excellent condition. At least, mine is. Well?"

Betty set down her coffee-cup with a little rattle.

"Here," she said, "chuck it! There's enough mysteries about this house without you makin' more. What does it matter about the silly old cigars? For the love of Mike let's be happy if we can. There's the old Johanna. I suppose it isn't in tune, but try to knock something out of it, Milly. That's to say if Nick don't mind."

"Rather not. I second it." Nick grinned at Milly and addressed her in a tone of parody. "Come and play your piece, Miss Hailsham."

He came and took her empty cup and saucer from her as she rose.

"Only," he continued, "play something lowbrow. Choruses we can all sing. I believe this old vault of a house has been getting on all our nerves already. Let's change the atmosphere a bit." The next half-hour was an almost unbroken period of music and song. It was interrupted at last by a tap on the door. Betty broke off, with a choked laugh and a hand over her mouth, to whisper:

"Blimey! His nibs has come to tell us to put a sock in it!"

Perringer indeed appeared in the doorway with his normal air of austerity.

"Yes?" said Nick.

"Excuse me, sir. I have come to ask if there is anything else that you may require to-night."

Nick understood the broad hint. Perringer wished to retire early, or at least to feel that the rest of the night was his own.

"No, I don't think so. Drinks in the dining-room if required? All right, then, good night. Oh, by the way, I suppose it's some time since anybody made a noise in this house? You could hear us, of course. I hope it didn't strike you as unseemly."

Next moment he was sorry he had spoken. Perringer might so easily misunderstand the last remark, the irony of which was directed upon the house and not upon the man. But Perringer smiled.

"Indeed, no, sir. We—that is to say I—I have been enjoying it very much."

He went. Basil cast a sardonic glance at the closing door.

"Now," he said, "why did he say *We*—as if there was more than one of him—and then correct himself?"

Betty shot him a vitriolic look.

"There you go again! Enough to drive anyone barmy. Goin' to make a mystery out of *that* now, I s'pose. Very likely the man's daft and thinks he's the King of Constantinople. Or else he imagines he's goin' to have a baby."

CHAPTER VIII
DR. BLIGH TALKS

It was Thursday morning. Nick, not always the most energetic of the four during the first hours of the day, happened on this occasion to be first down the stairs. The gong had started to thunder as he left his room, and he found all ready in the small morning room which they used for breakfast.

But he did not immediately sit down. The sunlit windows invited his gaze, and no sooner had his gaze responded than his attention was diverted to something less abstract than the weather. A postman was trudging sturdily in the direction of the front door.

For the past two or three days Nick had been awaiting, rather restlessly, the coming of letters, so he walked out and into the outer hall to intercept the postman. There was no letter-box in the massive door, but Perringer, it seemed, had already unfastened it to let in the air, and in closing it again he had slipped only one bolt. Nick was thus enabled to open the door before the postman had time to reach the bell, and the man—uttering a cheerful "Good morning, sir!"— unburdened himself of a small percentage of his load without an instant's delay.

All the letters save one were addressed to Nick. He glanced at the envelopes in turn, frowned over one of them and then gave a second glance at the cover of the letter addressed to Perringer. This last he left on a corner of a table in the inner hall, and as Perringer suddenly appeared, called out to him:

"'Morning, Perringer. Letter for you."

Perringer said nothing beyond formal thanks, but Nick, in spite of sudden preoccupation, fancied that he looked mildly displeased. The fleeting impression passed to return later, when he had leisure to think, and meanwhile he sat down and began to slit open envelopes.
It often happens when one has been expecting various letters for some time that they all arrive by the same post. And when they are satisfactory letters they make a good beginning for the day. One of them, which Nick grinned over, contained a pink slip of paper which—when he had written his name on the back—would be worth quite an appreciable amount of money.

He was still reading when Basil followed the two girls into the room. It seemed that they had met on the floor above, and had been chatting at the head of the staircase before coming down. Nick exchanged good mornings, then muttered an apology and went on reading.

"Remembered your existence at last, have they?" said Basil when Nick looked up at him and grinned.

"Not half! Letter from the Gallant Soldier. And cheque. Yes, cheque, my boy. Just a bit to go on with in case I'm short. Very soon, it seems, I'm going to get balance due—plus, probably, an account about as long as the Magna Charta. Very thoughtful, though, to send me this."

Basil crossed over to inspect dishes on the sideboard.

"Anything about us?" he inquired with his back turned.

"Plenty. Matthews must have dropped him a line. Or Perringer. Or both. *Quite* against my late dear uncle s wishes— having you here. However, judging by the tone, he feels he can't do anything about it. Hopes for my sake that the expressed conditions will be complied with to the letter. No expressed threat, but there's a sinister smell to the ink. Ominous hint, too, about making my personal acquaintance in the near future. That means that he is going to burst upon us when least expected."

"Well, you won't mind that, will you?" said Milly. "I think when you've seen each other it will make things easier for both of you."

"And when he's seen you he'll know that everything here, after all, is just as uncle would have liked."

"'Cept for me," said Betty. "I'm what they call an acquired taste. Shall I make him take me on his knee? I'm rather good with old gentlemen—straight I am."

"Old Matthews' love-letter is pitched in much the same terms.

He pretends to be afraid that I'm in danger of queering the will. Wants to see me soon to have a business chat. Think I'll get him over to lunch some day. Shall I?"

"Don't ask us." Basil's tone was airy. "*You're* the boss. Heard from the County, by the way? Cricket, I mean."

"Yes. Awfully decent letter. Not a word of reproach. I'd written, of course, explaining how things were. But they want to know if I can play in two or three matches from which I could get back here every night. Well, we're not so far out of London, and there's games at Lord's, Leyton and the Oval yet."

"You'll want a flivver for that," said Betty.

Nick stared at her and laughed.

"Taken the words out of my mouth, bless her!" he said. "Directly I saw that cheque I had a vision of a packet of trouble on four wheels. Have to go easy at first, though, until cheque's big brother comes along. Pick up something second-hand for the present."

Milly looked round at him at once.

"Somebody in the village has a Morris for sale. Bargain. Three years old. Perfect running order."

"How do you know?" her brother inquired. "Had a run in it?"

"That's what it said. There's a notice on a post card stuck up in the post-office window—alongside five shillings reward for a semi-Persian, male, with half an ear missing."

Nick, with a little money to burn, and ready to buy the first second-hand car he saw, grew brighter still.

"Good. Well, I've got to go down the village this morning. I'll look in and ask about it."

Shortly before eleven o'clock Nick was standing outside the shop-cum-post-office. The notice, written in an educated hand, was still there. Inside, the woman behind the counter gave him the required information.

"Oh, yes. That's Dr. Bligh's car. I'm sure you'd find it in good order. But he told me he'd got two cars and hardly room for one, let alone both. I should think you'd just catch him if you go along now. It's on the other side of the road, only about fifty yards down. You'll see his plate outside."

Nick went. A maid ushered him into a reception-room, and, without asking his name, departed to find her master.

Dr. Bligh appeared to be young, breezy, broad-shouldered and of athletic carriage.

"Oh, the car?" he said. "You can see it now, if you like. Or I'll tell you what. I've got to run out a couple of miles with a bottle of medicine. I can take you along in her. You—er— don't live near here, do you?"

Nick smiled.

"Well, yes. Since a few days. The Manor."

The young doctor raised his eyes slowly and his look became a stare.

"You're not Mr. Rockwell, are you?"

"Yes. And glad to make your acquaintance. Rather glad of the excuse for calling. I think you knew my late uncle."

The young doctor moved towards a chair.

"Sit down, won't you, Mr. Rockwell. I am very glad to meet you. We—my wife and I—were going to call in a day or so. My wife, because I believe you have ladies with you. Your sisters, are they not? You are not married, are you?"

"No. They're visitors—permanent visitors, I hope. An old friend of mine and his sister and an old friend of theirs." He laughed. "I think you may tell Mrs. Bligh that we're quite respectable, although of course there will be a lot of talk."

Bligh laughed.

"You bet there will! Well, it *is* a bit Arcadian, isn't it? But I don't blame you. Who could have expected a young man to live in a place like that by himself?"

"My late uncle seemed to expect it. So did Perringer. So did his lawyers and executors and old Uncle Tom Cobleigh and all. But I'm not having any if I can help it."

The young doctor nodded and sat silent with an air of expectancy for a minute or two.

"Well?" he said at last. "Can I help you in any way? Anything I can do? Anything I can tell you? Anything you can tell *me*—in strict confidence, of course?"

"Well," said Nick, "first of all I'd like to know if my late uncle were mad."

It was a blunt question, and it was as bluntly answered.

"Oh, undoubtedly," said Bligh cheerfully. "All right, you needn't get hot and bothered. I'm not suggesting that he was so mad that his will could be set aside. There are degrees of insanity, you know. You're slightly mad. I'm slightly mad. That fellow Perringer is just more than slightly mad. And your late uncle—as sensible a man to talk to as ever I met—was just about one more degree unbalanced. Sorry, but you asked for it."

"That's all right," laughed Nick, knowing that he was going to like Dr. Bligh. "What sort of madness would you call it?" Bligh passed over a box of cigarettes.

"Now, my dear sir," he laughed, "you're not going to nail me to anything. I'm a G.P.. I am—not a specialist in diseases of the brain. I might have called it religious mania, but there are one or two factors that negative the theory. A number of mild manias accumulate into a lump of Something.

"Let me try to assess him by what I know of his life. He was a rich bachelor. I am not suggesting abnormality because he remained a bachelor. From something he once hinted to me I believe he once thought of marriage and was disappointed. There are men who don't put themselves in the way of that sort of disappointment twice. And possibly it was that disappointment which unbalanced him.

"He was a deeply religious man. Well, I'm a Christian, and I don't suggest that religious people are mad. But when a man goes out and tries to reform the morals of a South American Republic—well, I ask you!"

Nick had heard and read sufficient of Spanish America to cause him to laugh.

"That what he did?"

"Ask old Perringer! And here's an odd thing. Your late uncle was conventionally religious—a great church-goer here— while his chosen companion on all his travels, and afterwards, proves to be an atheist. Perringer, I mean. I know, because Perringer said so at the inquest. He was excused the oath and allowed to make an affirmation.

"Well, to continue. Sir Anthony buys the old house here and settles down. There's a silly story about it being haunted. Of course, Sir Anthony immediately sees the ghost, and advertises it pretty generally by sealing up that room. That's another straw in the wind."
Nick looked across at Dr. Bligh.

"You don't believe in ghosts, then?" he asked, smiling.

"I rather annoyed Sir Anthony by telling him that if he would show me his ghost I should be happy to remove its appendix. Now don't be annoyed. Weigh all you may know already, and all that I am telling you, against the possibility of Sir Anthony— nice man and true gentleman as he was—being mentally normal."

"Well," Nick grunted, "putting it in that way "

"Oh, but you haven't heard the worst yet. This is in the strictest confidence. I mean that it didn't come out at the inquest. Dr. Wooding of Arunford did the P.M., and saw no reason to tell the court what I'm going to tell you, so out of delicacy he didn't. But he told me, and I think perhaps you ought to know."

Nick began to fidget.

"Well?" he asked nervously.

"Well, then—his body was dirty and he was a great deal more than half starved."

Nick started and uttered a short laugh of sheer amazement.

"What!"

"That is a fact. It amazed me when I heard it. I knew your uncle as well as he allowed anybody round here to know him, but I never attended him. He was one of the sort that think they can do without doctors. Well, what do you make of things now?"

"Phew!" Nick uttered a soft whistle. "That's amazing! Are you—er—are you really sure?"

"Oh, yes. Wooding wouldn't—and besides it helps to fit the puzzle together. Religious mania. Some of the saints of the Middle Ages starved themselves and dodged the bath-tap as forms of penance. Well, that's all in the way of kinks, I think. All that I know of, I mean. Perringer may know of others."

"Ah, Perringer!" said Nick. "What do you make of that fish?"

"Just what I was going to ask you. Been with your uncle for years and over half the world with him. I understand. Perfect servant of his kind—or at least your uncle seemed to find him so. You may see another side of him."

Nick laughed.

"He's not altogether a servant to me: he's also a kind of policeman. I might like him better if it weren't for that. According to the terms of the will I can't get rid of him—at least, not without leave of the trustees. D'you know what I believe. I haven't read the will through, but I shouldn't be surprised if Perringer can't get rid of *me*. I've a pretty strong idea that he's been left some sort of income for so long as he remains in my service, and he forfeits if he gives me notice." The young doctor shrugged and smiled.

"Binding you together in a kind of unwilling alliance. Well, that would be another straw in the wind. Symptomatic of another kind of mania. And the trouble is that if either you or he took any legal steps to set part of that will aside the whole balloon might burst."

"Quite! If a man wants to benefit at all by a will he'd be a fool to attempt any legal steps on the assumption that the man who made it was Bats. Chancery's waiting with its mouth wide open for titbits of that sort. Well. Dr. Bligh, thank you very much for all you've been able to tell me." Bligh detected something like a hint in that last remark, and made a gesture which motioned Nick towards the door.

"Not at all. If you're ever in any difficulty in which you think I might be useful—if I can help you in any way—I should be glad if you would let me know. Meanwhile I am sure my wife will unload some cards on your good ladies—which may silence the tongue which talketh evil. And now I suppose you would like to try the car?"

The car proved to be in perfect running order and it had just been decarbonized. It was Nick's— and at a very moderate price—before the morning was over. He drove it back, and it proved a welcome distraction for Basil and Milly, both of whom could drive. They tried it out in turn between the house and the lodge gates, having for a passenger Betty—who was humorously pessimistic about strange cars bought of strange doctors.

It was thus that they were all at the luncheon table, and Perringer safely out of earshot, when Nick told his companions the result of his inquiries. It was Betty who, with less reserve than the others, expressed in her own language the opinion of all.

"There you are, my dear," she said to Nick. "He was Bats. Only, of course, as the doctor said, it doesn't do to say so. Don't think I'm runnin' your fam'ly down, or anything like that, Nicodemus. Dessay he was all right before he came to live here. It's this house that did it on him—this dreadful old vault of a house with its ghosts all under locks and keys which aren't any good with ghosts. We'll all be Bats if we stay here long enough."

"Oh, shut up!" said Milly, aware that Betty was only half serious.

Betty pulled a dreadful, imbecile face and rolled her eyes.

"But we will. 'Member that bit Juliet has to say when she's thinkin' about what a jolly time she's goin' to have when she wakes up in the vault? Shall I not play with my forefathers' joints? Or pluck the mangled Tybalt from his shroud?' I had to do that bit once at a dramatic class: that's how I know it. Well, we'll all have gone that way before we're through."

Nick and Basil had cause to remember her words before many hours were past.

CHAPTER IX
THE SOMNAMBULIST

Perringer was removing the sweet plates from the luncheon table when he coughed and spoke apologetically to Nick.

"Excuse me, sir. We were talking of revolvers and revolver practice the other day. I have cartridges and two spare weapons, and I have made some serviceable targets. There is a bank at the end of the kitchen garden where a target could be set with safety—whenever you, sir, and Mr. Hailsham would care to try a shot."

"After lunch?" said Nick, looking around. "Right! You come, too, Perringer."

And after lunch he accompanied them, bringing three automatics and some cardboard targets. These were of about the size used on a miniature rifle-range, and had been made with the aid of compasses, a paint-brush and a lavish quantity of black ink.

Perringer halted his party a dozen yards from the bank, set one of the targets and loaded the weapons.

"These, gentlemen," he said, "are an American pattern, and they work on a hair-trigger. You don't take two pressures as you do with a rifle. You will probably find a slight kick upward and j to the right, and it is a good plan, gentlemen, to learn the little ways of your gun. Once you are on the bull, gentlemen, you ought to be able to stay on it, or near it." lie handed one of the squat, heavy little firearms to Nick and another to Basil.

"It would be better, sir," he added, addressing himself to Nick, "if each of you gentlemen kept to his own weapon. Know your gun is a good proverb. Are you taking first shot, sir? Then may I show you? Don't point your weapon by bringing it down to shoulder-level with a jerk—as I fear they do on the stage. It is less dramatic but more effective, sir, if you raise it from your side, looking down arm and hand and barrel until you are on the bull."

"You're a sardonic devil, Perringer," Nick laughed, and in response to a glance from Basil he prepared to take first shot.

He fired six times and landed only two shots on the target. "Rotten," said Basil, and, when his turn came, hit the target only once. "Damn' sight worse," he remarked, grinning ruefully. Perringer, however, remarked that it was not so bad. "Having regard, sir, for the fact that the target is smaller than a man's head. It should be remembered, however, that a living target is different and is seldom so obliging as to remain entirely still."

"You have a go now," said Nick.

Perringer fired six shots—rapidly and without much apparent care. The first was low down on the edge of the target, the next five were all in or touching upon the bull. A crown piece would have covered them.

"Gee!" said Basil. "The man's a trick shot."

"Hardly that, sir. Perhaps a little above the average. But then I have had a great deal of practice."

A gleam of humour came into Nick's eyes.

"Ever shot a man, Perringer?"

"Sir," said Perringer with enormous dignity, "if that were put to me in the House of Commons I should say, with great respect, that I required notice of the question. And if I were asked the same question in a court of law I should answer, with equal respect, that no man is required to commit himself."

"And if I were the Judge," said Basil, with a glance at Nick which belied the deep gravity of his tone, "I should say: 'A very good answer—I will make a note of it.'"

Perringer listened without smiling and without a ruffle. It was, as Nick said afterwards, like trying to pull the leg of Mr. Gladstone's statue. Then the man addressed himself once more to Nick.

"With your permission, sir, I will leave with you two gentlemen a weapon each and a box of ammunition. Also the targets, which can be repaired with stamp-paper. If I may say it, gentlemen, I should like to repeat my former remark about not firing unless it is urgent and in self-defence. In England you may not shoot even a burglar unless your own life is in peril. There was a case, I believe, of a respectable householder who served twelve months for manslaughter, having fatally wounded a man who broke into his premises."

They promised Perringer, however lightly, to bear his advice in mind, and as they were turning back towards the house Nick found something more to say to him.

"I suppose you've noticed that we've just got a car? Do you think my uncle would have disapproved?"

Once more the irony splintered on Perringer's armour.

"On the contrary, sir. He would have approved it, I am sure, so long as you kept it immobilized—if that is the word—at night. The doctor's car, if I am not mistaken, sir?"

"Yes. I made his acquaintance this morning—and learned one or two strange things from him. What's all this about my late uncle having starved himself almost to death?"

Perringer started and half turned.

"That, sir," he said, "is something which I shall never understand. I had difficulty in believing it when Dr. Wooding spoke to me privately. I can still hardly believe it. Mind you, sir, bachelor gentlemen are notorious for getting into careless ways, especially when they have to fend for themselves. But no mother could have taken better care of her child than I took of him. I prepared his meals with the greatest care, I took away the empty plates and dishes. That is all that I can say. I can only suggest that he must have secreted most of the food and disposed of it without my knowing."

Nick uttered a sudden laugh. It would take little now to send him into a fit of bewildered merriment.

"But why the devil should he do that?"

Perringer seemed to give the question deep consideration—as if it had never occurred to him to ponder it before.

"He was, sir," the man muttered, "in some respects a kind of saint. And the saints of other days"

"Quite," agreed Nick. They had reached the outside of the house by now and had paused on the terrace. "Exactly what Dr. Bligh was saying. But you know, Perringer, the mediaeval holy men didn't go barging around the world with guns in their hip-pockets."

"Did they not, sir? Perhaps they had to deal with another kind of sinners. And if I may venture to remind you, sir, St. Peter himself—if we are to credit the story—carried a sword and used it. I his, sir, was painfully apparent to the Servant of the: High Priest—when he began to search around the Garden for his ear."

Nick laughed again, this time with unaffected amusement.

"You win, Perringer," he said. "If we ever joined the same debating society I should try to be on your side. Thanks for the gun. I think I'll keep it in my bedroom."

"It would be best there at night," Perringer agreed, "where you can put your hand on it at a moment's notice, sir."

The rest of the day and—so far as Nick and Basil were concerned—the ensuing night passed uneventfully. But Nick, who was down first on the following morning, was shortly afterwards confronted by a clouded face—which was Betty's.

"'Morning, duck," she said briefly and hurriedly. "Here, I'm glad I've got you alone for a minute. Want to talk to you. Something a bit serious."

"Serious!" he repeated.

"All right. Don't get the breeze. Nothing serious has happened yet. But something might. I don't know whether we ought to tell her—or whether we ought to tell her brother first. It's Milly. She walks in her sleep."

"Milly! Oh, yes, I know she used to as a kid. She and Basil were talking about it the other day. What's wrong? She hasn't been—"

"She has." Betty turned away in the direction of the window and stood frowning. "Not a safe thing to do at the best of times—or in the best of houses. And in this creepy old mouseolinoleum, with you three fellers talkin' about whether it's right or wrong to shoot on sight, it don't seem good enough. Of course I know you'd act like a perfect gentleman. After you'd put a bullet through her you'd drop on one knee beside her and say, 'Pray, forgive me, Milly. I'm most fraightfully sorray. I mistook you for a burglar or else a ghost—reahlly I did.' But it doesn't seem hardly good enough."

"Well, tell me what happened," said Nick, grinning in spite of himself.

"Oh, sometime during the night something woke me. Can't say what it was. May have been Milly rustlin' out of the room. Anyhow, by the time I was wide awake and lookin' around I was all alone in the room. Her bed was empty.

"Well, I didn't think much of that at first, but as I waited I grew a bit anxious. So after a while I got up and nipped down the passage. Nobody in the bathroom-place and the door standin' half open. That flummoxed me a bit. Didn't know whether I ought to call you or Basilco, but I decided to wait a bit. Milly would be mad if there turned out to be no reason. So I went back and got into bed and waited.

"After a few minutes I heard a sound outside. Then in she come—like Lady Macbeth. I didn't see what it was at first, and asked her wherever had she been. She didn't answer, although she was looking straight at me. Might have been a duchess handin' a polite raspberry to some lad who'd tried to get fresh with her. Then I cottoned to what it was.

"She got into bed somehow head first, kind of sorted herself out like a snake, gave a sigh as if she'd just swallowed a quart of iced lager, and went on sleeping like Muwer's Little Luv. That's all, duck. I haven't said a word to her about it yet. Thought I'd better get a spot of wisdom from old man Solomon before opening my head."

Nick nodded gravely several times.

"Yes, it's awkward. Might scare her to remind her. We'll see what Basil has to say. If she did that sort of thing as a kid they probably had some way of stopping her."

Betty grimaced.

"Shovin' a tanner's worth of jellied eels down her neck wouldn't be bad," she remarked. "But they say it's dangerous to wake them with a shock. Still, they say it's a shock if you wake them anyhow. And a bigger shock still, I dare say, if they fall out of a third-storey window. So what are you to do?"

It was impossible to ask Basil's advice on the subject forthwith, for when he appeared he entered the room on Milly's heels. Milly looked tired and rather jaded—as if, Nick thought, her night's rest had done her little good. She caught herself yawning, covered her mouth quickly, and laughed.

"Didn't you sleep well?" Nick inquired.

"Yes, I think so. But I had a beast of a dream."

Betty and Nick exchanged glances.

"Pastry at night," Nick said lightly. "Your own make, too—with old Perringer, who thinks he knows everything, hopping about on one leg and dying to show you how. What did you dream?"

Milly sat down and helped herself to tea.

"The Sealed Room. I dreamed I had to go there for something or other, and in my dream I knew that there was somebody in that room. I found myself standing outside the door, frightened to death, but I had to go on. Promising start for a nightmare, wasn't it?"

"Well, go on. Did you go in, or did Bogie Man come out?"

"Neither. It's rather tame to tell, but it was pretty beastly all the same. I knocked. No, the door didn't fly open and I didn't hear any hellish shrieks. But a voice answered me. A man's voice. An educated voice. Quite a nice voice. It said something like this: '*Yes, what is it? What's happened? And how many times must I tell you not to come here at night? Why didn't you go the other way?*' "

"Quite sensible words in a way, except of course that they didn't apply to me. All the same they scared me to death. I got the real nightmare then. The galloping in the ears and all that. And then I suppose I dropped off into ordinary sleep." Nick was careful to avoid Betty's gaze.

"Well, I'm glad the ghost didn't come out and chivvy you with a carving-knife. You'd better take his tip. Don't visit him any more in dreams."

"It was beastly." Milly shivered. "I wonder what he meant, though. Why didn't I go the other way? What other way?"

Her brother made an impatient face at her.

"Don't be such a mutt! As if the voices you hear in dreams ever say anything sensible."

Betty winked at two of her three companions, and proceeded to play the part which might have been expected of her.

"Might mean something," she said. "I'll look it up. I got a dream-book somewhere. Given away as an advertisement for somebody's do-me-good. And there's a calendar, and the multiplication table, and the dates of the kings and queens of England all mixed up with it."

Thus she swerved around a dangerous corner, carrying Nick with her: but he was far from happy. And shortly after breakfast Milly, by leaving the other three, gave them the opportunity to discuss her.

"Tell Basil," said Nick shortly.

Betty did so, and was interrupted several times by exclamations. "Yes," said Basil at last, "I know she did that sort of thing occasionally as a kid. When she'd got something on her mind—lessons or something of that sort, you know. We were wondering how to break her, and then she seemed to break herself. It's a trifle awkward. Dangerous, too. Good idea might be to drop a few tacks on the floor of your room."

"Thank you!" said Betty, and then suddenly changed her tone. "Look here, Basilco, there's one question I'd like answered, and I guess Nicodemus would like to hear it answered too. When she walked in her sleep—*did she go to that sealed door or didn't she?*"

Basil hesitated, seeing whither he was being led.

"I think she probably did," he muttered, seeing she'd got it on her mind."

"Then did she dream she heard that voice—or—or—*did she really hear it?*"

CHAPTER X
IMPORTANT VISITOR

The suggestion, framed as a query and uttered in a tone which could hardly be ignored, conduced to a moment or two of the most uncomfortable sort of silences. It was as if some unforgivable word had been shouted in the presence of the refined and hypersensitive. On those occasions it is the custom for everybody to sit tight, trying to look as if they had not heard, and praying that the power of speech may return to somebody else.

Basil at last approached Betty, threw an arm around her shoulders and drew her close against his side in a little hug.

"Now, old girl," he said, "don't you start trying to give everybody the jims. What on earth's the use of taking notice of dreams? Other people's dreams at that. She heard it when she was asleep, didn't she? Ergo—as they say in the classics—she dreamed it. Q.E.D."

Betty allowed her head to touch his shoulder.

"You can hear real voices through a dream," she said. "You know that. Sometimes they start the dream going another way. What do you say, Nick?"

"Tell you the truth," Nick answered, "I'm not a bit happy about the whole business. None of us are. What's the use of any of us pretending? I had an eye on Milly, poor girl, while she was trying to peck a bit of breakfast, and I think I'm like both of you. I think she did go to that door in her sleep, and I think she heard something which got through to her normal consciousness and partly woke her. Perhaps a rat stirred inside the room—there are plenty of rats here—or perhaps she heard a cat squawking in the grounds. Anything like that.

"As for ghosts—well, Basil, old lad, you and I don't believe in them. The tale Betty told us about her father—well, that's rather on a different footing. I don't believe in the kind of ghosts you meet in Christmas numbers of the magazines.

"Now the ghost that's supposed to haunt that room is the supernatural bit of a gentleman who died in sixteen-ninety-something. Are the words which Milly heard typical of a man of that period? Of course they're not. I've read some of the State Trials covering that time, where the exact conversations of ordinary people arc reported. They didn't say Gadzooks and Oddsbodikins and stuff of that sort, but their speech wasn't quite the same as ours. Can't imagine one of 'em saying, "How many times must I tell you not to come here at night?'

"'Nother thing, my chicks. The ghost ought to have known that it was the first time he'd addressed Milly, yet he adopted that I've-told-you-twenty-times sort of tone. *That* doesn't make much sense, does it? Couldn't be much of a ghost if he mistook her for somebody else. They can walk through doors—or the best sort can—so I suppose they can see through them. Now let's see where we are. Seventeenth-century ghost sees Milly through door, addresses her in ordinary modern English, and wants to know why she's done something which he's repeatedly told her not to do—while all the time he ought to know that he's never spoken to her before. No, no, no, it doesn't make sense."

"Oh, of course it was part of Milly's dream," grunted Basil. "We all know that."

"Yes," Nick agreed. "Yes, probably. But, just to give us all the creeps, suppose it wasn't? We don't know what's in that room all the time, and we don't know what may be in it some of the time. Suppose my very eccentric relative had some secret which he didn't propose to unload on the world just yet awhile? Suppose that's where he kept it, and where it still is? Suppose Perringer knows all—or a great deal—about it? Well?"

Basil shrugged.

"But taking the line that somebody was in that room and that Milly actually heard a human voice, whose voice could it have been?"

Nick was in the act of lighting a cigarette, and his sudden chuckle brought a little cloud of smoke about his face.

"Oh, that's an easy one. Nine-tenths asleep she wouldn't have recognized it—from the other side of that thick door. Also she'd never before heard it speak in that querulous tone. Perringer's voice, my sweet children."

Basil frowned and shook his head.

"Then how the devil did Perringer get in there?" he demanded.

"Not such an easy one. But not a complete floorer. How did Father Christmas come when he brought you the rocking-horse? Nice wide chimneys here—and that one probably swept clean in preparation. Failing that, there may be some other way into the room. Might easily be secret passages in a house as old as this. Those are two possibilities that I can think of."

Basil snorted, clenched his fist and brought it down on his left palm.

"Right! Say it was Perringer. Say Perringer has a way of getting in and out of that room. It isn't remotely likely, but it's not quite impossible. Well? Who did Perringer think had come to knock on the door?"

Nick had been expecting the question in its turn and had the answer pat.

"Oh, friend of his. Somebody from outside. Accomplice might be the right word for all I know. Listen. Here's my theory. It may be all wrong, but at least it's a theory of sorts. It makes sense and fits in places.

"Suppose my uncle had been engaged on some secret life work in that room, and Perringer enjoyed his complete confidence. Naturally if he died before it was complete he'd want Perringer lo finish it for him. But it wouldn't and couldn't be secret long if I and my friends had the complete run of the house, including that room.

"Why didn't my uncle leave everything to Perringer so that he could work undisturbed? Well, Perringer, however much my uncle may have liked and trusted him, was only a servant. Blood's thicker than water. He wanted some relative to have his house and the bulk of his cash, although I don't know why he picked on me. Perhaps he was fond of cricket or something. Well, what about it? How do you like the theory so far as it goes?" Basil smiled uncertainly.

"Well, old man, I suppose it fits where it touches. It's an idea of sorts. But all the same it's just wild guess-work, isn't it?"

"What do you say, Betty?"

Betty nibbled at a fingernail.

"May be guess-work," she said, "but it's a reasonable sort of idea. I mean, it's a bit more cheerful to believe that it's something like that than to think there's a roomful of ghosts and horrors. Even if it's not the right idea the truth may be something just as simple—if only we knew it."

"Just so. Let's get away from the ghosts. Wild guess-work is it? Well, I'll show you two bits of the jigsaw puzzle that fit beautifully.

"Say Perringer's up to something in that room and he's afraid of interference from outside. That would account for his arming us, and the pistol practice, wouldn't it? And say he has an occasional surreptitious visitor who is in his confidence and helps him in some way. That would account for his anxiety about our shooting any supposed burglar on sight. Those two bits of the puzzle fit perfectly, I think."

Betty's face cleared and she smiled and clapped her hands lightly and almost silently.

"Sure they do. There's brains! Thank you, Sherlock. Your methods amaze me. Straight, though, I'm on your side. I'd like to lay it was Perringer in that room last night, and the next thing is to find out how he gets in and out. Then you can get in and learn the whole bag of tricks without upsetting the jolly old will. Not me, though! Might find the dead bodies of some of your | uncle's wives. I played in *Bluebeard* once."

For that occasion nobody seemed to be listening to Betty's cheerful prattle, but the two men let her finish without interruption. Then Basil spoke, turning his gaze on Nick.

"More I think of your idea," he said, "the better I like it— although it suggests a spot of danger. Anyhow, if you're right, the danger—if any—is from outside. It would be pretty uncomfortable if we couldn't trust Perringer."

Betty had a word to say there.

"What's pretty uncomfortable," she said, "is the idea that Perringer can't trust *us*—or *you*, rather, Nick. Still, it's nice to think the old glue-pot isn't up to anything shady. Rather sticky if you found out that he was a traitor within the gates. Because even if you found him out you couldn't chuck him out on his ear without leave from those two blokes who're holding your uncle's L.S.D. And they, if you don't mind me sayin' so, are probably daft—or they wouldn't have been buddies of his. Everybody, seems to me, is daft in this damn' outfit."

"Except you, Betty darling," said Basil.

Betty retorted in a colourless voice that she was not so sure, that she was looking around for a little clean straw to twine in her hair, and that she would probably end like Ophelia in a nice cosy duck-pond.

"Tell you what." said Nick suddenly, "let's get out somewhere right now. Get away from it all for a day. We've got the new old—or the old new—bus. Anyhow, I've got to get some tennis stuff. There's a lawn good enough for playing on straight away. Only needs marking. I wonder if any of the gardeners know how to mark a court."

"The gardeners?" Betty caught at the word. "Yes, I've spotted one or two pretendin' to work. Where do they come from?"

"There's three of them," said Nick, "but I don't think any of them live very close handy. Anyhow, they all come on bikes. I suppose Matthews has been paying them up to now. I wonder how much I'm expected to give 'em. Perringer of course would know. Well, look here, let's all breeze over in the flivver to Arunford, get some lunch there and do a day's shopping. Tell our august and, I hope, faithful servitor that we shan't be back before dinner."

The proposal was seconded and carried. Milly's vote was taken for granted, and when she returned to the room a minute later—having already dressed to go out—she received the suggestion with enthusiasm.

Perringer was summoned and informed. His manner, as he entered the room and then inclined a deferential ear to listen, was courteous and unperturbed as ever. Yet all the four who saw and heard him were vaguely aware that all was not well with him. Something had happened to put him out of humour, and the same thought leaped simultaneously to three minds. The man, no doubt, was wondering which of the four had knocked on the sealed door during the night, what had been the result of the inevitable discussion, and why the affair was not mentioned to him. Doubtless too he was wondering if his voice had been recognized, although, Nick thought, he need have no doubts on that score—for who but himself could have been inside that room? It was with a secret and joyous sense of mystifying a maker of mysteries that Nick kept the man for a minute or two on tenterhooks. Doubtless, Nick thought, he had some story or a total denial on the tip of his tongue and was more puzzled than relieved because he was not given the occasion to utter it.

"Back to dinner, sir?" he said urbanely, drops shining on his forehead. "Yes, sir. Very good, sir." And as soon as he was gone from the room Nick threw an arm around Basil's shoulder and began helplessly to laugh.

The attractions of Arunford on an ordinary weekday were soon exhausted. It was too small, and not far enough from London, to be a good shopping centre. But shops there were, and good hotels and garages, and the High Street which stood on the main London road was busy with traffic. The sight of the little town in summer sunlight was cheering to the eyes of the two young men and the two girls. All four were conscious of a sensation—which none could have described—of returning to workaday modern England not merely from another age but from another world.

A short interview with Matthews was productive of a letter, which Nick took to the bank which was almost next door. After a few words with a most agreeable manager he opened an account by paying in the largest cheque he had ever handled, against which—through the sponsorship of Matthews—he was allowed immediately to draw. He rejoined the rest of the party outside, feeling rich and almost carefree, and unobtrusively slipped a thickish wad of folded paper into Basil's hand.

"Month's doin's in advance," he muttered. "Yours and the girls'. They may want to do some shopping. Hope it's enough."

Basil thanked him shortly, jerkily and sheepishly. He stowed the notes away without looking at them. But this act of delicacy had sooner or later to be annulled by inspection, and a little later in the morning he sidled up to Nick with a deprecatory air which I was not entirely hypocritical.

"I say, you know, Nick, we can't possibly take all this."

"Oh, rot! You all want clothes. Apart from the climate there's a law about that, I believe. And anyhow, my dear chap, I'm getting a darn sight more for staying in that frightful house—and I don't suppose I could stick it if it weren't for you three." They found a sports outfitters' which actually had a tennis net in stock, and was also able to supply balls of a famous make and four rather inferior but still quite serviceable racquets. By lunch-time the car was already somewhat overloaded.

Save for one or two trifles which could be easily and quickly acquired, the four had completed their shopping by the time they sat down to lunch, and the prospect of the afternoon loomed up not quite so attractively. There were two cinemas due to open at three o'clock, but they advertised ancient and familiar films. Nor was there much fun in the prospect of aimless driving in a car which was now uncomfortably full. Rather prematurely, it seemed, they were threatened with that ennui which corrodes the pleasures of the Idle Rich.

They sat long over lunch, and at last went out to see the town, leaving the car garaged at the hotel.

Arunford was neither modern nor ugly, but it contained nothing outstanding to attract an eye for beauty, nor did it offer much to the historian and archaeologist. Before departing for Mardstone Manor they had spent some days within its boundaries and seen all that it had to show to the superficial gaze. The girls' talk became listless and desultory. After a while Basil, glancing at Nick, saw that in his eye which encouraged him to make a suggestion.

"Not much to do here," he said. "What about getting back? Get the net up and mark the court."

"That's odd. I was thinking just the same thing. Funny—when this morning we were so damned glad to get away from the place. Only one snag, but I don't suppose it matters."

"Yes?"

"Nothing. Only I told Perringer that we wouldn't be back until dinner. He'll feel a bit let down if we go trooping back now."

"Not he. Besides, if he takes an afternoon nap he can go on taking it. Girls can get tea. I can give them a hand, but there's nothing to do except boil a kettle and sling a few things on a tray."

"All right," said Nick doubtfully, "only I don't want Perringer to think that we've swooped back suddenly to take him by surprise."

"Let him think it." Basil's tone was vindictive. "That man asks to be spied on. I'm damn sure he spies on us."

So a little later they drove back. As they approached the house and Nick was slowing down the car he grinned suddenly, nodded and went on to stare at something that had caught his eye.

"Old man Perringer's improving," he said. "'Member the fights I've had with him over that door? Look, he's actually thrown it open himself to let in some of that nasty fresh air he's so much afraid of."

The approach of the car made little noise and, as if the sight and shadow of the house had already subdued them, its four occupants alighted almost in silence. They were thus already in the inner hall—and might have gone farther—before Perringer became aware of their arrival. Had he been in his accustomed quarters he had hardly heard them at all, but just at that moment Perringer happened to be elsewhere.

The door of the dining-room burst open, and through the aperture Perringer emerged in a rush. He was sweating, and his grey face was the face of a man in fear and distress. But that look dissolved and merged into one of relief at the sight of Nick.

"Oh, it's you, sir!"

"Well, whom did you think? We're back early, but you needn't worry. Get our own tea."

Without much curiosity he was wondering what Perringer had been doing in the dining-room, but since Perringer's manifold duties gave him the run of the house it seemed to him that a question would have been unkindly inquisitive. Yet the unasked question was strangely and promptly answered.

Nick had turned towards the dining-room door when, to his mild astonishment, he found Perringer planted in his way.

"I beg your pardon, sir. Not in there, sir! Please, sir."

The look in the man's eyes—an anguish of fear and pleading— startled Nick and extinguished a spark of anger.

"But of course I'm going in there, Perringer. What's the matter with you?"

"If you'd only give me a moment, sir, to—"

He was interrupted—but not by Nick nor by any of his three companions. A strange voice spoke from within the dining room. It was a cultured, male voice, rich but high-pitched. Clearly it was the voice of an educated man, and it suggested a gentle and most agreeable personality.

"Oh, that's all right, Perringer. I can announce myself—or rather introduce myself."

Perringer opened his mouth as if to reply, but said nothing. Then, while Basil and the girls effaced themselves by strolling across to the drawing-room, Nick crossed the threshold which Perringer now left open to him.

Some inner warden had prepared him to be surprised, and he was thus able to look upon the eccentric figure which confronted him without any betrayal of good manners.

The man was tall, sparely built and elderly. His frock-coat of an ancient cut was almost green with age. His hair, almost white, was plentiful and worn rather long. He wore the drooping moustache affected by many retired Army officers of a bygone day. But he had not the eyes nor the skin of a man who was much past the prime of life. A tailor and a hairdresser would have set him back several milestones on the lost way to Youth.

The face seemed vaguely familiar to Nick. Somewhere and at some time he was sure that he had seen it before. But the occasion and the circumstances eluded him and lay hidden among all the dusty lumber of early experiences. Perhaps the stranger's photograph had once been published, or perhaps in a London street or indeed anywhere.

"Mr. Rockwell, I think?"

Nick, suddenly hearing himself addressed, inclined his head.

"Yes," he said. "Won't you sit down, sir?"

"Thank you. Thank you." The stranger fumbled behind him for the chair he had just vacated. "I don't think Perringer—excellent man—told you whom to expect. You know, I think, that when I—or when Dr. Whitemill—visited you we should come as—ah—as thieves in the night. Although, I hope, with less inconvenience to yourself. You have already received my letter, and no doubt you hardly expected me to follow it so quickly"

"Colonel Sandingford?" said Nick, as his visitor seemed to pause.

The other inclined his head a little in assent.

"And," he remarked pleasantly, "delighted to make your acquaintance and congratulate you personally on your good fortune—if you consider it to be good fortune in spite of the somewhat onerous conditions."

"Thank you, sir. But—excuse me—you'd like some tea, would you not?"

"Oh, no. Please don't hurry on my account. You and your friends have just come in, have you not? I was about to go, fearing that I should have to miss you for this occasion. I have—ah—examined the seal on the door. I trust Perringer is serving you well. There is just one—just one remark, though, that I should wish to make."

"Yes? " said Nick.

"Those friends of yours. My poor old friend—Sir Anthony, I mean—I know he would not have approved. You see, I knew his wishes and, although there is nothing in the will to prohibit It. You understand what I mean?"

Nick smiled in spite of himself.

"Do you really mean to tell me, Colonel Sandingford, that he expected me to live here ail alone?"

The older man spoke rapidly when he answered, as men will when they seek to gioss over an absurdity.

"Oh, no, my dear sir, not alone. Not alone. There is already Perringer. I could have found you other servants, perhaps. Good servants. Trustworthy servants. However, the mischief —if it be mischief—seems to be done. No doubt you would have found it lonely—oh, no doubt. But these friends of yours—they thoroughly understand the conditions of the will, do they not? That door, you know—"

He paused again, eyeing Nick with sudden intensity.

"If they should—if you should—I mean in some fit of curiosity—natural curiosity, perhaps—I think I ought to repeat that the consequences to yourself would be extremely serious. You would lose everything, Mr. Rockwell."

Nick lowered his head, then raised it to look straight before him for a moment.

"Colonel Sandingford," he said suddenly, "you seem to have been my uncle's friend. Also, if I may say so, you do not seem to be a gentleman who would enjoy making a mystery out of nothing or—or one who would believe in a fantastic ghost story. Then will you kindly relieve us all by telling me—as confidentially as you please—the meaning of all the absurd nonsense about that sealed door? "

Sparks seemed to kindle for a moment in the Colonel's eyes.

"Mr. Rockwell," he answered coldly, a sudden harshness in his voice, "I am at liberty to tell you exactly nothing. No, I am wrong. I may tell you one thing—and one thing only—and give you my word of honour upon it. I swear to you that that condition is no madman's whim. It is vital—and vital not only to yourself."

CHAPTER XI
STRANGE DISAPPEARANCE

Nick said nothing. He was conscious, and not for the first time, of one of the advantages of age over youth—an advantage which, like many others, may be used unfairly. But already he knew the terms of the will and, while he rebelled against all the seeming absurdities which hedged him, he was irritatingly aware of being treated according to the letter of the law.

Blindly he had accepted some eccentric conditions, blindly he must fulfil them or lose all.

"The friends you have with you," Colonel Sandingford continued suddenly. "Kindly tell me about them."

"I'll call them in if you like, sir," Nick said.

"Presently. Presently. I should like to hear something about them first."

So Nick described them and told him their late circumstances, adding, of course, that he had been at school with Basil.

"You might find Betty," he concluded, "rather a child of nature—which is odd, coming to think of it, since she's an actress. But she's one of the best, although she may not belong to any type that you know at all intimately. She's engaged to Basil, by the way, and I'm sure you'll like Basil and his sister, sir."

"H'm. Well! So long as they're not likely to interfere with that sealed door."

"They won't do that, sir. They know the consequences to me."

Colonel Sandingford was looking past him, frowning at a thought.

"I'm very glad to hear you say it. But curiosity, you know, is a grave temptation. And one step so very often leads on to another, until the fatal step is taken. Hasn't there already been a—well, an instance?"

Nick, looking straight at the other, knew that he knew— although how he knew was but another of the lengthening list of mysteries.

"Yes." he said. "That was Milly—Miss Hailsham. I don't know how you knew, unless Perringer has a habit of listening at keyholes. As a fact. Miss Hailsham did not know what she was doing. She was walking in her sleep."

It seemed to Nick that Colonel Sandingford suddenly stiffened and whitened.

"Good Lord!" he ejaculated. "In *this* house! Listen—I mean this very seriously. That sleep-walking has got to be stopped."

"It's going to be!" Nick responded. "Her brother is equally firm on the point. He's had to cope with it before." He paused suddenly to laugh. "I don't know exactly what Basil proposes to do, but I heard him mutter something about drawing-pins."

The Colonel, however, did not smile.

"So long as the means are effective!" he said grimly. And now you have told me all about your friends it would be only fair if you told them about me. And then I should be grateful for an introduction."

Nick took instant steps to comply, closing the door behind him. He found Basil and the two girls exactly where he had expected to find them, and addressed them breathlessly, telling them of what had just passed between him and his visitor.

"Not a bad sort, I should think," he said, "under the starch and red tape. What beats me, though, is how he knew about your somnambulistic act, Milly. Unless Perringer risks a cold in his ear at keyholes."

Basil shook his head.

"Just happens," he said, "that I make a point of never saying anything I don't want Perringer to hear until I've heard him walk right out of earshot. I'm rather nervy about that. So nervy, in fact, that I'd notice it if anybody else did it, and I'd probably start shushing. And I shouldn't think the girls—"

"Milly and me have never said a word that he could cotton to," said Betty hastily. "Have we, Milly?"

"No, I'm sure we haven't!"

"And that," said Basil, "proves something. Does it not, my little loves?"

"Proves what?" Nick demanded irritably.

"That while Milly was undoubtedly walking in her sleep it wasn't all quite a dream. There *must* have been somebody in the sealed room—Perringer himself or somebody he's in close touch with. Otherwise Perringer couldn't have known and Perringer couldn't have told the Colonel. This isn't just another of the jolly little mysteries of this house—it's a new light on an old one."

"Oh, come along," said Nick impatiently, "before we find any more of these 'ere bafflin' problems."

But he was just about to find another.

Having thrown open the dining-room door, he looked beyond before standing aside for the girls to pass him. The room was empty.

"Bird flown," he remarked, seeing on the instant a simple explanation. "Gallant Colonel no doubt gone to remove the stains of travel before meeting ladies. Anyhow, he looked a bit moth-eaten. Range yourselves tastefully about the room and form a pleasing tableau when he enters. Betty—I beg her pardon— Miss d'Havrincourt—will oblige us all by not addressing the gallant soldier as Old Cock."

Betty screwed up her face and then flickered a serpent's tongue at Nick.

"You go and fricassee your feet." she said.

They waited, bandying like pleasantries, while the minutes passed. Presently Nick, who had been growing restive, rose and tugged at the bell. After a short interval Perringer knocked and revealed himself under the lintel.

"Oh," said Nick, "you might find out, as discreetly as possible, whether Colonel Sandingford is taking a bath."

"Colonel Sandingford, sir," said Perringer, with massive imperturbability, "is gone."

"*What!* But that's impossible!"

"Nevertheless, sir, I saw him in the hall a few minutes ago. He said good-bye to me rather hastily, sir, and seemed in a great hurry. He had the air, sir, of a gentleman who had suddenly recollected something of paramount importance."

In the following silence Nick was well aware of what the other three were thinking.

"Very well, Perringer, thank you," he said quietly, and did not utter another word until Perringer's footfalls had receded. Then be spoke again.

"But it's quite impossible! It's ridiculous! He wouldn't— he couldn't have gone like that. He knew I'd just gone to fetch you. He seemed anxious to meet you. Here—there must be something wrong."

He was making for the door when Basil called out to ask where he was going.

"After him in the car. He must have gone towards the station. Didn't come by car or we'd have seen it outside. Can't let him go without a cup of tea."

Obviously Nick's hospitality was a secondary consideration. He was mystified. Visitors do not normally depart in that manner, and not only was Colonel Sandingford rather obviously a gentleman, but one who seemed to belong to a bygone age when manners were manners. There was a railway station in the not-too-distant village, and Nick drove to it without overtaking his late visitor. The station proved to be entirely deserted save for an Invisible Being behind the closed shutter of the booking-office. Nick presently roused the Invisible Being, and learned that the forsaken appearance of the station was due to the fact that he had arrived in the middle of an hiatus—two and a half hours long—between trains of any description.

Nick thought again and made an inquiry. Yes, there was a bus service into Arunford, and one due about now. Nick drove away and actually saw the bus halt to put down a passenger and pick up two others. But Colonel Sandingford was not on board. So Nick drove on to Arunford. Most of the drive was superfluous so far as the chances of overtaking the Colonel were concerned. Had the latter essayed the journey on foot—which was most unlikely—Nick must have overtaken him fairly soon. Had he been accommodated with a lift there was no chance of overtaking him at all.

And at Arunford station he drew another blank. There had been no London-bound train which his late visitor could possibly have caught.

Nick was now maddened, partly by the absurdity of the situation and partly by the stark problem—*what had become of Colonel Sandingford?* He scratched his head—which was as near as ever he went to tearing his hair—and drove down to the office of Matthews, the solicitor.

Matthews received him cordially and heard only the beginnings of the story when he interrupted.

"Colonel Sandingford—I did not know that he was down this way. He always comes in to see me."

"Perhaps he meant to this time," said Nick ill-temperedly. "Only the devil ran away with him first."

Matthews heard the rest of the tale in patience, and during the recital his face changed its expression more than once.

"Well, Mr. Rockwell," he said gravely, when Nick had finished speaking, "I hope you are going to profit by this experience. It begins to look to me very much as if it were not Colonel Sandingford at all. In your peculiar circumstances it is most unwise to let strangers into that house unless you are well aware of their identity and their purpose."

"But damn it—sorry, Mr. Matthews—we didn't let him in. We were all out when he arrived. Perringer let him in."

"Oh, of course!" The lawyer's brow suddenly cleared. "And Perringer saw him go? Just so, just so. Well, in that case, Mr. Rockwell, you have nothing to worry about. Nothing whatever.

Except...."

"Except what?"

The lawyer was silent for half a minute.

"I'm afraid," he said with a deprecatory smile, "you won't find my advice particularly comforting—or illuminating. I'm still not happy about those friends of yours, excellent as they may be in every way. So my advice is just—Watch Your Step. And watch theirs too."

Nick stood up as if to go. However, he remained standing to face the lawyer, who had not yet risen, and felt that he had some strange psychological advantage in thus towering above him.

"Mr. Matthews," he said, "I think I could put up with things a great deal more easily if I felt that I was being trusted. It isn't quite pleasant, you know, to be living in a haze of mystery. Everything's odd and queer and twisted about that damned house. There's the Sealed Room, the way my uncle died, Perringer, this Colonel Thingummy and Dr. What's-his-name who're allowed to jump on me and spy whenever they please, the revolver practice, which is Perringer's latest idea of fun, his quaint advice—or instruction—not to shoot a sitting burglar unless the latter is armed and menacing. What is a sane man—or a madman for that matter—to make of it all?"

Matthews smiled with an irritating calm.

"My dear Mr. Rockwell," he said, "I am almost as mystified as yourself. The little I know I may not divulge. I know perhaps a little more than you—and that little more enables me to guess a great deal. My advice to you is just not to worry. Carry out the conditions set forth in the will and you cannot go wrong."

"Yes, but—"

"Ah, I know!" Matthews raised a hand, and held it palm outwards as if in benediction. "Arduous and unnecessary conditions they may seem to you. Lunatic conditions if you like. But consider what you gain in return—and what you stand to lose."

"Oh, I know! " Nick grunted. "I should be a fool and a coward if I chucked it up. And it isn't only for myself. There's my three friends. Lord knows what they'd be doing if I hadn't had this stroke of—well, call it Luck."

"Just so, just so." Matthews' tone was patient and kindly and understanding—almost parsonical. "And there's somebody else to be considered, you know."

"Who's that?"

Matthews picked up a pen, looked closely at the nib and dropped it again.

"Your late uncle."

Nick laughed. He could well imagine that the sound jarred upon the lawyer, for it jarred upon himself.

"Do you really think, Mr. Matthews, that the dead really care a damn about what goes on in the world they've left forever?"

Matthews, idly picking up the pen again, answered him in three short sentences.

"God knows. I don't." There was a little pause. "Nor do you."

Nick drove back. Whatever his feelings they seemed not as yet to be shared by the others— who had, after all, less cause to be disturbed as yet—for laughter came across from the lawn selected for tennis. Already the net was up, and Basil was at work with a marker which they had bought together with the other accessories.

"Found him?" Basil sang out.

Nick, who had left the car and was then walking across, shook his head and drew near before he spoke.

"Didn't come by car, didn't go by car, bus or train. Either from here or Arunford. Just whiffled into thin air. So I went to see old man Matthews. Thought a nice wise old head might have something in it to soothe my worried young mind."

"And had it?" Milly inquired. "I mean, did he?"

"In one way—yes. 'Nothcr way—no. He seemed a bit hot and bothered himself at first, and then told me not to worry. Believe he suspected at first that it wasn't Colonel Sandingford at all. Then, while I was getting the whole story off my chest and it came out that Perringer had let him in, he looked relieved and started the Don't Worry stuff. One thing's rather a comfort."

"Ah!" said Basil. "Well, I'd rather like to know what that one thing is, I could do with a spot of comfort."

"Old man Matthews trusts our Perringer."

"Does he?" croaked Basil. "More'n I do. Meanin' that if there's any Queer Business going on about the house—and there seems plenty—nice-mannered Mr. Perringer is right up to the neck in it."

Nick passed a hand over his damp brow.

"My uncle trusted Perringer," he said.

"Yes, dear old lad. And where's your uncle now? Got knocked down by a car at night, didn't he? Nobody could have pushed him in front of it, I suppose?"

Nick frowned and shook his head.

"Perringer—no, my uncle was alone. Besides, the driver of the car would have seen."

"Driver of the car, me lad, doesn't seem to have seen anything at all. Half canned, very likely. Just felt something. Then when he found he'd got a bent wing he thought he'd better go and report. I wish I'd been a passenger in that car. Might have noticed a bit more than the driver spotted. And there's another thing worth remembering."

"Oh, yes?" Nick groaned.

"Taking things by and large, it rather looks as if your uncle expected to come to a sudden and sticky end. Queer to have a premonition like that—and then to get nudged by a bus outside his own gates!"

Milly laughed in spite of herself.

"Oh, shut up!" she said.

It was Betty who saved a situation in which frayed nerves were only too evident. She tripped up to Basil, put an arm around him—or so far as it would go—and, standing on tiptoe, put her face close to his.

"Didums!" she said. "No, don't you shut up, dear. You let it rip. Good for you. Doctors say so." With her face still close to Basil's she spoke to the others. "He don't need anybody to psycho-paralyse him to get at what's on his mind. Does it all himself."

They all found an excuse for laughing, but the sound called no responsive echo from the sad old mansion behind them. It was not made to echo laughter. And the windows stared at them with blank, offended eyes.

CHAPTER XII
"IT SUGGESTS A LOT"

Basil played the last card and took the last trick.

"Fifteen to me, eleven to you, and four the diff. That's another bob you owe me. Nicodemus—making two-and-nine in all. Want to lose some more or shall we chuck it?"

Nick felt lazily in a pockct and produced half a crown and twopence.

"Chuck it, I think," he said. "Owe you a penny. I want to think."

"Bad thing to do in this damned house. Sorry—your house, of course, and all that. But I don't take it back."

"It's just occurred to me that it hasn't been such a bad house lately. Let's see, it's a week to-day since the gallant Colonel vanished into thin air. And he must have materialized again elsewhere or the papers would have been full of his vanishing. How he slipped away—and why—still defeats me. Well, that's a week gone by and nothing's happened since. The House of Queer Things hasn't been doing its stuff. D'you know, I think I'll slip up to town tomorrow."

"Eh?"

"All right, me lad. Daddy isn't going to leave you. Want some clothes and several other little things. Be back by dinner."

"That what you want to think about?"

Nick yawned.

"No. Not specially. General review of things. Nothing happened for a week, but something going to happen soon. Feel it in my bones."

It was getting late. The girls had gone to bed an hour since, and the male half of the quartette had embarked on a series of games of single whist—which requires memory, patience and a certain amount of judgment.

"Y know," said Basil, "for a week we've been leading sane, healthy lives. Tennis and buzzing about in the car and all that. Milly hasn't been doing her Lady Macbeth act, or if she has she can walk barefooted on drawing-pins without discomfort. Don't you think that's got a bit to do with—er—nothing having happened. I don't mean that nothing happened before. I mean that if we hadn't been getting plenty of fresh air, and finding something to laugh at between whiles, we should have had a queer fancy or two between us by now."

Nick made a non-committal noise and lit a fresh cigarette from the stub he was about to discard.

"Well, I've got a queer fancy on me to-night. I don't like letting sleeping dogs lie. No, I don't quite mean that. I mean that I want to make quite sure that they're asleep."

Basil balanced the five of clubs on his thumb and flicked it over against Nick's chest.

"Yes?" he said. "What dogs?"

"Dog. In the singular. Perringer. I wonder if he's really got a way into that scaled room, and monkeys about there sometimes when he ought to be getting his beauty sleep."

Basil's eyebrows went up.

"Thinking of going there and knocking?"

"No. The occupant—if any—wouldn't answer. Not after Milly's little exploit. I wish we could be sure that she *did* hear a voice. Oh, I know she's certain she did, but she was walking in her sleep and *we* can't be so sure."

"Well," grunted Basil, "how can we find out, then?"

"If little Perringer's in his bedroom little Perringer can't be in sealed room. If Perringer's in his bedroom it won't prove anything. Must be in bedroom some of the time. But if we find he's not there it'll be a scrap more food for thought."

Basil laughed.

"Suppose Perringer's all stretched out on his virtuous couch sound asleep, what's going to be your excuse for digging him out?"

"You," said Nick, "are going to be the excuse. You thought you heard a noise down here. Fanciful old woman you're getting, Basil. So armed to the teeth with one of Perringer's guns you came to roust me out. Having armed myself I accompany you to roust out Perringer. Perringer snug in his room?—right-ho! Perringer's room empty?—what ho! If Perringer's there it won't prove he's always there. But if he's not there it will prove that he's sometimes somewhere else."

"Couldn't have expressed it more lucidly myself." Basil continued to grin, but some of the banter died away from his tone. "Well, let's suppose his—er—little chamber is empty—as the great Pitcher 'once wrote. What would be the next move?"

"I suppose a spot of scouting would be indicated. Do you think you could get around the house making less noise than a train coming out of a tunnel? At the same time holding your gun in such a way that you won't blow my head off if something startles you?"

Basil's reply was to the effect that he was willing to have a stab at it.

"Right! Let's go and get our guns. Not that we're likely to want them, but they'll be eyewash for Perringer."

They turned to quit the room. Basil, however, paused suddenly in the doorway.

"Just one point. What sort of noise did I hear? Better get that settled."

"You thought you heard a thud somewhere downstairs, and then somebody call out—you great, nervy lout."

Five minutes later they were back in the same room, each self-consciously fingering an automatic.

"Beginners, please!" said Basil, grinning. "Just like a ruddy rehearsal, this is. Fit?"

"Don't really much care for this," Nick grunted in a low voice. "Spying on one's own servant—what?"

"Laddie," returned Basil, "if we're up against anything at all—and p'r'aps we're only kidding ourselves—it's something that moves and fights in the dark. Queensberry Rules no *bon* for that sort of thing. Gentlemanly stuff a wash-out.... All right, go first if you want to. Then you won't be so likely to blow my head off if you get fussed."

They knew the way to Perringer's room, for—quite fortunately as it seemed now—he had insisted on showing it to them in case he should be wanted suddenly in the night. They negotiated the back stairs with scarcely a creak, and silently fumbled their way along a passage to a door, outside which they halted.

Nick, wincing slightly at his own undignified posture, bent his head and lowered his ear to the keyhole. After half a minute he stood upright and whispered.

"Not q sound. No breathing. No nothing."

"Well?"

In answer to the question implied Nick turned the door-handle and pushed. The door gave. Nick stepped quietly into the room and paused.

"Sorry, Perringer," he said in a quiet and steady voice.

Having received no answer he flashed an electric torch and stepped forward, Basil following. Save for their two selves the room was empty. The bed, neatly made, had not yet been occupied.

"Jove!" said Basil, speaking in his normal tone. "He's still in the servants' hall. Hasn't been up here at all yet."

"Oh, yes, he has. Look!"

He pointed to a pair of old patent-leather shoes which lay beside the bed. They were the shoes which Perringer wore of an evening when he came to serve dinner.

"Ruddy things are old, but they still squeak," Nick commented, "and Master Perringer knows it. Master Perringer been up to his room, but not to his downy couch. Query, where's Master Perringer now?"

"Sealed Room," said Basil simply. "I bet he's got some way of getting in and out of it—seal or no seal—that we know nothing about. Going to try it?"

"Yes."

"Knock on the door, same like our famous performing female somnambulist?"

"I think not. Shouldn't get an answer this time. Last time must have caused a scare."

"What then, Skipper?"

Nick touched his friend's arm and began to move away.

"Oh, just oil up to the door like a brace of cats after a sparrow. Sit mum outside and listen. If the bird is in the nest it's bound to make a twitter of some sort. Quite safe on the outside of that door so long as we keep mum. I'm sure it's not possible to get in and out that way—so long as that seal remains intact."

They were half-way down the back stairs when a thought struck Basil.

"Suppose Perringer's got the seal? So if he's got a key he could get in and out when he liked." Nick shook his head.

"No. Besides, if he's inside when we get there the seal would have to be off the outside of the lock—wouldn't it?—and I bet it isn't. Besides, when I first saw it—and when I last saw it, for that matter—the wax looked old. No, if he uses that room there's some secret way in. Not so unlikely—an old place like this. Come on."

But they did not go so far as the sealed door that night. There was no occasion.

At the foot of the back stairs they were about to cross to the service door which gave access to the hall when Nick suddenly halted and stiffened like a pointing retriever.

There was nothing unusual in the fact that the door leading to the cellar stairs stood open. It was normally so because of a strong upward draught and a defective latch. The only way to close it effectually was to lock it. But now a sound from below had fallen on Nick's ears. He felt behind him for Basil's arm and pinched it eloquently.

Yes, somebody was moving about in the cellars, and now there was a light which spread up from the bottom of the stairs and, without playing directly upon them, faintly illumined their faces. Then came soft ascending footfalls.

Basil, waiting to see what Nick would do, received a gentle but eloquent push. Another soft push directed him towards the door leading into the hall. They tiptoed thither, Basil passing through it first with Nick upon his heels. Then Nick swung about and pushed back the door, but he did not quite close it. He left a chink about an inch wide and applied his eye to the chink.

Basil, standing back, could see nothing through the chink but a light which grew steadily stronger as audible footfalls mounted the cellar stairs. Then, as the footfalls fell on level floor, the light became almost dazzling for the moment. An instant thus and it dimmed again as it was borne into the kitchen. Then it faded out.

As Nick straightened himself Basil heard somebody breathing heavily, and he was not quite sure if it were himself or Nick. A soft shove and a whispered half-word directed Basil to turn about. Still on tiptoe they returned to the scene of their card-playing. Nick, without a word, sat down and swept a scattering of loose cards into a pack, his brow heavy with a frown of pre-occupation. Basil closed the door as if his life depended on the silence with which the action was performed. Then he turned and uttered one word, still in a whisper.

"Perringer?"

"Who else?" said Nick, raising his voice a little. "He was flashing the torch before him, of course, but the light spread enough to show me his outline. And I saw what else he was carrying."

"Oh?"

Basil, waiting for more, came and stood beside Nick, drumming his fingers softly on the card-table.

"Well, Chatterbox? What else was he carrying?"

"Oh, tray. Plates on the tray and cup and saucer, and I think a glass. Can't swear to the glass, though. Light too uncertain and I only had a glimpse. Well?"

Basil was silent for ten seconds.

"Either" he began and stopped.

"H'm. Either x or y."

"Just so. Either friend Perringer has a taste for taking his meals in the cellar—which would be quaint but not unlawful—or he's been feeding somebody else."

"Which," Nick commented grimly, "might be both. Suppose that's the case—where are we? And where do we move on to?"

Basil said nothing at first, but after an interval he spoke again.

"Reminds me of something," he said.

"Yes?"

"You know my—ahem—household duties sometimes take me to the dust-bin?"

Nick suddenly threw up his head and laughed.

"Ah! Now we're going to hear something! Every good detective loves a dust-bin."

"All right, don't rag or I won't tell you. I couldn't help feeling that old man Perringer did himself rather well. Of course he's got his wages besides what you allow him for his keep. All the same—fresh lobster, you know! I noticed it because I knew we hadn't had lobster since we've been here. Nice one it must have been too, when the shell was full."

There was another spell of silence.

"You know," said Nick suddenly, with the air of one already embarked upon an argument, "you know, that lobster shell doesn't *prove* anything."

"I know it doesn't," Basil answered quietly. "But it suggests a hell of a lot. ... I say, old man! Eh? Oh, I was going to say, what about turning in? I want to think."

"Me too," said Nick. "You don't suppose *I* haven't any thinking to do?"

CHAPTER XIII
THE STARS LOOKED DOWN

Nick fulfilled his intention of going to London on the following morning. Basil drove with him to Arunford—whence a better train service was obtainable—in order to take the car back again. With some minutes to wait at the station Nick looked up a return train.

"Six-eighteen Victoria, seven-thirty-three here. That'll do me. Get back just in nice time for dinner—if you care to drive in and meet me."

"Sure. Seven-thirty-three."

And by seven-twenty-five that evening Basil was at the station, and had only ten minutes to wait—for the train was punctual— before Nick bore down on him from among a sprinkling of freshly arrived passengers. And at first glance Basil knew that something was wrong.

There was a small buffet on the station. Nick indicated it with a motion of the head.

"Time for a drink?" he asked shortly. "Want to talk to you for a minute before we get back."

"Yes, plenty of time," Basil said cheerfully. "Grub won't be on the table until eight-thirty. Girls thought you'd miss your train or else it would be late or something. Real optimists. But I didn't say anything because I thought you'd like a quick beer after your journey. Damned hot, isn't it?"

They had the buffet almost to themselves save for the young woman—who seemed to be in deep mourning—behind the counter. Basil carried two glasses of luke-warm beer to a little table which looked like a fossilized target.

Nick drank his beer before Basil had started, and went over to the counter for two more glasses. Then, reseating himself, he said:

"I've seen Colonel Sandingford."

"What! Again?"

"No, not again." Nick spoke in a low voice and clipped his words. "Wasn't Colonel Sandingford paid us that visit. Not real one. Thought as much. Dunno who the devil it was. Beats me. And beats me how he disappeared. No smell of sulphur either. Was there?"

While Basil was taking a long draught a sudden suspicion occurrcd to him.

"Sure it was the right one you bumped into to-day?"

"Oh, Lord—yes! Tell you how it happened. Went to my tailor's in Bond Street. Whitaker—that's the name—they've been dressing my people for over a hundred years. Still a Whitaker running the show. Actually had him to attend to me this morning. Rather like getting the Archbishop to show you over the cathedral, but it happened that way.

"Dccent fellow, Whitaker. Knows how to charge, but never expects to see his money in less than two years. If he saw it at the end of the quarter he'd have a mild seizure: and if you wanted to pay cash he'd think you were a cad and wouldn't want your custom. Came in handy that did, during the hard-up days.

"Well. I was talking to the High Priest in his temple, while his acolyte was brooding over my legs with a tape-measure, when it occurred to me to ask him a question. You see, I knew he'd been my uncle's tailor, too, for my father had introduced him years ago, before I was born. And since my uncle and Colonel Sandingford were buddies I thought it just likely that he might have decorated the gallant Colonel with trouserings, coatings and vestings at some time or another.

"You can guess part of what's coming. It seems he had. Colonel Sandingford was a pet customer. Wore his clothes with an air of distinction. Not like that sketch that vanished in a cloud of sulphur t' other afternoon. With that sketch in mind I couldn't understand it. Thought there might be two gallant Colonels with the same name. Said so. Then old man Whitaker clinched things by uttering correct address. So that was that.

"The High Priest presently waffled off and left me to his myrmidon, who asked me questions about minor details as to suiting. Later, when I was just on my way out across the precincts—you can't call the place a shop—I saw High Priest talking to nice-looking old boy with weeping-willow moustache. High Priest called out to me.

"'Excuse me, Mr. Rockwell—sir. By a strange coincidence Colonel Sandingford stepped in the very minute after you had mentioned him. I took the liberty of informing him of the coincidence, and he was most interested to learn that you were on the premises. Pray allow me—if I may do so with propriety— to perform the introduction.'

"Which, my boy, he proceeded to do—rather in the manner of the Lord Chamberlain in a pantomime introducing Prince Charming to Little Bo Peep. And I can assure you the introduction was necessary, because I was goggling at a total stranger.

"The right Colonel Sandingford this time? I'd say he was! Couldn't have known much more about me if he'd been the Recording Angel. Asked me how we were getting on down here, and seemed damned uneasy about something. Said he'd been meaning to come and look us up—and was coming soon in any case. Then without knowing it he clinched his identity even more by asking me to lunch at his club.

"Once inside that mausoleum—which was then almost empty and only ten per cent full at lunch-time—he bore me off to a dark corner under half an acre of canvas which, when clean, had represented the Martyrdom of St. Sebastian. And over two glasses of the high-and-dry he began to fire questions at me.

"What were you and the girls like? Didn't care for your being there at all, but he supposed it couldn't be helped. How was I getting on with Perringer? Seems that his quaint taste compelled him to like Perringer. And was the seal all right? *That* was most important. And I answered all his questions in a smart and soldierly manner."

Nick paused and grinned feebly. Basil then put in the question he had been itching to ask.

"Tell him about his understudy?"

"We-ell," said Nick, "tell you the truth I was in two minds about that. Then something whispered to me—or perhaps it was something in his manner—but I had a queasy feeling that he knew already. Had an idea that Perringer—if Perringer were not up to something on his own account—would have written and put him wise. And that, I'm sure, Perringer did. Well, thank God Perringer seems to be on the level after all. So I outed with it all. Same like as if I didn't know he knew already."

"Ah!" Basil, wishing he had been there to see and hear, began to laugh.

"How did he take it?"

"Pretty seriously. He told me that in this instance it didn't matter. Perringer had, of course, recognized the impostor as such, and must have given something away without meaning to, because the impostor bolted. But he said it showed that I should have to be very, very careful. Because if Perringer had happened not to be about something very serious might have happened." Basil laughed shortly and went on to question.

"Well? Did you ask him what it was all about? The sealed room, the queer conditions, everything?"

"You bet I did!" Nick answered almost vehemently. "Well, me lad, I'll tell you just one thing. When we had lunch a little later we kicked off with oyster soup. Tinned oysters, no doubt, for the fresh 'uns aren't in season. And the oysters in that soup were garrulous compared with that old badger."

"Got nothing out of him?"

Nick bent his brows.

"Well, not quite nothing. He told me I'd probably understand some day—if I lived long enough. And he warned me that there might be danger—but what sort of danger he wouldn't say. Except—he must have caught this from the gipsies—he was anxious that dark-skinned persons shouldn't cross my path. I've got to beware of 'em."

Basil gasped slightly.

"Phew! Niggers did he mean?"

"No. I gather that he had in mind the sort that walks about with flashing teeth and dark ear-rings with half a yard of cold steel up its right sleeve. Gentlemen of one or more of the Latin tribes. Couldn't get more than that out of him, but I knew he meant the South American species of dago. My uncle having spent so much of his time out there, you see. And that brings me to the point."

"Ur? What point?"

"Girls," said Nick. "Now we know there's danger—danger for certain—they'll have to be shunted. I'll find the money and you can let them think it came from somewhere else. Park 'em in a seaside boarding-house or somewhere for the time being. Let them have a bit of real holiday. As for you, old boy—well, you'll please yourself what you do."

Basil sat still, staring at him.

"If," he said, "I thought you were serious in suggesting that I should leave you to it I'd slug you one on the jaw, here and now."

"But there's the girls, you damned fool!"

"All right, you damned fool, well I'll put it to them, if you like. Tell them all about the dangers we know nothing about, and add all the trimmings I can think of for luck. And after that, if anything short of dynamite can shift them from your ruddy old haunted mansion I'll eat my hat—maker's name, ribbon and all."

Nick warmed to the words, but while he was comforted he was also troubled in spirit. Two voices were there.

"All the same " he began weakly.

"You see," said Basil, "we're all like links in a chain. Betty wouldn't dream of going while I was with you, and even if I were such a skunk as to go I should never hear the last of it. She's a grand kid—Betty. I know she's made you want to laugh at times—both with her Melisande stuff and as her natural self —but you've always been too decent a scout to waffle an eyelid. D'you know, I think she sees that and appreciates it. We don't use the word Gentleman much in these days of Sahibs and Decent Blokes, but I think Betty recognizes the rare bird when she sees it. Poor little waif, what chance has she ever had? Yet—I can say this sort of thing to you if to no one else—I know she's straight and has always been straight. And—next to me, I hope—she thinks the world of you."

"Oh, she's one of the best," said Nick, in a tone which sounded indifferent—because he was suddenly and strangely touched.

Basil eyed him, and, reading him like an open book, grinned to himself.

"Right! Well, then, there's Betty and me strapped on to you, whether you like it or not. Then there's Milly."

"Yes," said Nick, and paused uncomfortably. "I should get her out of this if you can. Er—I should feel pretty rotten, you know, if—er—anything went wrong with her in that house. Phew! isn't it hot in here?"

"That's because you've been in the train," said Basil with a cynical grin. "Harking back to Milly— of course she likes you and all that. Couldn't help it after you've been so awfully decent. She'd think it would look bad, too, to leave you in the lurch. And she wouldn't like leaving Betty and me—we're all she's got in the world. So if you want her to go—I mean if you think she ought to go for her own sake—you can damn' well tell her so yourself."

"Eh? " said Nick listlessly. "Tell her? All right, yes, I will. Well, look here—better be getting back now, hadn't we? "

They rose. Basil was now grinning openly at Nick. He dropped a hand on Nick's shoulder as they approached the door.

"Anybody ever tell you you were a damn' fool?" he asked pleasantly.

"Dunno. Plenty of people have inferred it, I dare say." His voice was quite colourless. "Very likely they were right."

"Um! And did you go to see an oculist while you were in town?"

"'Course not. Nothing wrong with my sight."

"Isn't there, by gad!" said Basil.

They drove back—to find the two girls awaiting them in front of the house. It was Milly who called first in greeting.

"Come on, you two. Had a good day, Nick? Dinner's all ready."

"Thanks. Good." Nick was climbing out of the car. "Weil, I'll go and have a sluice. Basil, old lad, you'd better spill the beans to them before you go in. Walls and Perringers have cars. Tell 'em the bit of news I've brought back from town, and then there needn't be a word about it at table."

So it happened that Perringer—even if he were not above listening at keyholes—learned nothing instructive about Nick's visit to town. But after the verbal testimonial given by the real Colonel Sandingford most of their distrust in the man had vanished. Whatever doubts and mistrustings may have existed among the five inmates of the house were all lodged in one mind, and that the mind of Perringer. Nick, in pauses between talk, dallied with ways and means of getting the man into the open, talking to him freely and frankly, and giving him complete and unreserved confidence.

The restraining thought was shaped by the fact that the confidence would probably be one-sided and therefore, from Nick's point of view, almost useless. If Perringer knew things which were unknown to Nick and his friends—as no doubt he did—he was probably pledged by some nebulous loyalty, such as an ill considered promise to his late master, not to divulge them. Meanwhile the present unfair conditions bade fair to continue. In return for the ninety per cent trust they had in Perringer they could look for no more than a dubious fifty per cent of the man's own confidence.

They sat long over dinner, but the long June evening was still light when they rose from the table. The girls were standing in the drawing-room when the two young men joined them. Nobody had suggested a stroll in the gardens, but they stepped out as if by some tacit prearrangement. And after a minute they found themselves paired like partners at a dance.

Nick picked up Milly's small hand and tucked it inside his arm.

She let it stay, and Nick felt just the least responsive pressure while he talked of his trip to town and his reactions to the real Colonel Sandingford. Suddenly they found themselves alone, and Nick remarked on it.

"Not a mysterious vanishing this time," Milly laughed. "Really, you know, they don't get many chances, those two. Either I'm with Betty or you're with Basil or we're all four together."

"Well, I'm grateful to them this evening," said Nick gruffly. "Want to talk to you. Basil and I have been talking things over. May be—well—danger of some sort here. Don't know what sort. Perringer's sort of flashed the red light, hasn't he? And the old Colonel made no bones of it. I told Basil I was afraid this house wasn't the best place for you and Betty. He said— well, he said if I wanted you to go I'd better tell you so myself. So—so I'm—not very tactfully, I'm afraid— putting it up to you."

"Meaning," said Milly in a very small voice. "that you want me to go?"

"Yes," he answered in a short, dry tone.

Milly very quietly withdrew her arm from his.

"Very well," she said tonelessly. "I'm sorry. I should be sorrier still if I weren't sure that it was all your fault. You could have shown me—couldn't you?—that you didn't want me, instead of waiting and then having to tell me. It's all through being too polite, I suppose. Because, you know, you made me think—"

He swung round on her, his frayed nerves snapping for the moment.

"Are you off your head," he demanded, "like everybody and everything else in that damned house? Can't you see that I'd cut off my hand if that would help me to keep you here with me in safety? I haven't yet told you that I love you. Having eyes and a little intuition I thought you'd know—and understand why I hadn't told you. It's because, although I'm not poor, it would mean asking you to share this ghastly house with me—the very place I want to get you away from.

"In any event I don't suppose it would make much difference. I wasn't such an ass as to imagine that you might care for me. Only—only don't accuse me of trying to get rid of you, because that's just unbearable. Now do you understand?"

By this time Milly was walking half a pace behind him. After a pause she spoke in her cool, clear little voice. And now that voice was slightly vibrant.

"Nick. Nick, dear. I want to tell you a story. A long time ago—or so it seems—a very plain little girl, all over freckles, was taken to a Speech Day at her brother's school. And on the lawns she was introduced to—oh, yes, introduced *to*—her brother's friend, who was the most important boy in the school. He wasn't important because of his work, but he was ever so good at games.

"And directly the ugly little girl saw him she said to herself: 'Bags I. That's mine.' She actually fell in love with him at first sight. Oh, yes, she did. Of course she knew he wouldn't look at her just as she was, but she determined then and there to grow up pretty for his sake.

"Well, the strangest thing is that it wasn't just a passing fancy. She used to count the cherry and plum stones on her plate to find out when she was going to marry him, and when they said Never people used io think she was greedy, because she always wanted a second helping to try and change her fate. And she always felt a bit depressed if it had to be Never for the time being.

"And somehow he didn't fade out of her mind as she grew older. And then things went wrong at home and she had to go on the stage. She found herself there in another kind of world. Her looks had improved—at least, I think they had improved a bit. And she soon discovered that it wasn't so easy for a girl, placed as she was, to keep herself—well, nice.

"But she did it, and I know partly why. Do you know that story by O. Henry about a poor little New York working-girl who remained a good girl—at least for a time—because she had a picture of Lord Kitchener, and those sad, searching eyes of his were always looking down at her.

Well, this other girl—the one I'd been talking about—hadn't any picture, except the one she carried in her memory. But it served just as well, although she'd given up hoping to see that boy again. And when she did meet him, and by a wonderful chance came to live under the same roof with him, he wanted to send her away. Just because he thought he was in danger and that she might be in danger if she stayed. Danger—as if she cared for that when he was near her! As if she wouldn't—as if she wouldn't—"

It was as well that Nick's lips closed upon hers just then, for she could scarcely have uttered another word.

The sunset faded in the west and the moon brightened—as if the angel, whose job it is to attend to such matters, had turned up a wick. The stars looked down into the garden, quite coldly, quite callously, quite incuriously.

After all, they had seen plenty of this sort of thing before.

CHAPTER XIV
"Everything's crazy"

June had turned to July, July was in her third week, and nothing of importance had happened in or around the sinister old house since that evening in the garden.

Nothing of importance? Well, Milly wore a diamond and platinum ring on the third finger of her left hand—an eminently pawnable ring, as her brother said caustically, with recollections of the not so distant Bad Old Days.

Nick had bought it during one of his excursions to London. He had been going up for three consecutive days to play cricket for his old County at the Oval, for the distance permitted him to go and return by morning and night.

There had been callers—just the callers they had been half expecting and no more. These consisted of Dr. and Mrs. Bligh and the Vicar and his lady. All four of these good people wore an air of repression and all—especially the two ladies—were plainly bewildered. It was a shock to rural modesty to find two engaged couples living under the same roof with no chaperon other than Perringer, who, excellent as he was in so many ways, could hardly be adapted to the role. But these excellent folk, with their shabby little card-cases and their well-measured small-talk, were well aware that Nick was the victim—if that be the word—of a peculiar will. They could hardly expect the poor young man to live in the great house—a house reputed to be haunted, too—with none other than the somewhat chastening society of Perringer.

And Perringer, it seemed, was another thorn in the flesh. Mrs. Crossley, the Vicar's lady, repeated that which Nick already knew—about Perringer being a professed atheist and having refused to take the oath at his uncle's inquest.

"And after he'd been so long with poor Sir Anthony, too, and travelled half over the world with him!" said Mrs. Crossley in a grieved voice. "I'm sure Sir Anthony didn't know. Why,sometimes he used to bring Perringer to church with him. Well, I suppose the man thought it would be more than his place was worth to own up to his belief—or disbelief."

"I can tell you something very strange about him—in the circumstances," Basil laughed. "If you look closely at his neck you may get a glimpse of a thin silver chain. Well, on the end of that there's a little silver crucifix. I saw it once when he was working without his coat and his shirt came open."

"Ah," said the Vicar, "no doubt it was a gift from some dear friend or relative. Or perhaps he acquired it in South America, where such sacred symbols are much more common than here. Besides, I am afraid it is not unusual for holy emblems to be used quite superstitiously—as charms, in fact.

"I—ah"—he paused to smile—"I hope none of us here is superstitious."

"I am," said Betty promptly. "I'm not goin' to get married on a Friday—not if I know it. Are we, Basilco?"

Mrs. Crossley brightened at this hint of regularizing a possibly unholy union.

"Ah!" she said, smiling. "And when is the happy day going to be?"

Betty laughed.

"Search me! Ask Nick—er—Mr. Rockwell. We're all going to be turned off at once, aren't we, Nick? And we're going to have lots and lots of. babies, aren't we, Milly?"

"*Betty!*" cried Milly.

"Well, what's the matter with that?" Betty demanded, looking blandly into scandalized faces. "That's all right, isn't it—after the Registrar has said the Holy Words? In fact it's wrong not to have babies, isn't it? Anyhow. I once read a letter by a bishop in one of the papers, saying it was wrong and what was England coming to? And he ought to have known what was wrong, being a bishop."

The Vicar was instantly infected by the bad cough which attacked his wife. Betty regarded them with the blandest innocence, well aware of the effect of her speech, and particularly of her reference to the Registrar. But there was a wicked gleam in her eyes when she turned them upon Milly and Nick and her fiance.

"Betty," said Milly, when the callers had departed with troubled spirits, "go and stand in the corner. Or, no, you needn't. Come here and be spanked."

"Why?" Betty was smiling seraphically. "Oh, because, well, do 'em good. I talked like that for a joke, but anyhow I hate humbug. Mustn't say this and mustn't say that. What will the old chap do when we go to him to be spliced—as I dare say we shall? Why, he'll read us the marriage service. Yes, and I'll tell you this, if any foreign chemist round Leicester Square was to print part of the marriage service on a card and sell it for sixpence he'd do time."

Nick, who did not want to laugh outright, but hated giggling, was disturbed to hear himself giggle.

"Trouble with you, Betty," he said, "is that you're a child of nature."

It happened to be just what the Vicar, in all charity, was saying to his ruffled wife at that very moment.

They remembered that afternoon ever afterwards—not because it held anything of importance, but because it was the inconsequent prelude to tragedy.

After dinner that night they had a little impromptu music and played two dull rubbers of bridge. The girls went up shortly after half-past ten. Nick and Basil followed about twenty minutes later. And Nick, for one, began to sleep almost as soon as he was in bed. It was still dark when he wakened with a start.

The sound which woke him was instantaneous, but he knew what it was—or what it seemed. The acoustics of the old house were good, although the wainscoted walls held echoes. The echoes had not quite ceased when Nick leaped from his bed to the floor and seized his automatic. Somewhere in the house—and it seemed to him on the ground floor—somebody had discharged a firearm.

As he ran out on to the landing he heard another door flung open. A torch shot its flare upon him, then lit the floor for his feet. Behind it he became aware of the pyjama-clad figure of Basil. They wasted no words.

"Got your gun?" asked Nick.

"Yes. Downstairs?"

"Sounded like it."

They padded down into the hall and stood uncertainly at the foot of the stairs.

"Which way," began Nick, "do you think?" He paused abruptly. "What's that? Switch up the light."

There was sudden light just as the baize-covered door, which led to the back stairs and the servants' quarters, opened as if it had been struck by a gale. Nick lowered his pistol at the sight of Perringer—who showed him a white, distorted face.

"What's happened?" he cried.

"Don't know, sir. Keep back. Let me go and see."

"Keep back yourself," Nick growled. "Where was it?"

"Along here, I think, sir." Perringer still remembered to say sir. "Library or billiard-room it sounded like."

Nick outspaced both Basil and Perringer in a race for the library door. As he opened it a rush of cold air, striking full upon him, made manifest the fact that one of the tall windows stood open. He switched up the lights and for the moment he stood still and unnerved.

"My God!" he said, as Perringer pushed past him.

And he went on to stare with a startled, horrified fixity at the body lying in the middle of the floor and at the shapeless and growing pool of blood which still oozed slowly out of sodden clothing.

Perringer approached the still form swiftly and purposefully and without any apparent qualm. He knelt down and looked into the eyes while he picked up one of the wrists and began to feel for the pulse. Silently Nick and Basil crossed the room and stood one on either side of the body.

"Dead?" asked Nick in a voice he did not know.

"Yes," said Perringer, briskly and simply. "We couldn't help him, sir—even if we wanted to."

Nick heard him without taking his eyes from the body. The man was short and swarthy. Black hair had started to turn grey, but the face looked scarcely middle-aged. His eyes, from all that was visible of them, seemed black, but although they remained wide open the irises had rolled up under the lids leaving only thin crescents to be seen. Dreadful white eyes, like the marble eyes of statues, regarded the ceiling and the man who bent to look into them with the same sightless and stony unconcern.

This man was plainly of the Latin type and dressed neither well nor ill in a thin and bluish suit. He held something in a hand grotesquely bent, and Nick saw two or three inches of thin pointed knife jutting out below his sleeve.

Basil looked straight at Perringer. Nick turned to follow the direction of Basil's gaze. It was Basil who spoke next.

"Who—who did this?"

Perringer glanced at the open window.

"He's got away," he growled.

"You mean there were two of them?" Nick demanded.

"Must have been, sir."

"You mean that there were two burglars—"

"Better call them that, sir," Perringer interrupted quietly.

"—two burglars who broke in here and then one shot the other? But it's fantastic!"

"Facts, sir," said Perringer, "so often are. It may possibly have been an accident. Firearms are often discharged in that way. Or it may have been a case of thieves suddenly falling out. You see, sir, this man has a knife drawn in his hand. We can't tell—yet."

"All right. No. I see." Nick, trying to control a disposition to be flustered, was wondering what to do next. "You'd better get on some more clothes and then go for the police."

Perringer did not move.

"I beg your pardon, sir," he said quietly, "but I have certain duties to consider—duties to your late uncle, sir. Have you considered, sir, what such a proposal entails? Murder has been done here. They would demand to search the premises. *All* the premises. I do not think they would permit a room—*any* room— to remain locked and sealed. I am well aware, sir, of the terms of the late Sir Anthony's will. If that room is entered—whether through your fault or not, sir, and whatever the pretext—I need not remind you of the consequences to yourself."

The silence was so acute that the echoes of Perringer's voice seemed to linger in the room. Then Nick's voice, sharp like a knife, cut through the stillness.

"But damn it, man, we can't conceal murder."

"I was not suggesting it, sir. I merely venture to suggest that you do not act too hastily. Consider, sir, what can we do at this hour of the morning? Hunt for the murderer? Even if we could identify him we should have no chance of finding him in the dark. Inform the police? We are not on the telephone. The man in the village is probably out somewhere on duty. If he were found he could do no more than inform his superiors at Arunford. They would not send detectives here much before noon. And meanwhile, sir, great issues are at stake and much is to be considered."

Nick looked him straight in the eye.

"Perringer." he said, "I believe you know things that I do not know. I have discovered already that you have not always been frank with me. Yet on top of all this I have been told by some-body whose word I must accept that I may trust you implicitly. Rather reluctantly I do so. At least I will hear what you have to say. But come away from here. We can't talk freely in the same room with—this."

Perringer seemed satisfied.

"Leave everything as it is then, sir. We have not touched the body except to make sure that life is extinct. Will you lock the door, sir? And then we can talk elsewhere if you wish it, sir."

They went into the dining-room, where Nick mixed three stiff whiskies and sodas.

"Normally, sir," said Perringer, accepting a glass. "I am. as I think you know, an abstainer. However, on this occasion, sir—"

He drained a tumbler and continued in the same tone.

"Apart from the very grave consideration which I have already ventured to lay before you, there is something else. One may not shoot a burglar except in self-defence. Even then it may become a charge of manslaughter. But which of us three is going to plead self-defence when all of us are prepared to swear that we never shot him?

"Gentlemen, we are all armed. Let us examine one another's weapons so that you may swear— and I can assert—that none of these pistols has been fired to-night. We can, of course, give each other alibis. But that, gentlemen, would look as if we were acting in collusion."

Both Nick and Basil handed their automatics to Perringer, who passed his own pistol over to Nick.

"Now, gentlemen," Perringer continued, "we shall be none the worse for sleeping a little on our difficulties. It will be daylight very soon. Let us each go to his room and consider what is best to be done, taking every aspcct of the situation into account. Mr. Rockwell, sir, I suggest that you summon Mr. Hailsham and me to a conference in your bedroom at—say—seven-forty-five. Meanwhile, sir, I suggest that each of us studies this unexpected problem in all its aspects."

Nick glanced at Basil. Basil looked back at Nick, and presently spoke.

"It's up to you, old man. I think perhaps he's right. But it looks as if we'll have to inform the police whatever happens. Damned serious if we don't. Broad-arrow job, I should think."

"Very good, sir," said Perringer, plainly relieved. "Mr. Rockwell seems to agree with you and, unless he changes his mind in the course of the next few hours, the police must be informed." I hey talked on for another twenty minutes without coming a step nearer to a solution of their difficulties, at the end of which time Nick told Perringer that he might go to bed. Perringer went, leaving Nick and Basil to stare at each other.

"Girls heard nothing," said Nick at last. "They'd have been down asking questions. Going to tell them?"

Basil shrugged.

"Not until we've got to. Phew, what a mess! No common burglar, that, I'd like to bet. Dago. And what do you think of old Perringer's efforts to play for time?"

"Well, I thought I'd humour him. I don't know what the hell to do. If the police take a fancy to look inside that sealed room I shall probably be sunk, as Perringer said. Funny—Perringer being up and almost fully dressed at this hour. Didn't you notice?"

Basil grunted and tried to steady a swimming head by passing a hand across his brow.

"Must have heard the shot and put on his trousers and shirt in a hurry," Nick continued.

"Yes—or taken off his coat and waistcoat in a hurry. Wonder if he was eating lobster salad down in the cellar again."

Nick scowled at him.

"Shut up, man. Don't talk as if you're crazy."

"But I *am* crazy, old boy," said Basil in a tone of dreary resignation. "Didn't you know? *You're* crazy. The whole house is crazy. Everything's crazy."

CHAPTER XV
THE DISAPPEARING CORPSE

Basil entered Nick's bedroom shortly after half-past seven. He looked pale and jaded and his eyes were tired.

"Well, old man?" he said, planting himself with a soft thump at the foot of the bed. "Get any sleep?"

"A little—after I'd made up my mind. Whatever Perringer says we'll have to get the police. We can't connive at murder or homicide or wink at a fatal accident—whichever it may have been. We can't hide a body. If we were caught it would mean years in gaol, even if it didn't mean swinging. No, all the money in the world wouldn't be worth the worry and the risk."

Basil smiled and uttered a soft sigh of relief.

"I'm with you," he said. "But if you'd wanted to do the other thing I'd still have been with you."
"Thanks. I knew you would. That weighs with me too. Suddenly find myself with a tidy amount of responsibility."

Basil got up restlessly and strolled towards a mirror.

"Look here," he said, "don't consider anybody or anything but yourself and your future. I might just as well do time as go back to the stage. You do get regular meals in chokee. The girls are right out of this: they know nothing. Couldn't have heard anything in the night or they'd have been barging in. Last chance, old lad, if you want to change your mind."

He examined himself in the mirror.

"Gosh!" he continued. "I couldn't look worse if I'd spent fifty quid in a night-club. Damn it, I *look* like a bloody assassin. So, incidentally, do you. If we were arrested like this and photographed we'd never get a fair trial."

Nick laughed in spite of himself.

"All the same," he said, "I think we'd better make it a clean show. After all, our consciences are clear enough. And, coming to think of it, why should the police demand to enter that sealed room? The fact that it's sealed ought to tell them that they couldn't find anything there that had any bearings on this business. And it's miles away in another part of the house."

"In one sense, yes. In another sense, no. Take some time to get to it from there, but actually it's just above."

"Oh?" said Nick, considering. "Ah? Yes, I suppose it is. Hullo, I think this is Perringer."

He had heard footfalls, and these were followed almost immediately by a soft tap at the door, which was opened instantly to reveal Perringer.

Perringer was fully dressed and looked—for Perringer—slightly perturbed. In contrast to the dull eyes turned upon him his own eyes were almost feverishly bright.

"Good morning, sir. Good morning, sir." He greeted each in turn. "I am a minute or two before my time, sir, because—"

"All right, Perringer," said Nick shortly. "Sit down. Chuck me my dressing-gown and take that easy chair."

Perringer obeyed with quick, restless movements, but he seemed to sit unwillingly.

"We've made up our minds, Perringer," said Nick. "We ought to have done it then and there and acted accordingly. You were the stumbling-block, I am afraid, and Mr. Hailsham and I were too upset to be able to think clearly. We are going to drive into Arunford and bring the police back with us."

"Yes, sir? But why?"

Nick groaned.

"Oh, Perringer," he said, "you have spent too long in places where every prospect pleases but man is singularly vile. No doubt in San Analdo—or wherever it was you went with my uncle— you just buried any dead body you happened to find and walked away whistling. But you can't do it in England and get away with it. Really you can't."

"But, sir"—Perringer's own manner became slightly ironical—"suppose you can't produce your dead body?"

For the moment Nick and Basil both thought that Perringer had gone mad. The former answered him in a tone of wearied patience.

"I didn't propose taking it round to the police-station, Perringer. No, my intention was to call there in the car, collect a copper, bring him back, lead him gently by the hand to the side of the corpse, and then point to it and say, 'There, look at that!'"

"Yes, sir," said Perringer, in a tone of the deepest respect. "Only, unfortunately, sir—or fortunately as it may be—there isn't any corpse to show them, sir. The man who was killed—or the man we thought was killed—is gone."

A fit of coughing saved Nick from yelling aloud as he sprang out of bed.

"What—what the devil are you saying?" he cried, as he recovered his breath.

"I am trying to explain, sir. I went to the library a few minutes ago to make sure that all was in order. Very properly, if I may say so, you had left the roam exactly as it was for the police to inspect it—in view of the theory you then held of the necessity of calling in the police. That entailed leaving the window wide open.

"You had locked the door on the outside, leaving the key in the lock, so that I was able to inspect the room from the inside without troubling you. I entered, and everything was in order except that the window, sir, was still wide open. The body, sir, was gone."

Strangely enough, neither of Perringer's hearers uttered a sound. They seemed indeed to be holding back their breath.

"For the moment," Perringer proceeded smoothly, "I almost wondered if the events of last night—or early this morning— were a dream. But there was the open window. And between the open window and the spot where the body was lying there were bloodstains. Since I am a tidy man, sir—besides being, if I may say so, domesticated—I made haste to remove these by a simple method—"

"Oh, yes," snarled Nick, "I suppose that's about the first thing you learn in South America—how to remove a bloodstain."

"I acted on the principle, sir—no body, no murder. But a bloodstain, sir, is always an object of suspicion to the police."

"Yes," said Nick, "they've nasty minds. But where the devil *is* the body?"

Perringer spread out his hands as if in preparation to make a gesture showing that there was nothing up his sleeve.

"I have two theories, sir, if you will allow me to annunciate them."

"For God's sake, do!" said Nick.

"One is that the man was not dead after all. He recovered consciousness after we had left the room, and, suspicious of the hospitality this house seemed likely to offer him, dragged himself away."

"That's a wash-out!" snapped Basil. "The man was as dead as my Aunt Nelly, and you know it! You said so yourself."

"I certainly thought so," said Perringer, "but then I am not a medical man, and even doctors have been deceived by a cursory examination. I could not feel his pulse—but then I sometimes have difficulty in finding my own. I did not undress him to see where the bullet had struck him. Certainly the wound seemed to be in the region of the heart, but the heart, as you know, sir, occupies very little space. I have seen men before now with bullet-wounds in the chest who have been able to walk about."

"We'll have your other theory now, I think, Perringer," Nick said coldly.

"Alternatively, sir, I would suggest that the murderer—or the man's confederates—were for some reason unwilling to leave him there. His presence in the house, living or dead, might incriminate others. So they did themselves—and perhaps us—a service by stealing the body."

Nick was looking very hard at Perringer.

"Look here," he said sternly, "you didn't steal that body yourself, did you?"

"Sir," he said, "I take no offence because the accusation was hasty and therefore ill-considered. I own, sir, that the presence of the body would have been an embarrassment. Murdered bodies so often are. But you will admit, sir, that the hasty and effectual disposal of the same is almost an impossibility. That, sir, is why so many go to the gallows.

"Before you accuse me of having stolen the body—and I will admit that my expressed views might condone such a suspicion—! beg you to ask yourself what I could have done with it? Plainly I could not carry it very far, and if we should find a freshly dug grave in the grounds I give you my word of honour that I know nothing about it. Did I hide it about the house? If so, sir— for certain disgusting reasons which I hesitate to mention—you would be aware of its presence before very long.

"And now, sir, if you will allow me to say so, I think it would be doubly a mistake to inform the police. We did not kill the man. The body is gone. If we insist that there *was* a body there can be but one result. It is just possible that the police might not have insisted on entering the sealed room if the body were still where we found it. As matters now stand it would be their first attraction."

"By gad!" cried Basil. "He's right there!"

Nick said nothing. Dully he was aware that it was all wrong, dully he was aware too that he had been listening to a piece of sound reasoning.

Perringer stood up. His manner had suddenly changed.

"Shall I serve breakfast at the usual hour, sir?"

He spoke as if all were already settled and Nick, well aware of the liberty, condoned it. For his friends' sakes and his own sake too he was suddenly disposed to let Perringer have his way. It entailed going against the law, but nevertheless it was obvious that nothing he could do would restore the dead man—if he were really dead—to life.

"Thank you, Perringer," he said. "I feel that there's a great deal in what you have been saying. We'll leave it at that. . . . Er—what was it you last said? Breakfast? Thank you, yes— in about half an hour."

Perringer thanked him and moved towards the door, but suddenly halted and turned again. "I beg your pardon, sir, I think it would be as well if you advised me as to your intentions with regard to telling the young ladies."

"Not a word, Perringer, unless they ask. If they ask I don't yet know what we shall say. But I've a strong idea that they heard nothing."

"I hope not, sir. Very good, sir. And I shall have heard nothing either if they ask me."

The door closed upon him. There was dead silence within the room for some thirty seconds. Then Basil wandered to the door, opened it and looked out. Perringer was really gone.

"Well?" he said, closing the door again. "What do you make of things now? Did Perringer pinch the body—or didn't he?"

"I wouldn't put it past him," said Nick grimly. "But there are objections to that theory. Perringer rather glibly pointed them out. I'm not holding it up against him because he was so damned fluent and so damned lucid. He'd had hours to think out his position, same as we had."

"Ye-es," said Basil slowly, "there's a good deal in that. No use trying to fasten anything on to Perringer simply because one doesn't like him. One thing I'm not satisfied about, though. Could Perringer himself have done the shooting?"

"That's been giving me a headache, too," said Nick. "If it were even just possible I wouldn't hesitate to suspect him. But I don't think it was even reasonably possible. Look at it like this. We were pretty quick down, weren't we? No distance for us to the main stairs. Well, down in the hall we heard Perringer coming down the back stairs. Having shot his man he'd have had to make a hell of a detour to get where he was when we met him, and I don't see how he could have done it in the time.

"He wasn't out of breath and his gun, as we saw for ourselves, hadn't been fired. He might have had two guns, of course, but why should he? For there's one thing sticks out a mile—whoever killed that little dark-skinned bloke didn't premeditate it. And Perringer—if he did it—must have premeditated it to collect so much evidence in his own favour. Besides, how on earth could he have known that that fellow was going to break in?"

Basil looked at Nick almost admiringly and a broad smile illumined his face.

"Looks to me," he said, "as if Perringer must have bitten you. You're getting fluent and lucid too."

"I'm trying to be. It's a knotty problem, but there aren't so many ramifications to it. The right answer—a plain Yes or No— to three or four questions would give us the solution. If Perringer hid the body he did it for an obvious reason—that he didn't want the police in here and making some excuse to enter that sealed room. They could do it, of course, if they insisted. Well, that would be his motive. But did he do it?

"Had the dead man confederates? And did they afterwards enter by way of the window—left conveniently open for them—and remove the corpse? Well, it would be possible, but why should they? Because its presence in the house might implicate *them*? That would pass. But did they actually do it?

"If so, what did they do with it afterwards? Or, in the other event, what did Perringer do with it? Will it come to light again, and will some frightfully clever detective—one of the fictional sort materialized for our benefit—trace it to this house?

"Last, and not least, did it walk away under its own steam? "

"Like Lazarus?" Basil suggested irritably.

"I mean—was he really dead?"

Basil stared and puffed out his cheeks, pursing his mouth as if to whistle.

"Well," he said grimly, with a slight shudder, "he looked dead, didn't he? And Perringer examined him and said he was dead."

"Oh, yes, he looked dead. And there are men walking about to-day who've been pronounced dead by doctors. And Perringer isn't a doctor. Perringer felt for his pulse and couldn't feel any-thing. Can't always find my own pulse. I repeat—was he still alive after all, although badly wounded, and did he manage to get away?"

Basil laughed cynically.

"Did he go or was he pushed? And was he a common burglar or was he after something else? Well. I suppose one day we shall get the Yeses and the Noes to some of these—if we don't go Bats in the meanwhile."

"In the meanwhile," Nick echoed, "let's get ready for breakfast. Not that I feel like it, but I rather fancy the unruffled Perringer will be able to peck a bit, even if he hasn't been feeding his face already. So why shouldn't we?"

A little later the girls, arriving downstairs, brought with them bright morning faces and complexions in full bloom.

"My dear!" exclaimed Milly, looking hard at Nick after she had been kissed. "You don't look a bit well. Had a bad night?"

"Rotten," Nick grunted.

"Bad dreams?"

Nick smiled and then uttered a sudden laugh which sounded strange even to his own ears. "One of those darned silly nightmares," he said, "with no sense to them at all. You know the sort?"

"Yes," laughed Milly in all innocence. "I know what you mean."

CHAPTER XVI
PERRINGER AGAIN

It was part of Nick's innocent philosophy that a needle, cotton, buttons and a few bits of old rag were sufficient to keep any True Woman—or Girl—amused between breakfast and tea-time, allowing of course for a luncheon interval. But it is not within the scope of this chronicle to discant on the many things he had to learn, nor tell by what processes—painful or otherwise— he came to learn some of them.

But it chanced that morning that the girls lived up to his ideal of True Womanhood by finding that they had sewing to do, and a great deal of sewing at that. There was also shopping to be done, so that Nick and Basil were able to escape to Arunford in the car, with a list of requisites scribbled by Milly.

They began their shopping in the bar of the *Chequers* without having to consult Milly's list of requirements—for they were still feeling shattered, as Nick expressed it, by the recent events. The *Chequers* seemed to be a rendezvous of the better-to-do townsmen and certain aimless and casual gentlemen who drove in cars from the surrounding villages. Sympathetic listeners, hearing that they had had a lot of worry and a disturbed night, suggested interesting and divers remedies: and after the sixth prescription Nick said that he felt a bit better but had developed a headache, and Basil said that the headache from which he had been suffering was gone, but that uncomfortable symptoms had developed elsewhere.

These remarks occasioned the barmaid—a young woman with an original turn of mind and a taste for epigram—to remark that we are not all made alike.

While they were trying to devise an elixir of which one dose would be sufficient to banish all ills from all men of divers constitutions, their purpose was suddenly diverted by the arrival of Major Jones-Dobbins. They did not then know Major Jones-Dobbins, but his remarks to the young lady, while he was covering the distance between the door and the counter, instantly diverted their thoughts from their own minor ailments.

"'Morning, Nelly. Heard about the murder? A large Haig, please."

Nick glanced at Basil, who had just spilled some matches.

"Murder?" he repeated. "Excuse me, sir—did you say Murder? "

"Yes," said the Major cheerfully. "Only a few miles out here. Strangers, aren't you? Little place called Mardstone, if you happen to know it."

"We've just come from there," said Nick.

"Oh, really? Really? Well, you know Mardstone Manor?"

Basil spilled the rest of his matches and stood holding the empty shell of a box.

"Not *there!*" he breathed.

"No, no, no, no, no. I'm just trying to explain it to you. Half a mile this side of the lodge gates of Mardstone Manor there's a spinney on the other side of the road. Well, some people call it a copse, but I call it a spinney. Which would you call it, Nelly? That place where you go courting on your evening out?"

Inwardly fuming, Nick and Basil had to listen to laboured jest and clumsy repartee. And afterwards it was with difficulty that the Major was steered back to the point. A sudden intellectual urge to discover the precise difference between a copse and a spinney caused him to direct that one of the hotel servants should fetch him a small dictionary which he knew to be in a little bookcase in the drawing-room.

"Oh, somebody been shot," said the Major at last. "Just met our worthy Chief Constable and he told me. Looks a foreigner—the dead man does. They found him in the spinney—or the copse. Might have been done in by one of those race-course gangs, you know. He'd got some kind of burglarious tool in one of his pockets, but he doesn't seem to have broken in anywhere. However, we'll know more about that later on. Will you gentlemen join me?"

They "joined" him, but with more apparent apathy and less courtesy than they might otherwise have shown.

"Same, do you think?" Nick whispered to Basil, as a miniature dictionary was presented to the Major.

"Must be," muttered Basil, with hardly a movement of the lips. "Foreigner."

"Dictionary says that a copse is a small spinney," the Major announced in full voice. "Now let's look up Spinney."

"Then how the devil did he get there?" Nick whispered.

Basil hunched and dropped his shoulders.

"Search me!" he whispered back.

The Major flung the dictionary on to the carpet with a gesture of disgust.

"Bloody thing says that a spinney's a small copse. Now what good would that be to a poor blank of a foreigner who was trying to learn our blank language?"

"Well, one—er—sanguinary foreigner won't have to trouble about our asterisk language any more—if he really were a foreigner," said Nick. "Had your friend the Chief Constable any theory about him, sir?"

"Didn't say. But it sticks out a mile. Gangster business. Revenge. They didn't kill him there. Signs of his having been dragged there. Probably his friends took him for a ride. Shouldn't think the police will worry about it much—if they know the man. One more undesirable out of the way, and a damn' good job. Too many of 'em about. Serve 'em damn' well right if they can't learn English. Tell 'em a copse is a spinney, and then tell 'em a spinney's a copse. *Thai* settles—"

With the ex-Temporary Major firmly attached by his elbows to the bar, and looking as if nothing less than the sudden dissolution of the counter could remove him, the two younger men retreated a few steps and began to whisper. Basil spoke first.

"If the police come round now? Rather near us, you know, and they might—'specially as that chap had something suspicious on him. Well, what are we to say?"

"Nothing. We don't know anything. Our mental attitude has got to be that a man found dead in our house can't have—or at least needn't have—anything to do with another man found dead half a mile away. We don't know anything about this second man, and since the police don't know anything about the first we're not likely to be questioned on those lines."

"Right—I see!" Basil was looking extremely unhappy. "I've got a kind of complex, you know. Had one pretty foul sort of nurse when I was a kid. Always threatening to give me to the policeman when I jibbed at burnt sago pudding. Ever since then I've had a kind of horror of the police. I can't help regarding every copper I see as something even worse than burnt sago pudding. And, you know, they're not all fools, even in the country. They do find out things sometimes."

"Let 'em," grunted Nick. "I've got a one-track mind for the time being. I'm not going to see any possible connection between one foreigner who has the bad taste to get murdered in my house and another foreigner who has the decency to get the job done in privacy half a mile or so away. Nor will Perringer."

"Perringer!" Basil laughed aloud. "Gosh, no, I bet he's with you there! Wonder what he's thinking—if he's heard. Well, we'll all be on Dartmoor by and by, and meanwhile let the lunatic game—whatever it is—go on. And, just for the present, what about that shopping?"

"Yes. let's," said Nick.

They departed: and did their shopping after the casual fashion of young men, heaving their purchases callously on to the un-occupied seats in the rear of the car. They were driving home-ward when, in a tone that sounded casual enough. Nick said: "I think we'll give the car a bit of a clean when we get in."

The cleaning of cars was not much to Basil's taste and his comment lacked enthusiasm.

"Oh, she's not so bad. Had some oil this morning. Running parts all right."

"I wasn't thinking of that," Nick retorted, frowning. "Didn't you notice anything on the floor behind when you were shedding the groceries?"

"No. Can't say I did."

"Oh, well, I spotted something. Show it you when I get out. Great blob of something. Might be red paint, of course. Might be—something else."

Sudden light dawned on Basil.

"*Phew!*" he said.

"Yes. Now we know how the dead body came to wander so far. Good job Perringer's a careful driver, isn't it?"

"You think it was Perringer?"

"Don't know who else would have sneaked the car for a job like that—and brought it back again. Wonder we didn't hear him. But we were too hot and bothered, I suppose, and full of talk and theories. This ought to teach Perringer to be tidy— giving himself away like that. And it's nothing that we'd want the police to notice!'

Basil was resting his brow in one of his hands. His voice spoke from the neighbourhood of one of his sleeves.

"We can't prove that Perringer—"

"My dear old ass, who was so set in the first place against going to the police? Who wanted us to do nothing until daylight—and why? He knew he couldn't hide the body for long and he wanted to shift it to some place where it wouldn't compromise us—and him."

Basil grinned.

"Y'know," he said, "there are points about that move. If Perringer were twenty years younger, and only half as ugly, and belonged to the opposite sex, I'm not sure that I wouldn't want to kiss him."

"All the same I don't like flummoxing the police. I want the murderer to be collared. And from what our military friend let out, the police know already that the body wasn't killed just where it was found."

They drove on in silence save for a brief remark dropped by Nick as they passed the copse—or spinney—where the body had been found. A policeman stood at the roadside, having apparently nothing to do but smile contentedly at the blue sky. Two or three bicycles were in the ditch and a dark blue car stood empty a few yards up the road.

"Every picture tells a story," Nick observed.

They turned into the drive. Outside the house a flutter of blue and white disclosed itself—as the distance lessened—as feminine attire worn by Milly. She hurried a few superfluous steps to meet the slowing car.

"Have you heard?" she called out. "There's been a murder!"

"I know that one," said Nick cheerfully. "Somebody put water in the bishop's whisky."

"No—really!" Her manner became more urgent as the car stopped. "In that copse—over there."

"Copse, you see—not spinney," said Basil. "That settles it."

"Will you stop fooling, you two!" Milly actually stamped a small foot. "Of course you were out when the police came—so we had to cope with them."

Something like glee was surging in Nick's breast as he climbed out of the car.

"The police? What did they want? And what did you tell them?"

Milly's brief ill-humour had evaporated.

"Well, they seemed to think that the man who'd been killed was a burglar, and they wanted to know if anybody had tried to break in here last night. Perringer just laughed."

"I should like to have heard him," said Nick. "Scornful sound, was it? And what happened after Perringer had laughed?"

"Oh, Betty and I told him that there hadn't been any burglary here. And he asked if we were sure that there hadn't been any attempt. Because if we were sure, he said, he needn't waste his time and yours by calling again when you were in. So of course Betty and I swore solemnly that nobody had tried to break in here, because if they had we couldn't help knowing it by now. So then he—What's the matter with you, Nick?"

"Nothing, darling," said Nick, releasing her from his arms almost as suddenly as he had picked her up. "You looked so delightful that I just had to kiss you. Er—do you think you could find me a drop of warm water and a scrubbing-brush? The old bus is a bit untidy. . . . No, thank you, dear, I don't want you to help. . .

Milly went around to the yard behind to enter the domestic premises by a back door and fetch the articles required. She had gone half-way when she heard the car following her, and, catching other sounds, she glanced back at it over her shoulder and smiled.

"Like a pair of schoolboys," she thought. "I wonder what's made them so frightfully buckish all of a sudden?"

They had just effectually made short work of a small but important job when Perringer came out to them. Since it was a very warm morning he wanted to know if he should fetch up some hock for the luncheon table. There was no ice, he regretted, but the cellar was beautifully cool.

"All right," Nick responded. "And I say, Perringer."

He lowered his voice and looked straight at Perringer.

"I'd like to have heard you talking to the police this morning. Telling them that there'd been no burglary here!"

Perringer uttered a dry cough.

"I beg your pardon, sir. It was the young ladies who said so first. And I submit, sir, very respectfully, that it was not my place to contradict my betters."

Basil, who saw a lot of dry fun in Perringer, uttered a sudden hoot of laughter.

"You'll be the death of me one of these days, Perringer," he said.

"On the contrary, sir, if I may say it with all respect," Perringer returned evenly. "I may be the saving of you one of these nights."

He was gone before they could ask him what he meant, and they did not call him back. They had already learned that nothing was to be gained by questioning Perringer too closely.

CHAPTER XVII
"A GREAT DEAL TO HIDE"

The murder, while of course it became the most fruitful topic of conversation in the immediate locality, did not rouse the interest of the general public throughout the land—like many other murder mysteries, solved and unsolved.

The dead man was nobody known and respected. He was some sort of foreigner and plainly of a low type. In death he kept his anonymity as close as—it seemed—he had contrived to preserve it in life. No relatives came to claim the body. His photograph and finger-prints were unknown to the police. A brief burial-service read in charity ushered him into a nameless grave. And then charity gave place to speculative slander.

The man, whosoever he may have been, was better dead than alive. He was probably one of a gang, and on his way to "do a job" when one of his own kind had turned on him. At least, that was the view of the police as given to the crime-journalists, and passed on by them—with very few imaginative flourishes— to the public at large. A plausible theory was that his colleagues in crime had suspected him of being a prospective "squealer", and had thought it preferable to taka their vengeance a little in advance of the "squeal".

An irritating feature of the case to Nick and Basil was that although they had heard the fatal shot, and were on the spot so shortly afterwards, they were as much in ignorance as the general public as to who had fired it. They knew so much more than anybody else except Perringer, and they were just as much in the dark with regard to the actual murderer.

It was easy to accuse Perringer in their minds, and equally easy to acquit him. No evidence they could bring against Perringer—if they were minded to charge him—would be enough to secure a conviction. It was very doubtful if Perringer could have gone from the scene of the crime to the spot where they had encountered him without his passing through the hall. In which case they must have heard or seen him. And Perringer would have needed time to manufacture all the appearance of innocence after a deed which must at least have been unpremeditated. Perringer had presented them with a cold and fully loaded pistol. True, he might have made a hasty and temporary disposal of another weapon, but—regarding the hasty and obviously unprepared nature of the deed—it seemed highly unlikely.

But did Perringer know who had done it? That was another matter. Perringer's subsequent conduct said Yes. But if the deed had been done by one of the dead man's accomplices—and therefore another enemy—why did not Perringer denounce him and thus kill two birds with one stone?

Answer (according to Nick, and agreed to by Basil, after much discourse): (1) Perringer might know why the deed had been done, yet be unable to say exactly who had done it, or (2) Perringer was keeping quiet because he feared that, once the police were in the house they might be over curious about the Scaled Door. That was Perringer's expressed excuse for not immediately calling in the police and persuading Nick and Basil to "sleep on it". But one never knew what motives were at work behind Porringer's pallid brow.

When, two mornings later, Perringer approached Nick and urbanely and respectfully told him that he had a confession to make, Nick imagined for the moment that at last he was going to know the truth or listen to a new lie.

"Sir," said Perringer, "there is something that I must confess to you."

Nick was disposed to play lightly with him.

"Don't tell me you've mucked up the tennis net—trying to tighten it."

"Indeed, no, sir. It is quite another matter, and if I may say so, sir, a more important one. If, sir, I have deceived you, I shall ask you to believe that I did so with the best intentions."

"Yes?" said Nick grimly. "Well, I suppose you've been told where good intentions lead?"

"Yes, sir, it was Byron said it," Perringer answered rather surprisingly. "And Byron," he added thoughtfully, "of all men, should have known. He must have been a man rather like the late Sir Anthony, sir. Except that Sir Anthony's conduct towards the ladies, sir, was always above reproach."

"Delighted to hear it," said Nick, laughing, "and I hope I take after him."

"I am sure you do, sir," Perringer returned gravely. "When you brought another gentleman and two ladies here, sir, I will confess that I had some misgivings—particularly, sir, as they seemed to have been connected with the less serious side of the drama. But I am bound to say. sir—if I may say it with all respect—that this unconventional household has been a model of propriety. And as soon as you are married to that charming young lady, sir, my cup of joy will be full."

Nick laughed a little and wanted to laugh much more.

"D'you know, Perringer, I suspect you of being a prude. But you've been all over the world and must have bumped up against some pretty queer morals. Also, damn it, you're a professed atheist, so I suppose you ought to believe in free love."

Perringer sighed.

"As to what I may have seen abroad, sir, I tolerated much of it on the surface—for it was not my place to do otherwise. As to my being an atheist, sir, that is another story. I humbly submit, sir, that a man may change his mind—or have it changed for him by the Powers that be—and find a creed. So, sir, the clergy would have us believe."

"Go on, Perringer," Nick laughed. "You're a much better Christian than I am—which wouldn't be hard—and you said you were an atheist at my uncle's inquest to avoid lying on your oath." The thought had only just occurred to Nick, and he flung it straight at Perringer just as it came to him. For the effect it had on Perringer it might almost have been vitriol rather than words which he had thrown in the man's face.

"My God, sir!" Perringer cried, aghast.

Nick, too, was almost aghast at the effect of his words, which had been uttered quite tentatively and hardly in all seriousness. But he knew that they had gone home. At last he was rewarded by the sight of Perringer with his armour pierced. He followed up his advantage.

"However," he said, "I don't suppose it was that which you wanted to confess. So let's hear the worst."

Perringer moistened his lips before speaking.

"The gentleman you found in the house that afternoon, sir, and I told you he was Colonel Sandingford—well, it wasn't the Colonel himself, sir."

"Then what was he doing there? And what right had you both to say—"

"He was there, sir, with Colonel Sandingford's full authority, sir. Technically, sir, I did nothing wrong. I—we—did not quite know how to explain to you at the time. We were taken by surprise, sir. Colonel Sandingford himself, sir, is already aware of what happened. He is sorry about it, but he realizes that I am not to blame."

"I know he knows," said Nick grimly, "because I met him in Town."

Once more Perringer's jaw dropped.

"You—met—him!"

"Aha, my good Perringer, I've been holding this over your head for quite a while. It's a pity we can't trust each other, for I begin now to think that we are serving a common cause—you in the light, so to speak, and I in the dark, as it were. Had you been frank with me I might have been frank with you. But, you see, your distrust in me bred distrust on my part."

Perringer's lips moved for a moment or two before he actually spoke.

"Sir," he said earnestly, "I do trust you. I always trusted you. If there are certain things which I did not tell you—and do not tell you now—it is because of a promise I had already made to keep them secret. I think that you will be told all someday, sir, and then you will understand. And if in the meanwhile you should find them out for yourself—which I almost wish may happen—you will still understand."

Nick considered and inclined his head.

"Yes," he said slowly, "I'm willing to believe that. Colonel Sandingford—the real Colonel Sandingford—told me that I might trust you implicitly, as undoubtedly my uncle did. And—er—

just to cement the new-born confidence which we have in each other, will you be good enough to answer just one question?" The younger man's tone of light irony was almost playful, but Perringer knew him well enough now to be alert to a suspicious symptom. A very awkward question was on the way.

"If I may do so, sir, without any breach of confidence to— others."

"Then tell me what the devil you meant by borrowing my car without my leave and depositing that dead body in the copse?" A slow grin—almost the disarming grin of a boy detected in an act of naughtiness—spread over Perringer's adult face. Suddenly. and at least just for that moment, Nick found the man exceedingly likeable.

"I do not admit, sir," he murmured distantly, "that I did any such thing."

"Oh, you needn't admit it," said Nick cheerfully, "but I'll give you a damned good tip. Next time you take a dead body for a run in my car—the body of a man who's been untidily killed—don't leave a bloodstain like a map of Corsica on the floor matting. It's a wonder the whole bunch of us isn't in gaol."

Once more he was rewarded by the sight of Perringer's shattered face and the sound of Perringer's very uncertain voice.

"Did I—er—was there a bloodstain in the car, sir? Well, sir, I think I can explain that. I was giving the car a bit of a dust-out, sir, and I happened to have cut my hand and—look, sir, here's the place."

Nick looked and laughed.

"That cut," he said, "is a good many days old and it hasn't bled for at least a week. You go to hell and think up something better. But I don't blame you for refusing to commit yourself. You did a very serious thing, and I'm willing to believe that you had a sound reason for doing it."

He looked at Perringer and grinned, and was about to turn away when Perringer spoke again.

"Excuse me, sir. if I take a liberty. But there's one favour I should very much like to ask of you."

"Right ho, Perringer. Yes?" (After all, whatever it might be, there was no harm in being asked.)

"I should very much appreciate the honour of shaking hands with you. sir."

Nick held out his hand at once.

"Sorry to be theatrical and all that," he said airily, "but all the same it's true that I've never shaken hands with a man unless I believed him to be honest."

"I am only a servant, sir," said Perringer, "but since I have been an honest man myself I believe I can say the same."

Two clauses in that sentence contained food for thought which Nick assimilated as their hands met. He seized upon the first.

"Excuse me, Perringer," he said, "but you're a man of education, aren't you? You throw in a lot of Sirs and occasionally you make a grammatical lapse—I think on purpose. Still, I think that you're not quite what you seem. Aren't I right? But don't answer me if you'd rather not." Perringer moistened his lips.

"To tell you the truth, sir, I was practically sure of a First in Mods, at Oxford—but I was sent down for stealing."

Something exploded on Nick's lips and surprise gave him a physical and visible reaction. "And." Perrineer continued in a voice rendered almost toneless by suppression, "God knows what I should have become by now if Sir Anthony—God bless him—had not thrown me a life-line. So it's no wonder—is it?—that I should be ready to lie on his behalf and fight for him and die for him. My name was not always Perringer. My father was vicar of a fashionable church when I discarded the name which I had disgraced. He died a bishop, having gained much and lost nothing by his godliness. Your uncle, a finer Christian in every sense, did something more than intone services and preach. He gave everything, risking liberty, life—"

The man's voice broke suddenly and paused, but after a breathing-space he regained control.

"I don't think I need labour the comparison," he said with a wry smile.

Nick had been listening, much more deeply moved than he cared to show.

"Thank you for telling me all this," he said gruffly. "Just one thing more. My uncle's death, tragic as it was, doesn't seem to have been in any way mysterious or due to malice. The driver of the car that knocked him down came forward like a man as soon as he suspected that there had been an accident. It was all plain sailing. I can't think why the devil you had to get out of taking the oath by yarning to the coroner about your being an atheist. You had nothing to hide."

"Pardon me, sir," said Perringer, returning to his old manner, "I had a very great deal to hide—if I had been asked the wrong sort of questions."

Nick laughed in spite of himself, seeing Perringer prepared to close like an oyster if any of the wrong sort of questions were forthcoming now. Concerning himself, he had been engagingly and surprisingly frank, but there were other subjects on which he was not to be drawn.

"Very well—er—Mr. Perringer," he said, giving the older man the courtesy title for that single occasion. "Thank you for being so frank with me. Am I on my honour, by the way to repeat nothing of what you have told me to—er—my friends?"

"I have no right to ask it, sir," said Perringer. "No doubt they have a right to your full confidence. But I should like your assurance, sir, that it will not go beyond these walls."

Perringer had slipped easily and naturally back into the role of servant again. Nick let him remain.

"All right, Perringer," he said, gently and gravely. "I promise you that."

Basil was out and the girls busy until nearly lunch-time, so that it was not until they had assembled to wait for Perringer and the square mahogany butler's tray, that Nick told the others about his recent conversation with the man. Basil arrived first.

Milly heard that part which the girls were not yet to be told.

"No doubt now," he remarked, "about who shifted the body. But there never was much—after we'd found the bloodstain. Did he own up?"

"Not exactly. But he didn't deny it. He just fenced a bit."

"That's Perringer exactly," grunted Basil.

The girls joined them and were told the rest in snatches.

"Wonder what Porringer's real name is," Nick concluded. "Mind you, I believe every word he told me. Easy to catch him out if he weren't really an Oxford man. But fancy his being the son of a bishop!"

Betty wrinkled her impertinent nose.

"Was Perringer's old man an archbishop? " she inquired. "Or just an ordinary sort of bishop—like the one who once patted me on the head in Spa Road, Bermondsey?"

"Oh, just an ordinary sort of bishop, I suppose," said Nick. "Why?"

"Oh, nothing." Betty's expressive nose became all wrinkles. "Only I didn't think Perringer's father would have been anything so common."

She gained her laugh, for they had begun to laugh easily once more. It ended with Nick saying: "No frivolity this afternoon, Betty, my child. Nice demure clothes and nice demure behaviour. I rather think Colonel Sandingford—the real Colonel Sandingford—will be paying us a surprise visit to-day or to-morrow."

Milly gave him a quick glance.

"What makes you think that?"

"Well—er—Perringer must have heard from him, I suppose." Basil looked surprised.

"Mean to say he told you? Not a bit like him, is it?"

"Ah," said Nick, grinning, "but he doesn't know he told me. I'm just beginning to learn our Perringer. Anyhow, I thought the aged warrior ought to know of what had been happening here, so I dropped him a line. I dare say that would have brought him down in any case."

"What's been happening here?" Milly asked quickly: while her brother uttered a smothered groan and rolled his eyes at Nick. And Nick, in danger of being stumped, managed to slide his foot back over the crease in time.

"Oh nothing much," he said airily. "Just a murdered body found in a copse over there. Nothing to do with us, of course, but I thought it would cheer him up to know. And incidentally I thought I'd better break it to him that I'm engaged to be married."

Perringer appeared suddenly from below the stairs, burdened by his enormous wooden tray. Of any previous talk which had taken place between him and his young master there was rot the ghost of a recollection lingering in his eyes.

"Lunch will be served in one minute, sir," he said to Nick. "There is claret on the sideboard, sir, but would you wish me to get up some more hock?"

"I don't know what sort of bishop his father was," Basil commented within himself, "but he's about the best butler I ever saw off the stage."

CHAPTER XVIII
THE REAL COLONEL SANDINGFORD

Colonel Sandingford duly arrived at about a quarter to four that afternoon in a hired car from Arunford station. Any misgivings he might have had about the unconventional *menage* at the Manor were probably alleviated, if not dispelled, by the sight of four young people playing tennis. (Or three were playing and one trying to play, for Betty—whose childish athletics had been limited to hopscotch—was still in the novice class.)

Nothing is more innocent nor disarming than the sight of four young people, all in white, playing tennis. It would be difficult to observe such a scene and believe that the devil ever came near a tennis-court. A croquet-lawn is different. Sinister figures in frock-coats—long enough to conceal a barbed tail—used to be seen playing croquet.

No such parenthetical observations as these, however, passed through Colonel Sandingford's mind. He told the driver to wait for a few minutes. He was acutely conscious of the presence—in the back of the car—of a suitcase large enough to become the principal exhibit in a trunk murder trial. It suggested an obvious intention, and delicacy forbade him to expose it until he had had a few words with Nick.

Nick saw him as he alighted. The game stopped abruptly and Nick came hurrying across, swinging his racket and then holding it as if it were a sleeping infant.

"Glad to see you, sir," he said. "There are the others over there. Shall I call them over and introduce them?"

"No hurry," said Colonel Sandingford. "I shall be most pleased to meet them, of course, and I am sorry to interrupt your game, but I should like the opportunity of a chat with you first and possibly—if you will forgive me—one with Perringer. Perhaps they would be good enough to excuse us for a little while and improvise a game of singles."

"All right," said Nick. "Will you come inside?"

"Thank you. Er—in view of the gravity of your news I wondered if—er—I might trespass on your hospitality for a night or two."

"Oh, to be sure, to be sure."

"Thank you, Mr. Rockwell. I'm afraid I am not as young as the rest of your party, but—" He paused, laughed and laid a hand on the younger man's shoulder. "Let us go inside and talk, shall we? Your letter—not to mention what I have read in the papers about that oth—that murder so near here—has given me a great deal of anxiety."

After the suitcase had been lifted out and the driver paid, they entered the house and went through into the dining-room. The Colonel declined liquid refreshment and elected to wait until the usual hour for a cup of tea.

"Now," he said, accepting a cigarette, "will you be good enough to tell me, Mr. Rockwell, exactly what has been happening here sir.ee our meeting in town? Your letter was most disurbing. So was what I read in the papers about that murdered body which was found so near the house."

"Same body that we found in the library," growled Nick. "The one that disappeared."

"Did you see it? Are you sure?"

"No, I didn't see it, but I'm sure enough. Perringer stole the body and dumped it in the copse. Borrowed my car for the job and left a bloodstain big enough to convict the lot of us."

The Colonel started slightly, but kept his face and eyed Nick steadily beneath an imposing frown.

"Are you sure about this?" he asked heavily.

"Perfectly, sir. So, I think, are you."

"Exactly what do you mean by that?" asked Colonel Sandingford in the very gentle voice of an elderly gentleman who is anxious to preserve his temper.

"Excuse me, sir, but doesn't Perringer correspond with you?"

The Colonel's eyes narrowed, but suddenly his brows cleared again and he laughed.

"I can see," he said, "that I am dealing with a young man of some perspicacity."

Nick grinned, but not too good-humouredly.

"I've generally been considered rather bone-headed," he said, "and if I really were an ass would you consider it a virtue?"

"No." said the Colonel frankly, "but it might be deuced convenient."

He laughed again and his manner became more confidential.

"Perhaps I could clear up some of these mysteries," he said.

"I think I can safely promise that you shall know everything some day. Meanwhile there is one thing I can, and indeed must, tell you. It concerns your friends too. You are all in danger."

"So," said Nick, smiling, "it had begun to dawn on us. Something to do with the Sealed Room, I suppose."

"You have had one—er—burglar. He may be the forerunner of others. You are armed from what you tell me? So am I? For God's sake, don't shoot at sight. Don't shoot at another man—until you're quite sure he's going to make trouble. You might—well, you might make a very serious mistake."

"Such as hitting the man who came here and impersonated you that afternoon, sir."

Colonel Sandingford looked sharply across at Nick.

"What made you say that?" he demanded.

Nick, who had taken a shot in the dark, smiled to himself. It was rather pleasant to score against one who made himself so deliberately obscure.

"One important thing I should like to ask you, Colonel," he said, eluding the question.

"Yes?"

"Suppose we have burglars here again and suppose they force their way into the Sealed Room—what then? Am I still to keep outside?"

The Colonel drew in his lips. His brow was a maze of wrinkles. Obviously the problem was not new to him. Obviously all that delayed his answer was a choice of the form in which it was to be delivered.

"If they force their way in there," he said, "it doesn't matter much what you do. Nothing will matter anymore. It will all be over."

Nick hesitated to ask him what would "be over." He surmised that he would get no satisfactory answer, and he knew the irritation caused by too many useless questions. Still, it is possible that he might have asked another had not the Colonel reverted again to Nick's last utterances. "The Sealed Room—yes. I think, if you don't mind, I will go with you now and formally inspect the seal. Then—no doubt Perringer will be getting tea? I can go into the kitchen and have a little chat with him while he prepares it."

Nick, murmuring something that sounded politely acquiescent, rose and crossed the room, giving his visitor precedence at the door. Colonel Sandingford evidently knew the way to the Sealed Room, for he turned in the right direction and kept slightly ahead of his host.

They halted at last at the forbidden door, and the Colonel halted, legs apart and hands clasped behind him. Such an attitude, Nick felt, he must have struck while carrying out inspections of a much more prosaic sort in his old Army days. Something of the Army manner returned to his speech.

"Yes, that's all right," he said, in a voice pitched higher than usual.

It might have been his old manner of telling troops that their hut was in presentable order, but it seemed to Nick almost as if the words were intended to carry beyond his own ears. If, for instance, there had been someone on the other side of that door he must have heard every word and recognized the voice—if he already knew it.

They turned away and went back in silence to the dining-room. The sight of that door had previously acted as a brake upon Nick's speech—as if magic wings had borne him back to childhood and set him down outside that cupboard which was positively known to be the lair of the Bogy Man.

"You know, Colonel Sandingford," Nick said, rather sheepishly, "I've often felt that there's something on the other side of that door."

"So there is," said the Colonel shortly. "Otherwise there wouldn't be all this fuss."

"Some person, I mean," Nick amended, conscious of having said something rather ridiculous.

The visitor turned and glanced at him.

"Getting fanciful, are you? Well, you know why your uncle shut up the room."

It was exactly what Nick did not know. The reason given had never satisfied him.

"Surely, sir," he said, "you don't expect me to believe in ghosts?"

"If you did you would be in good company—with Stead, Hugh Benson, Bernard Vaughan, Conan Doyle, Podmore, Myers and a great many more brilliant men who have just passed on or still remain with us. To a long list of considerable names I could add your uncle's. He was no fool—and no dreamer."

Nick felt that the issues were becoming confused.

"The people from whom we seem to be in danger," he said, "and that foreigner who got in here the other night—surely it isn't the—er—ghost that attracts them?"

The older man looked at Nick again and his expression suddenly changed. Possibly he had a momentary vision of himself in Nick's place, for his expression grew kindly and almost playful.

"My dear boy—if you will forgive me—I do not intend giving you an unlimited number of guesses. You might ultimately arrive at the truth by the process of elimination—but I think it would take you a long time. I am sorry I am not able to be entirely frank with you, and I beg you not to press me.

"And now, if you don't mind, I will walk into your servants' hall and have a little talk with the excellent Perringer—while you go and tell your friends that the queer man who tells you nothing will be your guest, at least for to-night."

Nick said, not quite truthfully, that they would be delighted, and when they had reached the door of the dining-room once more he asked if he should ring for Perringer.

"No, no," laughed the Colonel, "I will go and draw the badger. I expect he has heard my voice. If not some other sense will have told him that I'm here."

Nick parted from him in the hall and went out again into the grounds. No game of singles was in progress and tennis seemed to be over for the time being. The three were squatting in line upon the court, plainly waiting his return.

"All present and correct," Nick remarked. "He's gone to swap vibrations with Perringer. That's how oysters converse, isn't it—by vibrations?"

"Like that, was he?" said Basil, grinning. "How else did he seem?"

"Oh, different from when I met him in Town. Grimmer and more portentous."

"I know!" grunted Basil. "It's this blasted house. Gets everybody. Dare say it's had a curse put on it by some holy man—after he'd been refused caviare at the back door. Did you tell him that our lord high bottle-washer is a bishop's son? That'd make him laugh."

Nick uttered an eloquent laugh.

"If you ask me," he said, "he knows a damn sight more about Perringer's past, present and prospective future than any of us is likely to find out. Nice situation, isn't it? He openly leaves his host to go and discuss him with the servant. And it doesn't seem in the least bad form. I believe the old boy's incapable of that. It's all in the crazy order of things that happen here."

They continued talking for nearly half an hour—all save Betty, who sat subdued. She was training herself for a prolonged spell of silence and reflecting upon the ordeal before her. Her notions of elderly military men of the officer caste were derived from stage misrepresentations and humorous pictures by artists of the baser sort, depicting ogres and purple faces and white whiskers swearing at broken golf-clubs.

When at last the gong sounded, and they made a move towards the house, the Colonel came out on to the steps to meet them.

"You really must try to forgive me," he said, smiling as he addressed Nick. "You see, I stand in the same relation to Perringer in matters of business as I do to you. I mean, of course, that he benefits by Sir Anthony's will. And since the present arrangement ties him to this house—well, the mountain had to come to Mahomed."

He looked at Nick while he spoke, but at the same time his gaze took in the Hailshams and Betty. Nick quickly performed the necessary introductions, and the party moved into the drawing-room.

Conversation was difficult at first, but Colonel Sandingford, gallantly determined to do his best and remembering the profession of Nick's three friends, began to talk about the stage. There, however, it was difficult to meet him on his own ground, since it appeared that the last "show" he had seen in London was a revival of *Trilby* in which the late Sir H. Beerbohm Tree had taken part. He meant well, but he was far from up to date, and Betty, sitting close by Basil, whispered to him to inquire if the Colonel had been present at the first performance of *Hamlet*.

Perringer, when he brought in the tea a minute later, wore a chastened air. Both the young men noticed it, and Basil, on his way to the table where Milly was preparing to pour out tea, found opportunity to mutter to Nick that Somebody looked as if he had been pretty thoroughly browned off. Their vague dislike of Perringer was born of a still more vague mistrust and their consciousness of his anomalous position in the household.

The air was suddenly cleared by Milly, who, picking up a thread of desultory cricket talk, mentioned a certain General Stackwell who had played for Hampshire in his salad days. The Colonel's attention quickened at once on hearing a reference to one of his oldest friends. Did Miss Hailsham know General Stackwell?

"He was my godfather," said Milly.

By that strange process of human thought which makes friends of two strangers in Montreal because they had both met a man named Smith in London, the Hailshams immediately underwent a change in the Colonel's sight. Hitherto they had been mummers, and therefore probably without caste and almost certainly immoral. But now it had emerged that their people knew old "Birdie" Stackwell, why, dash it, it proved that they must be all right.

He mellowed towards Betty too, strangely enough he had at first preferred her to Milly and Basil. Nice Little Gel, but why was she so shy and silent? He liked Little Gels who were seen and not heard—rare birds in these days—but dash it! one couldn't get a word out of her at all.

The truth was, of course, that poor Betty was afraid to open her mouth, having a strong intuition as to where her foot would go. The Visitor was undeceived about her a little later on the same evening.

The party had split up for a while after tea, and Betty, reentering the drawing-room, saw Milly and Nick and Basil grouped in the middle of the room. Colonel Sandingford had taken a seat close by the door, the opening of which had automatically screened him from view.

"Hullo! " she called out cheerfully. "Where's old Whiskers? " The sight of three faces and the sudden warning of some inner monitor caused in Betty's mind a sudden suspicion, which was confirmed by the sight of a highly polished shoe jutting out across her line of vision. She resisted an inclination to try to throw her skirt over her head and to scream. (She had had to do this sort of thing many times on the stage, at a similar contretemps which occurred in a Delirious Farce, but on those occasions she had had an apron to help her.)

"Dunno," said Basil indifferently. "Gone mousing, I dare say. Didn't see her at tea to-day, and she generally comes in for a spot of milk." And for the Colonel he added: "You fond of cats, sir?"

It seemed to Betty that, much as she had always loved Basil, she had never given him wholehearted adoration until just that moment. Indeed, Basil's speech was appreciated by all—without exception—of those who heard it.

To Nick in private converse a little later Colonel Sandingford said: "I like your friend young Hailsham."

"I'm so glad," said Nick. "Nice chap, isn't he?"

"Yes," said the old soldier, with a straight mouth but a gleam of laughter kindling in his eyes.

"Feller's got Tact."

The Colonel had been invited to select his own sleeping-chamber. It came hardly as a surprise to Nick that he should select one next to the Sealed Room. It was evident that he did not believe in ghosts, or, if he did, he had no reason to fear the proximity of that sinister chamber.

But he was apprehensive of something, and the fact emerged again when the girls had left the dinner-table that evening, leaving the three men to talk alone.

"I hear you've been having some revolver practice," he remarked casually. "Perringer says you're getting to be quite good shots, and praise from him is praise indeed."

"Are you a good shot, sir?" Basil inquired.

Colonel Sandingford answered at first with a deprecatory smile. He still wore the clothes in which he had arrived. Nick did not dress for dinner because Basil could not. Basil's only token of having once possessed "blacks" was a little square ticket bearing the name and address of an accommodating "uncle" who had scrawled a date and "£2" across its face. The situation had not been explained to the Colonel in full, but in response to a hint he had left his own evening clothes upstairs. He now felt in his hip-pocket and produced a little old-fashioned nickel-plated pistol with revolving chambers.

"Not much good with this toy," he said in answer to Basil's question. "But it should be serviceable at close quarters."

Basil laughed rather vaguely and asked him if it were his custom to go armed.

"Not usually," he answered, and added slowly and gravely: "But, you see, this is hardly a usual occasion."

Nick watched him slowly and thoughtfully expel a little cloud of smoke, and leaned towards him.

"I wish you could tell us a little more. Colonel," he said.

"My dear boy, I wish I could. I believe you are both brave men. I am sure you are. So let me put it in this way. If somebody were to hold lighted cigarettes to your bare feet and ask you certain questions you would probably give the answers—if you knew the answers."

Nick and Basil were aware of a little cold wave of horror sweeping over them both.

"I should for one," Basil laughed nervously. "Damn quick, too. Nick, old lad, you've got the wrong man with you in this show. You want a chap with a pair of artificial legs."

"But," proceeded the Colonel, "if you didn't know the answers you couldn't give them."

Nick's laugh was like an echo of Basil's.

"I should have a pretty quick shot at it," he confessed. "Or would they tell me that guessing didn't count?"

Colonel Sandingford regarded them with a faint smile in which there was both wisdom and deprecation.

"Really, you know, it isn't a joking matter. And that brings me to something I wanted to say. I wish—for their own sakes— you would get rid of those two charming young women. I don't know what may happen here, but—I feel most unhappy about them."

He saw Nick and Basil exchange glances, and heard Nick cough.

"We've already had it out with them," said Nick. "Can't get either of them to budge while Basil's here."

"I like that!" Basil retorted. "I know of one who wouldn't dream of leaving you here, and I doubt if the other would. But perhaps if Colonel Sandingford talked to them—"

"I don't think Colonel Sandingford will attempt the seemingly impossible." said the Colonel dryly. "But I should be glad if somebody could extract a promise from them not to investigate any nocturnal noises they may hear."

Nick had begun again to laugh.

"Sorry, sir," he said, "but you're giving both of us the creeps."

Their guest remained grave, but seemed to despair of imparting the whole of his gravity to his hearers.

"I assure you," he said, "that I myself am not suffering from the—er—the creeps. At the same time I am aware—as you cannot be aware—of the gravity of the situation. We are doing nothing contrary to the law, and yet we could hardly ask the law to help us without courting the most unfortunate results. Our police are probably the best in the world, but unfortunately they are not omnipotent, and they are hampered by the restrictions of a free country.

"It sounds like a paradox, but it amounts to this. If I went to a policeman and said that you had threatened to murder me, he would promptly ask if I had any witnesses. Having learned that I had not, he would shake his head and express his inability to take any steps until the murder had been attempted. Then, if it were successful, he would use his best endeavours to get you hanged, and if it were unsuccessful he would use the same endeavours to procure you the appropriate term of imprisonment. We are in the unfortunate position of having to fight those who are outside the law while at the same time keeping ourselves as far as possible within the law.

"You know, my dear Nick, what might be the consequences of calling the police into this house. Quite unconditionally, so far as you are concerned, that seal must remain intact."

Nick was suddenly aware that he was wearing a grin, involuntary and irrepressible. He saw the Colonel's eye upon him and felt apologetic.

"Sorry," he said. "Excuse me, but I couldn't help liking what you said about keeping within the law. We've already allowed the police to be hoodwinked about one murder. I suppose Perringer confessed to you that he took that body away and dumped it?"

The Colonel seemed to have become interested in the contents of an ash-tray. He began to frown over them and to stir them with the end of a spent match.

"Perringer, excellent fellow," he said slowly, "is not the kind of man to make embarrassing or unnecessary admissions. He told you something about his past, I believe, in order that you might understand his affection for—and loyalty to—your—ah—your late uncle. He did not tell me that the body which vanished from this house was the same body that came to light elsewhere, nor who had transferred it. On the other hand, I gathered from his manner, courteous as it was, that if I did not draw the right inference I should be a particularly obtuse and damned old fool."

He paused, smiled, and then added: "I may as well go on to say that if anybody else is so careless as to die with violence on these premises I sincerely hope that his body will come to light elsewhere—and if possible a little farther afield."

Afterwards there was music in the drawing-room, which Colonel Sandingford welcomed— perhaps because it was the one alternative to conversation. At last when the piano was still and desultory talk began he smilingly and apologetically confessed to being tired and begged leave of Milly to retire.

"Well," said Nick, glancing at Basil when the guest had departed, "what's the verdict now?"

"Honest but not brilliant," Basil answered. "The finished product as approved by the Army Council. They've got different names and slightly different features—if you look hard enough. But a jolly good type, as types go."

"What defeats me," said Nick, "is that he's obviously the kind of chap who'd cut his throat with a rusty razor before he had any truck with anything against his code. Yet here he is— up to the neck in some business which is, to say the least, decidedly queer, and prepared, if necessary, to step more than a yard or two outside the law."

"Ought to buck you up, that," grunted Basil. "Great comfort to me. We don't know what it's all about, but his 'ighly respectable presence sorter suggests we're on the side of the angels."

CHAPTER XIX
A LITTLE SURPRISE

Basil woke from sleep with a slight start which might have jolted him into a state of alarm if he had not heard Nick's reassuring voice.

"Sorry, old man. Make you jump?"

He flashed an electric torch as Basil turned upon his back and raised his head.

"What's wrong?"

"Nothing. At least, I don't know."

Basil, blinking away the effects of the flash, was now aware that Nick wore his dressing-gown and was carrying his automatic. He reached out for his own weapon, which was on a chair beside him.

"Break it to me, mother, dear," he said. "I'll be a brave boy and try to bear it"

"Nerves all tizzy-wozzy, I dare say. Thought I heard a noise."

"What sort of noise?"

"Can't quite say. Damn it, you can't expect me to imitate noises."

Basil began to raise himself.

"Well, where did it come from? What direction?"

Nick laughed softly and ironically.

"Need you ask?"

Basil did not at first think the question superfluous and thought hard for a moment before he understood.

"But Colonel Stannat-Hease is sleepin' next to that room. He'd have heard something if—"

"Just so. And for that very reason I think we'd better breeze along and see that he's all right. We don't want to have Perringer disposing of his body on somebody else's doorstep."

Basil began to climb out of bed.

"Beastly things you say," he grumbled. "Not funny—this time o' night. All right, let's go and view the corpse—before Perringer disposes of same."

Nick seemed to be singularly and suspiciously light-hearted for one who had been disturbed in the night and was full of dark suspicions.

"Might be Perringer's own body this time," he said, "and he couldn't very well dispose of *that*. Know where to lay hands on a spade?"

Basil glared at him searchingly and half indignantly.

"*You've* gone goofy now, have you?" he said, struggling into his dressing-gown. "Thought this damned house would get you sooner or later. See you in the looney-bin, Brother. Won't we have fun with the keepers!"

They set out silently in the direction of the room with the sealed door, pausing, however, at the door ofthe room next to it.

Nick rapped tentatively and had no answer. He rapped again, and then he looked at Basil, who raised his brows and hunched his shoulders. Then, without another word, he turned the handle and went a yard or two into the room, flashing his torch. Then he pointed at an empty bed and turned to whisper.

"Just as I thought. Don't like spying on a guest. Not British. Definitely not British. On the other hand, I don't like guests with quaint nocturnal habits. That's not British, either."

"Where is he?" Basil whispered, rather superfluously.

"Ask me another. Where's Perringer?"

"Ah!" Sudden enlightenment appeared on Basil's face.

"They're having a midnight confab."

"Not midnight. Seven minutes to two by my watch. Time good little guests—and good little menservants—were in bed."

"What are you going to do?" Basil whispered after a pause.

"Look up friend Perringer."

"Eh? What are you going to tell him?"

"Heard a noise."

"Same noise?"

"Same noise will do. Then we went to call the Colonel. Couldn't get an answer. That problem, though, will already be solved—if we find the Colonel perched on Perringer's bed-rail." Basil considered, frowning.

"All right, then," he said. "Bit awkward, though. I hate seeing people embarrassed. What's going to be the Colonel's excuse for confabbing with Perringer at this ghastly hour?"

"I shall talk about the noise—and we shall all go to investigate it straight away. Time we've discovered there was nothing in it the old C.O. and Perringer between them will have concocted a story. They weren't plotting anything or discussing Perringer's hobby of stealing murdered bodies. Oh, no! The Colonel had the megrims and went to borrow Daddy Perringer's smelling-salts."

Basil grinned uncertainly.

"Come on, then, Skipper," he said.

They made their way to the back stairs and so to the floor above. At Perringer's door Nick knocked loudly and boldly. Having heard no answer he turned the handle and stepped firmly inside—to be confronted by another empty bed.

"Well, I'm damned!" said Basil, over his shoulder.

"Looks to me as if they've gone for a walk—or gone poaching," whispered Nick.

There was no cause for alarm, but Basil afterwards owned quite freely to a tremor at just that moment. It was another twist of the unreasonable and inexplicable. In a flash he had begun to ask himself what was to happen if that ill-assorted couple had vanished forever. It would be all of a piece with the other crazy happenings.

"All very well," he said in a shaken voice, "but where the hell have they really got to?"

Nick was laughing at the apparently crazy inconsequence of it all, and in that mood he whispered:

"Let's hide under the bed. Then when old Perringer comes back we can pinch his leg just as he's going to—"

"Don't be an ass! What are you really going to do?"

"I think if we went back a step or two past the Colonel's room and kept quiet for a second or two, we should discover that the sealed room isn't quite so empty as it ought to be. Coming?" Basil nodded. They made their way downstairs again and were passing the kitchen when Nick suddenly halted, as he had halted once before. The door on top of the cellar stairs stood a few inches ajar, and both were aware of a muffled, indefinite sound which came up from below. It was followed by human speech, gruff, low and indistinguishable.

"Good Lord! They're down the cellar!"

Nick was unaware of having whispered the thought until he heard Basil breathe a corroborative "*Yes!*" And on the instant they heard a voice—the same or another—muttering in the depths below. Then, very softly, Nick shut the cellar door.

"Good Lord!" Basil breathed a second later. "What are you doing?"

At that precise moment Nick was doing nothing except grin. But he had just turned the key.

"Come along, dearie," he whispered. "Come bye-byes."

Out in the hall Basil clutched him by the arm.

"Man," he gasped, "you can't lock 'em up down there!"

"Can't I!" Laughter was mingled with Nick's explosive whisper. "Well, I've just damn well done it! Going round to see that everything was in order I discovered that the cellar door was unlocked. I prefer that door to be locked at night. Well?"

"Oh, all right," grunted Basil, "all right."

"If they want to get out they'll have to do a bit of heavy knocking. Then when I come to let 'em out I shall naturally ask a civil question or two. One doesn't expect one's guests to be entertained by one's servants in the cellar in the small hours of the morning. Let's go to my room and wait until we hear a few bangs."

Basil shrugged his shoulders. He had been a trifle awed by the Colonel and he was now vastly perturbed by the turn of events.

"Never hear from your room," he protested, and added: "We shouldn't."

"Oh, yes, we shall if they bang loud enough. And you bet they'll bang the adjective door down rather than spend the rest of the night there. They'll hold a council of war about it first, though. But they can't get out until somebody lets 'em out, and they'll be in the same fix whether it's now or to-morrow morning." They stood listening for two or three minutes, but heard nothing. Then Nick suddenly turned away and Basil followed him.

In Nick's room they sat and smoked with the door open, waiting and listening in vain. At the end of about half an hour Nick said: "Well, I'm going back to bed."

"What!"

"I say, Basil—swear that you won't go and let them out."

"Rather! And I'll swear never to uncage a tiger."

Left to himself, Nick, his mind made up—although made up very uncomfortably—went back to bed. He had no intention of sleeping, and he must have dropped off unaware while he was still wrestling with the tangled skeins which fate had thrust into his inexperienced hands.

He was wakened in broad daylight by a tap at the door. A moment later Perringer entered with a little tray and set morning tea on the bedside table. Nick stared at him and uttered a soft moan.

"Good morning, sir," said Perringer, brightly and civilly. "I hope you slept well."

The same courteous remark is said to have been made to the prophet Daniel—who replied that he had been slightly annoyed by some lions during the night. But on this occasion it was not the visitor who was surprised to see Daniel. The situation was in reverse.

"The Colonel's compliments, sir," Perringer continued half a minute later, as he drew aside a window curtain, "the Colonel's compliments, and he asked me to inquire what time it would be convenient for him to take his bath. I have had to explain, sir, that, owing to our present arrangements, there is only one geyser, and when the kitchen range is not in use "

"Have you seen the Colonel this morning?" Nick interrupted.

"I have just taken him his tea, sir."

"And—er—Mr. Hailsham?"

"Mr. Hailsham is apparently in very high spirits. The moment I appeared he uttered a loud shout of laughter and announced that all the world was mad. You know his—er—jocular manner, sir."

Nick knew it, but thought that on this occasion Perringer had selected the wrong adjective. Perringer had scarcely looked at him while speaking, but seemed to be casting about for some small service or attention which he might give. Seeing nothing, he retired quietly as upon any normal occasion.

Two minutes later Basil was in the room. Basil, it appeared, had come to stay for more than a few seconds if necessary, for he had brought with him his cup of tea, and the cup joggled in the saucer.

"Why the devil didn't you tell me at the time," he demanded, "that you were going to let those stiffs out of the cellar? I nearly had a child when old Perringer walked into my room as if nothing had happened."

"I was iust going to curse you for the same thing," Nick retorted. "Mean to say you didn't go and let 'em out? I swear I didn't."

"Then how the hell did they *get* out? No, I had nothing to do with it. You wanted 'em locked in. You're the skipper of this craft. Not for me to interfere."

He sat himself with a soft thud on the foot of Nick's bed and laughed blankly.

"Only one door leading down to those cellars," he reminded Nick. "Good stout door and good stout lock. Don't see how they could have bust it. You can't make a running charge at a door which stands at the top of steep stairs. Besides, it would have been a noisy business and at least one of us must have heard. I wonder if one of the girls—"

Basil shook his head vehemently.

"Not they! I don't mean that they're funks, but if they heard any bangs and crashes they'd naturally come along to see if we were in our rooms. Might be us that was making the shindy."

"Um! What about Milly? 'Out damned spot! ' The Lady MacBeth act again?"

Basil pursed his mouth as if to whistle thoughtfully. Then he shook his head.

"Betty's rigged up something—apart from drawing-pins, I believe—so that Milly would be bound to wake her if she got up in the night. Besides, the Sealed Door would be the centre of her attraction. No, I think we can rule her out. One possibility, though."

"What's that?" Nick demanded hopefully.

"Shouldn't be surprised if Perringer had some tools in the cellar. Shouldn't be surprised if our Oxon knows how to pick a lock. Learned the art in his unregenerate days when he was a thorn in the flesh of Papa the Bishop."

Nick nodded vehemently. There was at least sense in the idea. Indeed it seemed to afford the only possible solution.

"All right," he said, "I'll go and have a look at that lock as soon as I'm down. You can't mess about with a lock without leaving traces. But there's another little thing, dearie. A rather nasty thought, my pet."

Basil eyed him haggardly.

"Yes?" he grunted. "I'm listening."

"We know that the Gallant Ossifer and Perringer were not in their own or in the other's rooms. We know that somebody—more than one person—was down in the cellars, because we heard voices. I could swear that they were men's voices, but I couldn't swear that they were Perringer's and the Colonel's. Could you?" Basil uttered a little muffled shriek. It was a pantomimic effort, but at the same time it expressed what he thought.

"Hell's bells! That only makes it worse! I say, I wonder—ssh!" They both heard footfalls.

"Perringer coming back," Nick whispered.

And Perringer it was—bearing a letter on a salver. Having knocked and received permission, he crossed the room and presented it to Nick. Eventually it proved to be no more important than a request for a subscription to the village cricket club—made in the form of inviting Nick to become a vice-president.

"Hullo!" said Nick, taking it. "Post in already? Late this morning, aren't we?"

"Yes, sir," replied Perringer, and added with the most consummate coolness: "I thought, sir, in view of the sleep of all of us having been somewhat broken, that you might wish to be called a little later, sir."

Nick stared at the man's innocent, impassive face and groped in vain for words. Perringer, however, helped him out of his difficulty.

"On account of the high wind, sir."

"Wind?" said Nick. "I didn't hear it. Did you, Basil?"

"You are fortunate enough to sleep soundly, sir. I am a light sleeper. So it seems is the Colonel. The same noise aroused both of us and we went to investigate. It proved to be a loose window on the top floor which slammed in the wind and broke."

"Ah!" said Nick, busy with many thoughts. "All right. You'd better send for somebody to mend it."

Perringer allowed a short pause.

"I can do that myself, sir, after breakfast. We have some spare glass. All else that one needs is a yard-measure, some putty, a glazier's diamond and a little common sense. I think, sir, I can supply all of these."

Having spoken, he made an exit which appealed strongly to Basil's theatrical sense. It was Basil who began to laugh—or rather to croak.

"Ho, ho, ho, ho, ho!"

"Funny fellow, aren't you?" said Nick.

"Very. Don't you see it? Lovely alibi. Mystery over. Perringer and the Colonel weren't in their rooms, my blue-eyed boy, because when we went to look they'd got up to investigate loud crash which proves to be broken window."

Nick's face did not reflect the smile on Basil's.

"You know," he said, "you're a decent fellow, but a bit simple. I didn't hear a breath of wind stirring last night. Did you?"

"No," Basil admitted. "Mightn't take a very strong gust to slam a window, though. Besides, it might have died down again before we woke. When you get a commonplace and quite reasonable solution to a problem why not be satisfied? Why pick holes?"

"Right!" Nick answered him with a sardonic smile and a hard glitter in his eyes. "We'll agree if you like that the Colonel and Perringer were not in their respective rooms because they'd heard something go bang and went to investigate broken window in attic. Very good. *Then who the sanguinary Hades did we hear talking in the cellars?*"

Basil's jaw dropped again.

"Oh, hell!" he exclaimed.

The breakfast-table subsequently unfolded its meagre revelations to listening ears and watching eyes. Colonel Sandingford, who said nothing about the window, was brisk and cheerful. Possibly, however, he was a man who needed little sleep, and certainly he had just been refreshed by a cold bath. The girls, in answer to polite inquiries, both replied that they had slept well. Nick, looking into two wells of innocence which were Milly's eyes and at the unfurrowed brows of Betty as she laboured conscientiously with porridge, came to the conclusion that they were speaking the truth.

Nick, taking a cigarette out on to the drive after the meal, heard a faint tapping high up and out of sight. In endeavouring to locate it he walked around to the back of the house and discovered the cause. There was shivered glass at his feet, and high above him the handyman Perringer was tinkering with the framework of a small window.

It occurred to Nick that it was a little strange that a window which had been broken by slamming should have shed so much of its glass outside. And then he saw the probability that Perringer had knocked out the glass in the initial stage of his work. Not like the tidy Perringer, though. He might have been expected to let the glass fall inside the room on to a newspaper spread for its reception.

And then Nick laughed wryly at himself. He was becoming morbidly interrogative about the most negligible details. The atmosphere of the house was "getting" him.

But one problem remained. There *had* been men locked in the cellars last night. And if they weren't the Colonel and Perringer—as it seemed they weren't—then who were they? And it came to him as a sudden shock to reflect that they might still be there. He had been concentrating too much on Perringer's story about the window he was now mending, because it certainly seemed to provide the Colonel and Perringer with an alibi.

He stood aghast at having allowed himself to become mentally fogged. The vulgar saying "led down the garden" came home to him with uncomfortable force. It seemed that Perringer after all had taken him for a little stroll through the shrubberies to distract him from something that was going on upon the front lawn.

Nick, cursing a reasonably bright intelligence which for once had betrayed him, turned suddenly back, and at an angle of the house he ran into Basil, who had come out to seek him. Basil, it was soon evident, had shown more forethought, but the little gained by it was evident from the furrows in his young brow.

"Just been down the cellars, old man," he said, linking an arm in Nick's. "Tell you, I didn't fancy it much—going down there alone. But I didn't know where you'd gone—and I thought it was now or never, while Perringer was monkeying with that window."

"Well?"

"Well, I found the door at the top of the stairs locked, just as we left it. Only one way into the cellars, is there? You can swear to that. Oh, I know there's a trap outside—like you see outside old pubs—for letting barrels down. But the bolts inside are all corroded with rust and can't have been drawn for years. I had a good look at them."

"Well?" said Nick impatiently. "Get on with it."

"Well, we know there *were* men in the cellar last night, don't we? At least two men. The Colonel and Perringer—or Lord knows who. And we know they were locked in. We know they could only have got out by smashing or picking the lock—unless somebody let 'em out from the outside."

"Yes, yes.'" said Nick.

"Right ho, my bonny buck. Young Basil finds door locked, as we left it, and young Basil unlocks it and goes down—flashing electric torch and singing that ditty about two eyes of blew smilin' threw to scare bogy-man. Bogy-man just detests that song, and I don't blame him. And what does brave young Basil find?"

"'Beer, beer, glorious beer,'" sang Nick, falling into Basil's own manner.

"Oh, plenty drinks. Stacks. Bins full. But something more important. Nice fresh cigar-end. Nice fresh cigar-ash. I don't think cigar-ash left exposed would hold its shape for very long, and the cigar-end's neither soggy nor dry."

"Perringer—"

"Perringer says he doesn't smoke cigars. Somebody smoked a cigar down there last night. We heard voices—presumably while Perringer and the Colonel were investigating their broken window. We lock the Voices in the cellar, and the Voices get out again— without turning the key or leaving a mark on the lock. No, there isn't a scratch. Well, what do you make of it?" Nick grinned uncertainly.

"Colonel smokes cigars."

"'Course he does, old boy. And loves smoking them, no doubt, in the middle of the night in a nice cosy cellar. Now let's try to reconstruct. *Redncio ad absurdum.* Colonel, wakened in the dead of night by window crashing, puts on a fat cigar which takes forty minutes to smoke, and goes with Perringer to investigate bang. There's not a breath of wind blowing, but they find that the heavy gale's done in a window. Colonel then, instead of going back to bed, comes to the eccentric conclusion that he'll finish his cigar in one of the cellars. So he goes down, ignorant that a brace or more of intruders are there. Intruders manage to hide —like the Forty Thieves— and the Colonel finishes his cigar cosily among the cobwebs and goes back to bed, locking the cellar door after him. Does it make sense?"

Sudden light had come into Nick's eyes.

"No, but *this* does. Colonel hears voices in cellar, same as we did. He goes to investigate—same as we would have done if we hadn't thought we knew who it was—and doesn't see anybody. Why? Look at the number of the cellars, and he can only be in one place at a time. While he's investigating they nip up the stairs and out. Been a lark if they'd locked him in, but I dare say they didn't want to do anything to confirm the fact that they were there at all."

Basil shook his head and regarded Nick with a pained expression.

"Won't do at all, old boy. 'Sides, of course they'd have locked the Colonel in. Much the safest thing to do. And how did they get into the house—or out of it again? Did they smash a window under the roof—with such force that it brought two people immediately to the spot? And then did they run upstairs and jump out of the same window—and manage not to break their blasted necks?"

"Oh, hell!" groaned Nick, "I'm giving it up for the time being. It's just an unprofitable headache. All we know for certain is this. There were at least two men in the cellars. We locked them in. They may have been Perringer and the Colonel or they may not. Somehow they got out again without violence. Somebody in the house let them out or they'd got a trick up their sleeve that I haven't even heard of. And that's exactly all we know."

"Except," said Basil, "that the wind—what there was of it— bashed in a window upstairs."

Nick turned upon him in sudden exasperation.

"What the hell has a broken window in the attics got to do with some men getting out of a locked cellar?"

"Dunno, dear boy," Basil answered dryly and drearily. "Except that it happened in the same night. There's a fearful kind of inconsequence about everything that happens in this house. I'm beginning to believe in ghosts. I believe this place is haunted by spirits whose job it is to send people batty. Your uncle needn't have locked up that room. They're all over the ruddy place." He ended on the same disgruntled note, then suddenly and unexpectedly he laughed.

"Har, har," said Nick with heavy irony. "I'm laughing too."

"Sorry." Basil drew in the corners of his mouth. "I was only thinking that if only somebody had broken in on the first floor as well it would have been just like that old card-trick. You know the one I mean?—the old nursery favourite—the three Knaves and the Policeman."

They had been walking while they talked and were now close to the main entrance. Nick, looking down the drive, suddenly exclaimed.

"Talk of the devil," he said.

"Eh?"

"You said Policeman, didn't you? And here's one on a bike."

The sun was in Basil's eyes and for the moment he could distinguish no more than a uniform and shining buttons.

"Policeman my foot," he said a moment later. "Your guilty conscience, me lad. Common or garden postman."

"Both wrong," Nick growled, as the wobbling figure drew nearer. "Just a large telegraph boy. Wonder what he wants."

"To shed a telegram, I s'pose," said Basil innocently.

"But who's it for? I say, I hope they don't expect me to rush off and play cricket."

"Gentlemen and Players match starts to-day," Basil remarked, grinning. "Perhaps the Gents are one short."

Nick remarked that the amateurs would have to be more than one short, and that nothing less than a visitation of the Black Plague would get him a place in the team on his present form. And while he was saying it the boy drew nearer, grinned as he dismounted, and touched his hat with the buff envelope which he immediately extended.

"Cromer, sir," he said.

Nick's eyebrows went up.

"Sir Anthony Cromer is dead," he said, taking the envelope.

"I know, sir. Any answer, sir?"

It occurred to Nick that it might be necessary to hold a stance before that were possible, but he realized that such a remark might be mistaken for levity by the young official mind which was only doing its best to carry out the strict injunctions of the Civil Service.

"It isn't a telegram," he said a few seconds later. "I mean, it's a cable. From Stink Aroma, wherever that is. I suppose it's where the cheap cigars come from. At least, it looks something like Stink Aroma. Are you any good at geography, boy? Do you know where Stink Aroma is?"

"Used to import my cigars from there," said Basil, as the boy grinned and shook his head.

"Well, do you speak Spanish or Portuguese?"

"French," said the boy brightly. "*Avvy-voo lar ploom der mar tarnte? Jaim, two aim, ill aim.*"

"I'm afraid French isn't going to help us very much. And I don't see how to answer a cable to a dead man in a language which I don't understand. Never mind—here's a bob for you." As the boy departed grinning Basil said:

"I know where Santa Aloma is—if that's the place. It's the capital and chief port of a little state called San Analdo in South America."

"Yes, it says San Analdo as well. Take a look and see if you can make head or tail. You were rather good at Latin, if I remember. And they used to tell us that Latin was such a help with Spanish and Italian."

Basil scowled and smiled as he took the sheet of paper.

"Sent," he said, "by somebody named Alberico. Don't know if it's surname or Christian name or male or female."

"That's helpful, but perhaps the context will provide a clue. What does it say, my Latin scholar? I knew enough Latin myself to scrape through matric., but I've got to own -"

Basil frowned and struggled in silence for half a minute.

"I don't think it's Italian," he said. "Looks to me a good deal more like Spanish or Portuguese— and that's a good deal more probable. Not a bit like Dante."

"Can't you—?"

"Dear old boy, I've never seen anything like this before—except on the menu of a foreign restaurant in Soho. So I had to chance my arm. and I was between life and death for three days afterwards. Shouldn't wonder if it's in some sort of a code. So what?"

Nick considered.

"I suppose Perringer knows the language."

"Just what I was thinking. But could you trust him to tell you the truth?"

"Wondering about that, too. I think if one took him by surprise, and made him swear in advance—eh?"

"Perringer doesn't take oaths."

"And watched him carefully," Nick continued. "After all, however important it may be, it can't be so frightfully private. The telegraph clerk over there must know all about it. Besides, the Post Office have a copy of this, and I don't suppose any cable arrives here in a foreign language which doesn't get translated in official quarters sooner or later. Might be something rude or something seditious. And the Postmaster-General is always a model of patriotism and propriety. He goes regularly to church and prays according to a form which may be had post-free from the Stationery Department."

Basil's mouth suddenly became an O and then broadened to another smile.

"Try Perringer," he said, "and then try somebody else. See if the two versions tally. Test the brute."

They went indoors and upstairs. They knew the direction of the room where Perringer was still at work on the window, and the sound of scrapings led them to the door. Perringer turned as they entered.

"Nearly finished, sir," he said cheerfully. "Not a bad job, I think."

"No, not bad at all." Nick smiled and nodded approval. "On your travels, Perringer, did you ever strike a place called Santa Aloma?"

Perringer dropped a lump of putty.

"Er—er—yes, sir. Why?"

"You speak Spanish or Portuguese or whatever it is, I suppose?"

"A little Spanish, yes, sir. They speak Spanish there."

"Right. Well, I've just had a cable from there addressed to my late uncle. Would you be good enough to translate it for me, please?"

Perringer was now visibly a shaken man.

"Let me see," he said, half in a whisper, as he held out his hand: and the tone was almost peremptory.

"Just a minute. You have not always been frank with me, you know. Before I show you this I want your solemn word of honour that you will give me a correct verbal translation." Perringer swallowed.

"I promise you, sir—if I am able."

Still Nick hesitated.

"Why do you think that you may not be able?"

"It may be in code, sir. It was sometimes so."

"And you don't know the code?"

"No, sir."

"Very well." Nick held out the broken envelope which contained the message. "We must hope for the best."

Perringer took it and turned away to the light. They heard the rustle of paper.

"May I keep this, please, a little while?"

"No. Just hand it back, will you? What does it say?"

"It is in code, sir. But perhaps if I were to study it—"

"No, thank you. Just hand it back, please. I'll get an expert to look at it."

Perringer hesitated.

"If it is something very private, sir—"

"I can't help that. My uncle is dead. Anyhow, he seems to have led a blameless life. And there couldn't be many ghastly revelations packed away in those few words."

Perringer's manner seemed unwilling and a trifle absent. He was staring up at the ceiling while the paper rustled in his hands, and then with a little sigh he surrendered the buff envelope. Nick thanked him and turned away, Basil at his heels.

"Some stew our Perringer's in," whispered Basil outside the door. "Did you watch his face?"

"And some liar he is, too. I believe he read every word."

"No," said Basil, shaking his head. "Wouldn't want to keep it if he'd read it. Next move, skipper"

"Arunford in the car. Must be somebody in Arunford who can read Spanish."

Basil agreed, and ten minutes later they were in the car and on their way. On the outskirts of the town Nick slackened speed and brought the car to a halt beside a sauntering policeman, who turned and looked inquiringly.

The Mine of Information immediately yielded some of its wealth when Nick asked if there were anybody in the town who understood Spanish.

"Well, yes. There's the old Seen Yore. Can't pronounce his name, sir, but everybody calls him the Seen Yore. He's one of those Refugatives, poor old chap, trying to pick up a living teaching languages."

"Then he'd know Portuguese, too, if necessary. Where does he hang out?"

The officer gave them a number in the very road in which Basil and the two girls had been lodging when Nick encountered them. They went straight on—to encounter, after ringing a bell, a surly female who admitted that the Senor was in. She ushered them into an untidy apartment which smelled of fried onions, and after a few moments the Senor, in carpet slippers, shuffled in.

Probably he was not a very old Senor, although his hair was white and his dark, sallow face deeply lined. His chocolate eyes were young and grew almost merry with hope at the sight of two well-dressed strangers.

"Ah," he said, smiling, "you come to der right shop. Dat is der idiom, eh? Spanish, Portuguese, French, Italian, Dutch, German—I speak so perfect 'as I speak der English. Show him me and I translate him word for word and explick the sense if it have meaning different in Eenglish."

Nick handed him the envelope and watched him draw out and smooth the contents. Then the deep furrows in the Sefior's brow changed from the horizontal to the perpendicular.

"But," he said, "dis ees already Eenglish. Listen. Look. Two and a 'alf dozzen soft collars. Seex peejammos. One dozzen shirts—"

"Let me look," Nick exclaimed, suddenly interrupting. "Sorry, Senor."

The puzzled Spaniard presented him with a receipted laundry ' bill—at which Basil stared over Nick's shoulder while he thought the same unuttered profanities.

"Blasted Perringer's done it on you," Basil growled.

"Didn't know he was a conjuror, too," Nick growled back. "Palmed the cable and substituted this—right under our very noses. That's finished it. He'll have to go. I'll see the Colonel." He smiled apologetically at the elderly Spaniard. "Very sorry indeed, Senor. Been a mistake. But I had a cable this morning from a town in San Analdo"

"Ah!" The light of understanding shone in the Senor's eyes. "About der revolution. Eet is very sad. Eet is always sad, I t'ink, when der is revolution. Were it not for revolution I should not be here."

Something in Nick's subconsciousness, whispering without logic or haphazard reason, was trying to tell him that this news was of the highest importance.

"Has there been a revolution there, Senor?"

The Senor shrugged.

"One leetle paragraph in your Eenglish paper. It says not which party have winned. Dat, perhaps, dey know not yet in London. A Yankee gunboat is in der arbour. It will be well for der Eenglish and der Yanks. But dere will be bloodshot, no doubt—a leedle bloodshot and anotter Government, and nex' year, or nex' mont', anotter revolution."

Nick and Basil looked at each other in silence. Then Nick turned again to the Senor.

"Thank you so much, sir," he said, "and so sorry to have made a silly mistake and troubled you for nothing. Er—how much?"

The Senor smiled and raised a protesting hand.

"My good sir," he said, "bring me your cable when you find him. But I cannot ask payment for so small a service. What is it—just to read aloud?"

But Nick, it seemed, had already learned something from Perringer in the matter of sleight of hand. When he and Basil were gone the Senor came upon a pound-note, neatly folded and lying upon a corner of his table.

He had been wondering whence the next meal was coming, and now the diminishing—but still tormenting—odour of fried onions in the room would soon be reinforced. He kissed the note—as he had once kissed holy pictures in the convent where he learned his first lessons—and began weakly but almost happily to cry.

CHAPTER XXI
MESSAGE DECODED

Nick was about to garage the car when Perringer appeared in the yard.

"Excuse me, sir," he said. "Have you been in to Arunford?"

"Yes," said Nick shortly. "Why?"

"Oh, Miss Hailsham was looking for you, sir. There was a message—if you were going in, sir. Would you get some fish for to-night? But I fear it is too late now. Er—I have made quite a respectable job of the window, sir."

Nick was wondering whether he should pluck a crow with Perringer then and there, or let action wait on further consideration. By so doing he lost the initiative.

"Oh, and I beg your pardon, sir," Perringer resumed in not too heavy a manner.

"Yes?" said Nick.

"That cablegram of yours, sir. Here it is. I made an absurd mistake. My mind was very much preoccupied. I fear I handed you an empty envelope. I don't know how I came to do it."

"Nor do I," Nick retorted. "And it wasn't an empty envelope. I'm always glad to see a receipted bill, but I didn't expect to find that one just where it was."

Perringer permitted himself to smile politely and regretfully. "Well, I'm very sorry, sir. I really can't think how it came to happen. I suppose—"

"Have you taken a copy of it?" Nick demanded.

"Why, yes, of course, sir." Perringer's sudden frankness was disarming. "I thought you wished me to decode it if I could. I will try, sir, but of course I can't promise. I'm not much good at ciphers, even in English, and although I speak a certain amount of Spanish, it isn't like attempting something of the same kind in one's own language."

What was Nick to do? He could demand that Perringer hand over the copy he had made. And if he did so he could be sure of one out of two alternatives. For Perringer was obviously no fool, and if he were not already master of the cryptic contents of that cablegram he had taken more than one copy of it.

All his temporary sense of ascendancy over Perringer was gone. And there was Perringer smiling never so blandly, never so politely—but not in the least triumphantly—at him.

Moreover, by a kind of telepathy, he was aware of Basil's silent and not unsympathetic mirth. Nick had now the original cablegram in his hand. He put it away carefully in his breast pocket and turned to Basil.

"Well, I'll run back and get that fish," he said. "Coming? Where are the girls? Perhaps they'd like a run."

"I'll go and find 'em," said Basil, and climbed out of the car.

Five minutes later Milly appeared, hatted and gloved and carrying a handbag.

"Want me to come with you?" she asked.

"Rather! Where's—?"

"Betty and Basil aren't coming. Rather think they want to slink off somewhere and hold each other's hands."

"Don't blame 'em." Nick, who had stepped out of the car, looked about him, and then kissed Milly swiftly on the cheek, with the furtive air of a shop-lifter. He then whispered something which caused her to laugh and tell him not to be an idiot.

"But I do," he insisted aloud.

"Do you, dear?" said Milly. "I'm so glad. But don't think about me. Think about fish."

They got into the car and were already on the main road when Milly said: "You know, my dear, there's something in the air to-day."

"I know there is," said Nick, and he remembered that she had not heard about the cablegram. He proceeded to tell her.

"Ah!" said Milly. "That accounts for it."

"Accounts for what, darling?"

"Perringer *does* know what that message was."

"Eh?" Nick had suddenly to remember that he was at the wheel. "How on earth—?"

"About half an hour ago I went into the dining-room. I was wearing tennis-shoes, but I didn't mean to walk quietly. Certainly I didn't mean to eavesdrop. Perringer and the Colonel were in the room, and talking with their backs to me. I didn't shout out or cough. I—well, it never occurred to me that they might be saying something they wouldn't want me to hear. One doesn't expect a visitor to swap heart-to-heart confidences with a servant."

"Although," said Nick, grinning, "the Colonel isn't quite an ordinary visitor, and I'll be shot if Perringer's an ordinary servant."

"Well, I wasn't thinking of that at all. I was thinking about pepper and salt and wondering whether the cruets needed refuelling. The Colonel sounded as if he were frightfully bucked up about something. ' Well,' he was saying,' it's great news, it's great news.' ' Yes,' Perringer answered, * but the danger's not over yet. The worst may be to come. There's a double motive now for revenge.' Then the Colonel said: ' Well, you know 'em better than I do. I shouldn't think they'd go on taking chances for nothing. My impression is that they'll call it a day when they hear the paymaster's dead.'

"I'm telling you as nearly as possible the exact words they used. Anyhow, I know I've got the right sense of them. Well, Perringer spoke next. He said: * But they probably don't know he's dead. Nothing in the papers about that. And the very men who'd give them the wire may be dead too or under lock and key. I think the crucial time is just in front of us. One thing they can't help knowing—that things aren't normal at home. Their instinct may be to strike quick, if they can, and then beat it.'

"Well, just at that moment the Colonel turned and saw me. Just as well I'm an actress. Anyhow, he's not an actor. It wasn't until I saw his face that I realized I'd been hearing something he didn't want me to hear. But he got as much out of mine as if I'd been a wax doll. So he called out in that hearty, fox-hunting voice he sometimes puts on: ' Hulloa, Miss Milly! Thought you were out. Ought to be—a lovely morning like this, y'know.' And while he was talking the usual old-gentlemanly stuff about roses in cheeks and schoolgirl complexions Perringer literally slid out of the room. It was as if he were wearing roller-skates on a dance-floor and somebody had given him a good hard shove from behind."

Nick suddenly found himself grinning.

"Perringer all over. Our Perringer dislikes embarrassments. Well, there's a glimmer of light somewhere in the east. Seems in some queer way to depend on the success or otherwise of a revolution on the other side of the world whether some dagoes stop trying to steal something that we haven't got. Do you know what you're going to do when we get into Arunford?—and we're nearly there."

"Of course. I'm going to buy some fish."

"Right. I'll decant you at North's. And then you're going to have a nice cup of coffee and a dog-biscuit at the pastry cook's nearly next door. I won't be long. Then I'll come back for you and square up for the damage."

Milly eyed him with an air intended to convey that she was unaccustomed to taking orders. There were many wrinkles in her shapely nose.

"And what do you think you are going to do with yourself meanwhile?"

"I'm going to pay my second call this morning on Señor Alfonso Spagoni the Toreador. I've something really to show him this time."

So it happened that, a few minutes later, Nick was ushered again into the Senor's presence. The Senor had done some hasty shopping since Nick's former visit, and he was now praising heaven and eating kippers. He would have desisted from the latter exercise, but Nick begged him to continue.

"Always," said the Senor, "when I lose som'ting I say a ieedle prayer to de good St. Antonio. And always he find it if I pray enough. He never fail."

"Oh, yes? " said Nick, smiling. "English kids do that too— Catholics and High Anglicans. Only we call him St. Anthony."

"Good! You believe dees, then? Twelve year ago I lose a pound-note. It is moch to me, for always I am poor. So ever afterwards I pray to do good San Antonio to find him for me. Never I lose faith—never. But de good Saint he keep me waiting until dis morning. Dis morning I find once more der pound-note upon dees table—dere where I point. And so on Sonday I s'all burn for him a candle."

"Well," said Nick, "I've found what I wanted to show you, and if you can read it I hope you will accept something else from another St. Anthony. It really will come indirectly from another St. Anthony who hasn't yet been canonized."

The Senor took the cablegram from Nick's hand and glanced at it.

"Caramba! From der centres of revolution."

"Yes," said Nick, "but the telegraph service seems to have been running."

"But dees ees a siphon."

"A si. Yes, it's in code. But I think it decodes into Spanish. If you can manage it, and prove it letter by letter and translate into English."

"I do not know. I do my best. Always I have taken moch interest in such things."

"Well, Senor, there's another ten pounds from St. Anthony if you can manage it."

"Ten pounds: Ten *pounds*!" The little Spaniard laughed and uttered strange and not unmusical oaths in his own tongue. "And from San Antonio, you say? Dat ees vairy good—for it is to San Antonio 'eemself that I must pray, so that he show me 'ow to take monny from him. You will honour me, Senor, with your address?"

Nick took out a note-book and pencil and began to scribble on a leaf.

"Here you are, Senor, and I hope you'll succeed."

"I? Never! It will be de good San Antonio . . ."

Nick bade the excellent man adieu and went. "Except ye have the faith of a little child," he thought, and since these ideas are catching, he began whimsically to hope that the Saint, if not too much occupied in finding lost playthings for little children, would "do his stuff"—as he inelegantly expressed it.

Milly was drinking her second cup of coffee when Nick rejoined her.

"I've a fancy," he said, sitting down opposite, "that the Gay Cabalero will bring it off. The siphon, as he calls it, probably isn't a very difficult one to anybody who knows the tan.cnage. And I believe the old chap's thoroughly intelligent. He has a tremendous devotion to St. Anthony for finding for him the pound-note which he lost years ago. It may have been the very one I left on his table, and who am I to say that they're not the same? Anyhow, he's on a tenner if he pulls it off—and I should say that the Saint is on at least a dozen candles."

Milly gave him an answering smile.

"How delicious! I mean, to be able to believe that we have Friends like that to help us. And, after all, how do we know we haven't?"

"I've an idea." said Nick. "that we shall need St. Michael and All Angels before very long. To my way of thinking, something pretty big is brewing somewhere. I ran feel it in my joints and finger-tips."

They drove back, but not straight to the house. Milly remembered that she had forgotten to buy stamps in Armilord. And while Nick remained at the wheel, and as she was about to enter the village post office, Perringer came out.

Perringer stood aside, smiling politely as he uncovered his head. Nick called out to him.

"Hullo, Perringer! What are you up to this morning? "

Perringer approached the car.

"The Colonel, sir, wished me to send a telegram."

"Oh, he did, did he?" thought Nick. "Alarums and excursions. Telegrams and cables. And threats of coming danger. And somehow at the back of it all a revolution in a dago republic which half the people in England had never heard of until this morning." He was aware of a thin thread of consequence running through it all, but the thread was of gossamer and it broke when he tried to grasp it.

He did not know until a later time that Perringer had just sent an expensive cablegram to someone in Santa Aloma in the state of San Analdo—which was at that time beginning to recover from the two hundred and seventy-second revolution which had rocked that volatile little country since its severance from Spain.

It was a silent and thoughtful little party of five which sat down to lunch at the usual time. Colonel Sandingford seemed moody and on edge, and Nick and Basil, who did not feel too cordial towards him, made no effort to rally him. No doubt this self-invited guest was acting on the express authority of the dead man to whom, directly or indirectly, they all owed so much. But they had not his full confidence and they were humanly resentful of it.

Shortly after lunch the Colonel vanished. Nick had no idea where he had gone, nor that Perringer was not in his quarters, until he heard the sound of firearms from the improvised butts. The two were getting a little shooting practice. In another age, Nick fancied, he would have heard the sharpening of swords.

Tennis for the younger people followed a little later. Then tea and afterwards more tennis. The Colonel declined to play, having no shoes with him and possessing a foot some four sizes larger than Nick's or Basil's. But he sat in a deck-chair beside the court, and during some of the time he seemed to be asleep. However, if he were actually asleep, he heard nothing of sufficient interest to wake him.

After dinner, when the three men were left alone in the dining room, Colonel Sandingford turned suddenly to Nick with a question.

"What time are you fellows going to turn in?"

"About eleven, I suppose," said Nick, with a questioning glance at Basil.

"Suit me," said Basil.

"You couldn't make it a little later—one of you—I suppose? Say, just after one o'clock? Won't do for us all to be asleep at once. Perringer will be awake between one and three, and I shall be on the prowl between three and five. It'll be light before I'm through."

They nodded and agreed among themselves, knowing that it would be futile to ask him what was in his mind.

The evening was hot and pregnant with thunder, although they heard none nor saw so much as a flash of sheet lightning. But the humid atmosphere drove them to sit in the hall, with both its doors wide open, while dusk began to fall. The Colonel was interested in cricket, and Nick was telling him of an incident in the match between his county and the Australians, when he was interrupted by a shout from the drive outside.

"Put your hands up, damn you! Right up! "

It was Perringer's voice: and a moment later the same voice bellowed words in another tongue. They were probably the same words uttered in Spanish.

As the three men sprang to their feet they heard another voice answer in similar foreign accents. The tone was startled and protesting and then mollifying.

Nick and Basil noticed that the Colonel had his automatic with him. It was in his hand as he joined the rush to the steps. He paused, however, to bark over his shoulder: "Keep back, you two girls! Get right away! Go upstairs!" Twenty yards away they beheld Perringer flourishing a revolver in the face of a squat and elderly man who held his hands above the level of his shoulders and spat out unintelligible words as if they were machine-gun bullets.

"Hell!" cried Nick. "It's the poor old Seen Yore."

It was indeed. And evidently the sight of a gentleman of Latin origin—at that time and place— had been to Perringer as the red rag to the bull.

"Senor Rockwell—Senor Rockwell! Tell dees man not to shoot. Is he mad?"

"Of course he is." growled Nick savagely. "Awfully sorry, Senor. We're all mad in this damned house. Didn't you know?

"Perringer! For God's sake!"

"Do you know him, sir?" asked Perringer, without turning and without lowering the weapon.

"Know him? Of course I know him! Called on him this morning and asked him to do me a service."

"Oh!" Perringer's voice sounded shaken and disgruntled. "If you had been good enough, sir, to tell me that he was likely to call—"

"Why the devil should I? Besides, I didn't know. Thought he'd write. . . . Good evening, Senor— and a thousand pardons. Come in, won't you?"

The flustered Senor thanked him and then had trouble with his breathing apparatus. Nick began to shepherd him up the steps, but the Colonel—automatic still in hand—barred the way.

"Who is this man?"

Colonel Sandingford's courtesy had broken down under a strain of which Nick knew little. With a weapon in his hand and the scent of danger in his nostrils, the decent wrappings of gentility vanished and left the raw stuff of the fighting soldier.

"This gentleman," said Nick very quietly, "has been teaching languages in Arunford for some years. I expected to hear from him, but, although I am very glad to see him, I hardly expected him to call—or I would have warned that lunatic. You see, sir, I had a fancy to learn some Spanish. It might be a convenient accomplishment in this strange household."

He turned and addressed the little Spaniard in another tone.

"I'm ever so sorry, Senor. I believe you have a saying about 'mad dogs of Englishmen ', and I'm beginning to think we deserve it. Will you come into the dining-room and take a glass of wine? I don't suppose we shall be interrupted there. After all, this in my house, and I have a fancy to be master of it."

Nick just then was a very angry man, and the last remarks were flung for the benefit of another angry man. The Colonel, however, stood aside with a well-disciplined air of calm.

In the dining-room Nick closed the door, begged his guest to be seated, and—after more apologies—offered a variety of refreshments. The Seiior, still obviously shaken, asked for a leetle brandy.

While Nick was bringing a glass and a decanter—and also a siphon, which was politely scorned—the Seiior fumbled in his breast pocket and produced the cablegram and some papers of his own.

"Decs," he said, "has not been ver' 'ard. Der most common letter must mean der vowel *e* or perhaps der vowel *a* in our language. I find same word of three letters more so often than once with ser most common letter in der middle. I guess he must be *del*. So I have a *d* and a *l* besides and *e,* and so by guess I get more and more letters. And so I decode into Spanish.

"Now der English translation—eet is like this."

The Senor dabbed at every written word with the blunt end of a pencil.

"Der uprising is squash. Montes der devil is dead and his devilskins dead or vanquish. Thanks to God. A glorious welcome waits your return."

Nick thanked him almost absently, and then in silence he tried to digest it all.

"Thank you very much indeed," he said at last. "I am very much obliged to you. And now—I don't think I have ten pounds in cash—will you let me give you a cheque?"

The little Spaniard laughed and slapped his thigh.

"A thousand thanks, Senor. I take it if you wish, but any time —any time. To-morrow I am richer than for years. What do I do so soon as I have read der siphon? I telephone to a friend who does moch beezncss wit' der stocks and der shares. He pay me moch for what I tell 'im. For San Analdos are down, down —becausc of der revolution. To-morrow dey will be up, up again. Besides what he gif' me I tell 'im I am to have ten pounds, so he buy for me on—how you say it?—der margins. To-morrow I shall 'ave one hondred, two hondred—not less."
Nick suddenly burst out laughing.

"Good Lord!" he exclaimed. "Who on earth would have thought of that? "

"But you must t'ink of it, Seiior. To-morrow, early, perhaps der news will not be confirm. Eet is—what you call it?—monny for ham."

"Jam," corrected Nick, laughing. "But I'm an unlucky gambler, Senor. I won't hoodoo your chances of packing a parcel. And now I'll write your cheque and run you back in my car. And very, very sincere thanks."

They encountered Colonel Sandingford in the hall outside. The Colonel seemed to have recovered some of his lost humour.

"I'm just going to run this gentleman into Arunford," he said. "When you hear the car coming back you'll know it's me."

"Right," said Colonel Sandingford. "D'you mind hooting three times. Then there'll be no mistake."

"And," said Nick, looking straight at him, "there's a chance to make a fortune first thing to-morrow. Buy San Analdo government stock. It's right down now, but it'll shoot up again to-morrow. But perhaps you already knew."

The Colonel looked straight back at him.

"Yes," he said, "I knew already. I am hoping to net about a hundred thousand pounds. Only about ten thousand for myself, I'm afraid, and the rest for—er—a certain friend of mine."

He passed on with a quiet smile, leaving Nick speechless. But after all perhaps it was the Colonel's turn to score.

CHAPTER XXII
"SOMETHING'S GOING TO HAPPEN"

The night, during which the four men in the house took turns to keep awake and alert—without the girls having been informed of what was happening—passed uneventfully until the anticlimax of dawn.

Rain, beginning just before dawn, followed on the trail of distant thunder—a light but steady fall which lessened soon after breakfast and passed away just before noon, leaving a green and shining world in broad sunlight under a blue sky.

The postman ignored the house that morning, but shortly after ten o'clock the telegraph boy of yesterday appeared in a gleaming cape on the same bicycle. Nick went to intercept him, but found the Colonel on his heels.

"Sandingford." said the boy. presenting the envelope.

"Ah!" said the Colonel, and presented his back as he turned to open it.

Nick, no longer interested, turned away, but swung round again at the sound of the Colonel's voice. He said something which sounded like "Thank God!" and Nick wondered if the pious ejaculation—supposing he had heard it correctly—had been uttered in gratitude for the success of another gamble in foreign securities.

"Beg pardon, sir?" said the boy, who also seemed doubtful of his hearing.

"I said No answer, thank you," replied the Colonel, with a broad, mysterious smile.
Nick had already seen the morning paper. There was no official news from San Analdo, and since England was a long way off, and in general not in the least interested, a short paragraph was sufficient for this sort of negative information.

The day passed uneventfully and the summer evening seemed only late afternoon when they sat down to dinner, with the world outside still in the warm light of the sun. Milly commented on the length of the days, and Betty said:

"Yes: I've been reading that up the North Pole way it doesn't get dark at all this time of year."

"And in one sense," said the Colonel dryly, "it would be a great comfort to me if we were all living there just now."

"Hard luck on the courting couples, though," Betty remarked. "I bet those young Esquimaux don't like it much. Just imagine a boy and a girl sittin' on an iceberg and havin' to wait about four months for it to get dark."

"But they have a jolly good innings in the winter," Basil laughed, "so it cuts both ways. Gives the not-so-young girls a chance too. I dare say many a jolly little Lap has done his courting and got married entirely in the dark—and had to wait a good many weeks to see what he'd really got."

Nick smiled absently, having scarcely heard. His thoughts were centred upon Colonel Sandingford's remark. The Colonel had uttered pious thanks for something when his telegram arrived, but evidently the sense of danger still remained with him.

Later, when the girls had left the three men together, and Basil was holding a lighted match to the Colonel's cigarette, Nick said: "Same arrangement again to-night, sir?"

"Yes—same hours, if you don't mind. Perringer knows." Basil grinned and grimaced.

"Beauty sleep all going to blazes," he said. "Old and 'aggard before me time. Sorry, sir—all necessary and in a good cause, I know. But just out of curiosity—for grumbling is far from my noble nature—how long is this likely to go on?"

"Not long," Colonel Sandingford answered, almost brightly. "We are on the eve of battle if the battle's coming."

Nick sighed.

"I suppose," he said, "that even at this hour it's no use asking you what it's all about?"

The Colonel's air was apologetic and his manner more confidential than his speech.

"My dear boy, you are going to know very soon. It is not that you and your friend are not trusted. But if the worst should happen and you are made to answer questions on oath and at the pistol-point—or under other duress—you can answer them only according to your lights."

Basil grinned across at Nick.

"Jolly prospect, isn't it?" he said. "Like old Guy Fawkes. He never spilled the beans. Just died mysteriously in the Tower. And they kept some nice things in the Tower in those days to encourage frank confidences. Probably they overdid the use of the jolly old wrack, or whatever it was. You haven't seen a wrack lying about here, I suppose? Still, no doubt our friends will bring something along with them."

Colonel Sandingford smiled, indulgently rather than mirthfully.

"Glad you take it like that," he said. "One word more, though. Keep your weapons handy, of course, and if you hear anything in the night don't act on your own unless you're compelled. You know where to find Perringer and me."

Basil put up his hand like a small boy in a class-room.

"Please, sir," he said, suiting his voice to the gesture, "please, sir, are we to kill anybody, sir? Like Perringer did, sir?" Colonel Sandingford started slightly.

"I never heard of Perringer killing anybody. Certainly not in this country."

"Looks very much as if he did," said Nick, "and borrowed my car to dump the body afterwards. But perhaps he didn't go so far as to tell you that."

The Colonel smiled faintly and for the moment seemed to be absorbed in the study of his own finger-nails.

"Yes," he admitted, "I know all about that. But, whatever Perringer's subsequent actions may have been, it was not Perringer who fired that shot."

Nick groaned aloud and wrinkled his brows.

"But I don't see who else it could have been. Can hardly have been a question of thieves falling out among themselves. They'd hardly choose a room in a house they'd just broken into to settle their small differences—although that fellow had a drawn knife in his hand. Of course, though, it may have been an accident."

"Ah!" said the Colonel, suddenly laughing. "Perhaps that's what you'd better think—at least for the present."

They rejoined Milly and Betty in the drawing-room and sat talking moodily and disjointedly for a while until the girls went early to bed.

Nick and Basil followed them out into the hall to say good night, and in darkness at the foot of the stairs Milly drew Nick's head down to the level of her face as if to whisper. And whisper she did, after she had been kissed.

"Good night, my love. Take great care of yourself."

"Of course," he laughed lightly. "Always do. Why?"

"Something's going to happen. Don't you *feel* that something's going to happen? "

Nick had been feeling like that for some time, and there was little comfort in this instance of feminine intuition. But he only laughed again.

"Yes," he said, "I feel that old Basil—with what he's won from me at other card-games—can just about afford to learn ecarte. I'm going to teach him to-night before we go to bed."

CHAPTER XXIII
ENTER SIR ANTHONY

"That's four and six," said Nick. "Shame to take the money. Going to pay now or wait till we pack up? Your deal."

Basil dealt the cards, and in the absolute silence within the room the sounds made by his fingers and by the falling cards were plainly audible. Outside, beyond the shuttered windows which did not allow one knife-edge ray of light to escape, the world was as still as if time itself were suspended.

Nick, picking up the five cards dealt to him. obeyed a subconscious prompting to listen. He sat still for some moments and then, seeing Basil about to speak, checked him with a gesture.

"Sorry!" he said at last.

"You reminded me just then of a picture of the infant Samuel," Basil remarked in a low voice. "Nerves, old boy."

"No. I thought I heard something outside. . . . Hold on a bit and let's listen again."

Once more there was silence. Then Nick suddenly rose, crept to the door which stood open, and vanished noiselessly into the hall. Basil picked up the cards which remained undealt and sat in silence absently shuffling them. Suddenly, at the sound of a whisper outside the room, he dropped the cards and crept to the door, where he was met by Nick.

"I heard something." Nick breathed. "I think it's the library again. No shutters to those damned windows. Coming?"

Remembered instructions rather than irresolution caused Basil to hesitate.

"What about calling?"

"Mayn't be time. Fellow I thought I heard outside mayn't be the one breaking in. May be keeping *cave*. Don't want 'em all over the house before—"

"Come on, then," whispered Basil in another tone, but Nick had already turned and was a pace or two in the lead.

It is very well to be a man of action rather than of words, but the quality has its drawbacks. The allies of the man of action are not always able to anticipate, and act in conjunction with, his movements. Thus, when Nick without a word began suddenly to sprint, Basil was let t almost standing for a second or two and lost many yards in—as it proved—a race to the library door.

Nick flung open the door and sprang across the threshold. Instantly there were shouts in more voices than one. The door swung back as if upon a spring and slammed. Then, as Basil reached it, he heard the thud of something small and heavy striking hard upon the floor, and Nick's voice raised in an agony of warning.

"Beat it! Beat it! They've got me!"

It was the last kind of order or advice which Basil in such circumstances was likely to obey. He thrust open the door, automatic in hand, and leaped into the room—to become instantly conscious of artificial light. Then several things seemed to happen simultaneously.

There was a pain in his right wrist and his automatic was gone. His head bumped against the wall. Simultaneously it seemed that the floor had risen and struck him on the base of the spine. He found himself sitting, while the concentrated lights of two electric torches played on him. A third light played on Nick.

He raised his eyes and saw Nick standing beside him, his back to the wall. Nick seemed also to have been disarmed. He stood with his hands raised above the level of his shoulders, anger in his eyes and his mouth set in a savage grin.

"Lar-di-dar-di-dar," cried a voice, charged with savage mockery. "What you call a roughouse, eh?"

There were three men in the room, all armed with revolvers, all flashing electric torches. All were dark and foreign-looking. Two were short, thick-set and powerfully built. The third, a head taller than his companions, was of more slender growth but still of fine physique. It was he who had spoken. He, it seemed, was the leader.

"Now lis-ten, you two!" he said in a low and thrilling voice. It seemed that he spoke good English with a foreign accent. "We come not to waste lime. When we shoot we shoot to kill. We are not making a game. If you are fools you die—like dat!"

He stamped his foot as if to illustrate the suddenness of the death which might await them.

"Understand! We do not want you. You are nothing. Less than nothing. We want the Senor. Take us to him."

"What Senor?" Nick growled.

"The Senor Antonio Cromer."

"He's dead, you fool," said Nick.

"Aha, you know he is dead. He tell you so and you believe him. But if a man tell me he is dead I know he is alive. And I know Antonio Cromer is alive, and where he is this living minute."

"Then where is he?" Nick growled. "I haven't got him up my sleeve."

"He is in the room upstairs—the room so careful locked and sealed. Ah, we are not fools. Now there is anudder way to that room. It must be so. How else is he fed? How do he come and go? You show us der way and all is well for you. If not—"

"Don't know what the hell you're talking about," said Nick. The revolver pointed at Basil.

"Don't know any other way into that room," said Basil. "It's empty, anyway. And Sir Anthony Cromer's dead. You can see his grave and tombstone."

"N so dead as you may be at the end of one liddle minute—or less. Lis-ten. I go to count ten. *One— two—three—*"

"Oh, shoot and be damned, then," growled Nick.

The man counted slowly until he had reached ten. Then came silence. Basil, in an agony of apprehension, waited for the crash of a shot and the sight of Nick falling. But these things did not happen.

"Lar-di-dar-di-dar," chanted the tall man. "Is it so? Then we try som'tings else."

He spoke abruptly in Spanish. One of the smaller men handed him a knotted cord. Nick and Basil were afterwards left guessing as to what he intended to do with it.

Basil's horrified eyes, focused on the man as they were, could hardly take in the open window behind him. But a sudden apparition forced itself upon his gaze. Vaguely and without emotion he thought that another of the brutes was climbing in. Then suddenly his heart gave a great leap.

There came a crash, a spurt of flame, a scream, hoarse and startled cries, a body stumbling and leaning on the chair which broke its fall—and Perringer climbing into the room with a wisp of smoke trailing from the muzzle of his automatic. And all, as it seemed, in the passing of an instant.

Two weapons pointed at Perringer, but neither fired. There was a voice from the door almost at Basil's elbow. It was a voice which spoke English.

"Hands up!" it barked. And then, as if the speaker had recollected something, came two or three sharp words in a foreign tongue.

The two men, with their backs presented to this unexpected danger, stood quite still. Then one, and afterwards the other, dropped his weapon with a thud. Nick had not recognised the voice, and turned in amazement to see that the rescuer was a stranger—or so for the moment he seemed.

No, not quite a stranger. Nick had seen him once before— yes, once at least—when he had impersonated Colonel Sandingford. He was the man who had appeared once in their midst and so strangely vanished.

"Yes?" he said, speaking English again. "You want me, I think? You know me, do you not? Well? I am Anthony Cromer."

Neither Nick nor Basil noticed the ensuing silence. Indeed it was no silence for them. Those last words rang and repeated in their ears.

"Tony, my dear fellow, for God's sake!"

This was another newcomer to the scene, but neither Nick nor Basil had to turn to identify the speaker. Colonel Sandingford, however, passed across their line of vision.

"All right, Jack." It was the resurrected man who spoke. "It's better this way. I've got the situation well in hand, I think. Perringer—there's a good fellow—go and look at the man you've hurt. I hope it isn't serious. The poor man thought it his duty to kill me, no doubt. I, too, have shed blood, but only in self-defence. The last time I fired I did not mean to kill. You know that, Perringer?"

"But I'm damned glad you killed him all the same, sir," said Perringer, and looking at two backs he interjected quite inimitably the one word, "*Scum!*"

There was silence for a minute while Perringer bent over the man upon the floor.

"Not much bleeding," Perringer announced. "Just scraped his ribs. I think. More frightened than hurt. Bad shot. Meant it for his black heart. Can't see much for dirt. Last bath he had was given him by his mother's midwife."

The remark, coming as an anticlimax which until then had seemed highly dramatic, tickled the overwrought nerves of Nick and Basil. They began to giggle, then to laugh hysterically.
Sir Anthony then addressed the two smaller men in Spanish. They turned about and faced him with hangdog airs.

"Perringer," he continued, "go and get something to dress that man's wound. A bandage and some antiseptic and—yes—a little iodine, if you have them. Pick up those weapons first and hand them to me. Then we can all sit down. We may as well be comfortable."

Nick was looking at Perringer and the wounded man, and he started slightly to feel a hand upon his arm. He turned to look into a smiling face.

"Hullo, Nick, my dear boy. Sorry not to have had the opportunity of taking your hand before. But it's not too late now. Apart from one exciting occasion—when I was fairly caught out—we haven't seen each other since you were about five or six. You've grown, my lad, you've grown."

"I thought I'd seen you somewhere before," laughed Nick. "when you appeared on the scene to do your vanishing trick that afternoon. Though why you did it I can't understand. I hope you're well, Uncle Anthony, and I'm very glad to see you alive."

"And I'm very grateful to you and your friends for the way you've been standing between me and danger—although you didn't quite knew what you were doing. We'll have a long talk after we've got this little matter fixed. I'm afraid you have been rather mystified. Well, that could not be helped. And the explanation is so simple that you will probably wonder why it never occurred to you—if indeed it did not. I think you will understand, u:o, why I did not repose all my trust in you from the very beginning."

Sir Anthony's gaze wavered and passed on to the Colonel.

"Jack, my dear boy, have you got that cable which arrived this morning?"

"Yes." The Colonel was fumbling. "Here it is."

"Thank you." Sir Anthony, having taken the cablegram in its envelope from the Colonel's hand, turned once more to Nick. "The coded message which arrived yesterday for me —and which you very properly opened—would not have helped me to impress these men that their cause is now dead. I got Perringer to cable back and get it repeated in plain Spanish. These men will understand, too, that such a message would never be allowed to leave Santa Aloma or anywhere else in San Analdo if it were untrue." Perringer caused a hiatus by reappearing with a medicine-chest. The tall man's wound, which was inconsiderable although doubtless painful, was dressed and bandaged, and he was given the help that he scarcely needed to enable him to rise and then recline in a long and comfortable chair. Sir Anthony approached him, holding out the cablegram. He read and uttered no word, but an anguish of dread and disappointment came into his eyes and his mouth became suddenly limp and sagged at the corners. This man who had come with murder in his heart, and such courage as the assassin must needs muster, had become suddenly a poor thing whom children might have flouted and abused without reprisal.

The same flimsy sheet of paper was shown to each of the other two in turn. Neither seemed to doubt its authenticity, for they had had no news cabled to them from their own country, and no news for them at such a time was bad news indeed. They broke into lamentations in their own longue, and one dropped his head and held his face between his hands.

Sir Anthony then addressed them, and what he said to .them and their words to him were alike in Spanish. The Colonel and Nick and Basil were only aware that they were witnessing and hearing something moving and something strange. Afterwards Sir Anthony told them the meaning of what they saw and heard.

"You see," he said to them in Spanish, "—you see where you stand. You are now at my mercy in a strange country, sheep without a shepherd. The man who hired you and paid you the assassin's wage is dead. You stand within the British law, which knows how to deal faithfully with such as you. Men will say that blood shed in this country is upon your hands already. There was Juan—"

"We did not kill him," cried one. "He was killed in this room —God knows by whom. I was outside the window, waiting to climb inside, when I heard the shot, and then I ran away. And they found his body more than a mile distant in a wood."

"Yes, they found his body in a wood—an associate of yours who had been out with you on a business which you would find it difficult to explain. Stand up in the dock and tell that story to a British jury—and a British judge. To-night you came again, you broke in armed—to seek my blood. Oh, that is so easily proved. And the murder—would that be so hard to prove?"

They were guiltless of that at least, but no sense of wronged innocence oppressed them. They were concerned only with possible consequences.

"Senor," said the man whose face was still covered by his hands, "you came—you, a stranger—to our country and set it ablaze."

"God knows there was need for such a burning. I did not come as priest or missioner—a humble layman, I—but I believe that I carried the True Message in my heart and that it guided speech and action in all that I said and did. And I did not fail. When we ran, my colleague and I, with the hell-hounds upon our heels, my mission was already accomplished. San Antonio had purged itself by revolution. It had become another state—a state in which Decency could walk the streets without a blush.

"But the arch-devil escaped across the frontier—the Emperor of Vice in San Analdo. He was not financially ruined. He could still crumble golden messes for his hounds and whistle them across the world. He could pay for the blood of his enemy, the man who had brought decency and cleanness back to a fair country too long befouled.

"The hunted animal goes to ground, and so I prepared a lair for myself. As soon as I knew that I was in imminent danger— and I kept a line of communication with your country which was always open—I had a golden opportunity to disappear. A poor nameless vagrant lies in a grave beneath a stone inscribed with my name.

"But it did not deceive my arch-enemy. Any man, with cause to suspect—as I have realized since—must have smiled darkly to himself when he read the reports of that inquest. Perringer, who had to give his evidence and identify my alleged remains—for the poor face was so battered—had to declare himself an atheist to avoid lying upon his oath. Perringer an atheist! Well, they knew better than that in San Analdo.

"Still, lying in my retreat, which I could make some show of defending, seemed better than wandering about the world with a price upon my head. Our excellent police, I knew, could not help me much—even if they would credit such a story as I had to tell them. And I saw, too, that my retreat could become something more than a refuge. There was a trap ready made, into which one man had walked already, as you three have walked into it to-night.

"That, I think, is all that I wish to tell you. And now—what am I to do with you?—you who are hirelings without any more a master. You came here for my blood, and there has been a little blood, but it has not been mine. You have gambled on the side of evil and have lost the throw. You are castaways in a strange country, which will become a hostile country so soon as the colour of your hearts is known. Answer me then—what shall I do with you?"

And the man whose face was covered spoke through his fingers:

"Will you not have mercy, Senor, for the love of God?"

"Ah!" A strange smile played on Sir Anthony's lips and his eyes suddenly lit and softened. "You answer one question with another—and how shall I answer you again? I came to your country with the Christian message, or the simple gospel of human decency, if you prefer it so. Forgiveness stands high among the ethics of my creed. You have a car hidden somewhere close at hand, I suppose? Ah, that is well. And so I say to you. Go in peace, poor sinners, take your wounded friend with you and tend him, pray for me when you have learned to pray again, and sin no more."

There was a sudden buzz in the room. Nick had not understood a word of this speech, but he heard its authentic echo in half-inarticulate cries of relief and gratitude and saw all that he needed to see on three men's faces.

"Good Lord, Uncle Anthony! You're not letting them go?"

"My boy," his uncle replied slowly, "if ever I am allowed to pass into Heaven I know that I should hate to hear the voice of some superior angel saying to the Man at the Gate, 'Good Lord, Peter, you're not letting him through?'"

"Oh!" said Nick. It was all that he could say, and, not yet knowing the import of his uncle's words, he thought: "The house has got him too. We're all lunatics here."

The door had remained open. Sir Anthony turned to it again to widen the gap, perhaps as a gesture of dismissal. But instead of facing about once more, he stood still and exclaimed aloud: "Why! What are you doing here? And what's that poker for?"

"We thought—we thought," faltered one of the dressing-gowned intruders in the voice of Betty, "—we thought that there was danger."

"And so there was, and we wanted you well out of it. But it's over now. And how much did you hear?"

"We heard you say who you were," said Milly simply.

"And that," added Betty cheerfully, "is about all. Me no spika da Spaniola—tum-tum. Don't mind me. Nick's right, and we're all mad. But is the shooting over yet?"

CHAPTER XXIV
SIR ANTHONY EXPLAINS

"No, please, Sir Anthony," said Milly, "tell us all about it now. What possible chance shall we have of sleeping if you don't?"

It was half an hour later. The uninvited visitors were gone. All the inmates of the house, Perringer included, were in the same room with all its windows now closed. Perringer, that saintly character, had not been present all the time. Having speeded the parting guests, he had recognized a general need and brewed a large pot of tea.

"Yes, come on, Uncle," cried Nick. "I second that—if you're not too tired."

"Well," his resurrected relative returned good-humouredly, "I can't drink boiling tea at a gulp, and I think I can answer about a thousand questions in the shortest possible time by telling you a plain narrative. And I'd better begin by telling you in English—to the best of my memory—what I said to those poor tools of an evil man who have just slunk away."

And forthwith he gave them the gist of the speech which had wrought such an effect upon his foes.

"Now," he continued, "for the rest. I do not wish to seem a prig—you must think what you like of me—but always, since I was a very young man, I had a strong religious sense. Also—I could not help myself—I was very rich.

"I saw a picture once—it was a copy of one hung in the Royal Academy many years ago—which depicted the Young Man who turned sadly away. The picture was entitled 'For he had Great Possessions.' And I, too, had great possessions—much more, Nick, than my will disclosed, but I shall explain that later. Also I dreaded that metaphor about the Camel and the Eye of a Needle.

"You may wonder why I did not take Orders. I thought of doing so. But one day, half in fun, I put on the surplice of a friend of mine and looked at myself in the mirror.

"Possibly it was foolish—although I do not think so—but I seemed to see then and there that the thing was not possible. I don't suppose I looked a queerer sight than a host of other men. But I saw, and saw clearly, that I was not meant to wear it. I must give my service as a layman.

"I need tell you nothing now of my early blunders. It is not that I am ashamed of them, for at least they were well meant, but they do not come within the scope of the present story. I had worked, so much in vain as it seemed, for years: been sponged on, duped and nearly driven to despair, when I fell in with the gentleman whom you know as my servant, Perringer."

"You saved my life, sir," Perringer interpolated, "and I think you saved my soul."

"Perringer, as I know, has told you something of his story. I will not add to it except to tell you that, as a convert, he was at first no small embarrassment. He assessed me high above my worth. The man's humility was almost a nuisance. I wanted him to become my secretary, since I needed one. Socially he was my equal, but he would become my body-servant or nothing. I—well, at least I knew better than to waste that kind of devotion. I let him have his way.

"I was a younger man then and Perringer not much more than a boy. We were both enthusiasts. We planned to make the world a better place. We travelled much in many lands as lay missioners. We had our small successes, our heart-breaking failures.

"And then we heard of San Analdo. We heard of it from a man who had just retired from the Consular Service there. I need not repeat what he told me about that sink of iniquity. We went to see for ourselves—only to find that his worst tales were understatements.

"Now I do not wish to slander the mass of the inhabitants of the little state—mostly of Spanish descent and a great deal of Indian blood as well. Nor is it for me to enlarge on the old theories of the effect of climate upon morals. The underlying sin, from which all the other vices sprang, was laziness.

"It is understandable—in a climate where it is necessary for people to sleep behind drawn blinds for part of the day when only mad Englishmen go abroad—that a certain torpor should creep into the blood of a people and that they should become morally as well as physically lazy. Most of them were good people—or meant to be—who were jealous of the sanctity of their own homes, but incapable of cleansing the streets outside or purging the evil house across the way. And the good people were falling fast because temptations were so frequent and so obvious and so unrestricted.

"I will not tell you a hundredth part of what Perringer and I found in Santa Amada, the capital. The sale of dope and maddening drinks was rampant. So was the white slave traffic—and worse things still.

"To give the priests their due they preached and laboured continuously but in vain. I heard when I arrived that they were the worst of the lot. but I soon nailed that lie. It is the kind of slander that you hear on all dirty tongues and in all countries against the clergy of all denominations, and it is seldom hard to see what lies behind this malice.

"The local clergy could do only what local clergy can do elsewhere—they could preach only to the converted. And so the decent people, who still kept their heads above the mire, dozed in the shade which protected them from their eternal sunlight, and groaned in their sleep, and waited the coming of a prophet.

"Well, I didn't fill the bill in that regard. I was just a bluff Englishman and not even a Roman Catholic. I could touch them little on the religious side, nor was I qualified to attempt it. But I had one great asset in their eyes—I was an Englishman.

"I found that they had a great respect for the English, and had tried to adapt certain English customs. Football had almost ousted bull-fighting as the favourite sport—although I am bound to admit that football, as they played it, made the brutalities of the bull-ring seem tame by comparison. But I dare say a footballer, playing under a tropic sun, is easily irritated—which explains why the referee invariably goes armed.

"Still, you know, even that kind of football was a sign of incipient grace. And there was grace in that dreadful city under all its mire. The decent people needed somebody to wake them, and slowly they let the mad heretic Englishman do it.

"I soon discovered that most of the organized and commercialized beastliness originated from a syndicate headed by a man named Montes. He was a living and open disciple of the Fiend, many times a millionaire already, and protected by the Government which he seemed to hold in the hollow of his hand. Getting rid of him meant revolution and the slaughter of many vested interests. But they're used to revolutions in San Analdo. They had already had two hundred and seventy-one since they cast off the yolk of Spain. And this—with seventeen inter-state wars and three inquisitions—is no bad record for a lazy people

"Well, we worked, Perringer and I, and not in vain and not without danger. Between us we survived eleven attempts at assassination—eleven, I mean, that we knew of. And one day the Generalissimo of the little army came to see me. He annoyed me by kissing me on both cheeks, but he delighted me by telling me that all his commissioned officers were squared and that he was about to march on the Capitol and sling out the President.

"This feat he duly performed, and although I deplored many of the three hundred and fifty-four executions which followed, I regretted that Senor Montes was not among the victims. Montes, inside a Ford car, was already across one of the frontiers.

"So far, so good. The new president was a decent man and began to do his best—and not a bad best either—to clear up the various messes. But although Montes was out of the land he was still a power in it, and a host of men in his pay were within the frontiers. I had a slight knife-wound in the back from one of them, which might have been more serious if Perringer hadn't given me a shove before turning to break the fellow's neck.

"That was about two days before President Callino paid me the compliment of a personal visit. He urged me with tears to leave the country. He was doing his best to protect me, but I had too many secret enemies. Montes, with his ill-gotten millions, was biting his nails at no great distance, and still had a ragtag, un-uniformed army within the state. He was resolved to spare neither money nor the lives of his paid creatures to settle his score with me.

"Well, Perringer and I had done our job and—speaking for myself—while I was willing to take the risks I had never aspired to the Crown of Martyrdom. And so we returned home, leaving trusted friends to warn us of any approaching danger, for we knew that the world held no safe place for me while Montes lived.

"I was looking for a place to settle when this house came on the market. I went to see it, and probably would not have acquired it but for outstanding reason. The owner gleefully told me the ghost story —which enhances the value of any old property —and showed me a discovery he had just made in the room alleged to be haunted.

"This, as I dare say you have guessed, was the entrance to a secret passage—or, rather, to secret staircases, for as you will see it consists mostly of these. There's a neat little door in the panels which looks like a bit of jigsaw puzzle when it's open. It leads to the roof and to the cellars. The cellars are stone, as you've noticed, but one of the squares of stone in a dark corner, daubed with whitewash like the rest, is actually wood when you come to examine it closely. On the roof there's a most blatant trap-door. Hundreds of workmen repairing that roof in the course of the years must have seen that trap and imagined that a loft, or more latterly a cistern, lay beneath it.

"Weil, there was my hide-out if it ever became necessary. But I didn't fancy living in a narrow passage or on a mouldering staircase. So I resurrected the ghost story and had the room sealed up. Nobody, I thought, could imagine that I was living in a sealed room if it became necessary for me to disappear. And my problem was how to appear dead for a time without being actually so. A dead man has to leave his body somewhere.

"Well, somehow I thought that I should manage to appear dead and I took certain steps. I placed certain large securities in the safe hands of my old and trusted friend. Colonel Sandingford, and the residue of my property, all my known assets, I willed to you, my dear Nick—on conditions which must have puzzled you.

"Why did I select you and why impose the conditions? That is simple. I was afraid of what actually occurred. If I achieved my plan my enemies were still likely to smell a large rat. It wasn't fair to let Perringer face the music alone. And I had a poor young nephew—of whom I had heard good reports—who was a County cricketer, and therefore, I assumed, of the nerveless athletic type.

"Well, I'd had my warning for nearly three weeks when there came a chance which I seized with both hands. An unfortunate tramp of about my own build was knocked down close to the lodge gates at night by a car which failed to stop. I actually heard, although I did not see, the accident, for I was coming out at the time. The man's face had struck the road and was terribly battered. I saw the chance, dragged the body into the lodge, and rushed to find Perringer. We dressed him in my clothes, with some of my property in the pockets, and carried him back to the road.

"It seemed to dispose of me—and yet it did not in the sight of my enemies. Perringer refusing to take the oath at the inquest was a glaring pointer, and if only the papers had suppressed the fact all might have been well. And unfortunately the story of the sealed room—which I had deliberately allowed to become public property—would suggest a great deal to anybody who knew that I had cause to hide.

"But I think for a time I partly deceived my enemies. I cannot be sure. At the most they could only suspect. I see now that I made one grave blunder. I ought to have let them break into the scaled room and find it empty. They would never have suspected a door in the panels.

"Well, now, I think you know nearly everything that happened. Twice I nearly gave myself away. Once, when I heard that you were not expected back until dinner, I came out and was nicely caught. I had to pretend to be the Colonel—while all the time I had the embarrassment of knowing that you were certain soon to see the Colonel himself.

"On another occasion a certain young lady walked in her sleep and knocked at my door. That was a dreadful business! For I thought it was Perringer and answered: and afterwards I wasn't sure if she had heard my voice through her dream.

"There was another awkward occasion and a very recent one. Perringer had come to sec me at night and attend to my wants and brought the Colonel along for a chat. Meanwhile somebody had locked the door at the top of the cellar stairs and made prisoners of them both. They could get on to the roof, of course, but that did not seem likely to help them much at first. However, it did, for Perringer risked his life by some climbing and made his way in by breaking one of the upper windows. Then, of course, he went down and unlocked the door.

"Well, that is bringing me very near the end. And before I go on to other and important matters I should be glad to know if there is anything about which you are not clear."

He looked at Nick, and Nick answered promptly.

"Yes, Uncle. Who killed that man in the library?"

There was a pause. Sir Anthony looked straight back at him.

"I did. I heard the fellows—there was more than one, although only one entered—I heard them at work on the library windows below. Nobody else in the house had seemed to hear them. I did not know what they might do if they got in. I behaved quite illogically, of course, but I had some hope of scaring them away before they forced an entry. So I went down. But I was too late. One of them was already in the room, and he had a knife in his hand. I am a poor shot, I am afraid, and I swear that I did not shoot to kill. But my life depended on wounding him, and I did so—fatally.

"Perringer, as I suppose you have guessed, disposed of the body, because it would not have done to have the police rambling over the house and haling me out of my retreat to give evidence at the inquest. I do not think that I should have had to face any charge, that drawn knife found in his hand would have answered it for me. And indeed I think I have been punished enough, for I have no light regard for the sanctity of human life.

"Well, well, that answers all things, I think, and the worst of a very awkward business is over. Nick, my dear fellow, I will own that I was a trifle unnerved when I found that you had brought friends with you. I found that, by an inadvertence, I had only provided against your bringing your own servants. But Perringer reported well on them, and soon I was very glad indeed. I feel that I owe much to all of them for the way they have stood by you—and me—throughout some very trying experiences.

"Now, as to the future. You must have been worrying a little over that, I should think, my poor Nick. You saw me only once before, and that when you were a child, so that you wouldn't be human if you rejoiced over my coming to life again. Well, have no fears. Sir Anthony Cromer is dead for ever. There would be too many complications—legal and otherwise—if I came to life again. The Colonel here has been sitting on my nest-egg—a sum made over to him before I made my will and a larger one than you have as yet inherited. So all that you thought you had is still yours, and—er—go on being a good boy."

Nick began to say something. He was conscious of doing his best and of being conspicuously unsuccessful. His uncle cut him short.

"Sorry, my boy, but I haven't quite finished. I should like—I am old enough, I think, to say it without offence—to make some practical tribute to your very good friends. If you could tell me —"

"Well, I'm going to marry one of 'em," said Nick. "She'll be getting her—hr'mm—reward."

The older man smiled questioningly at Milly and saw her nod.

"My dear," he said, "I am delighted." And he went on to pour forth congratulations.

"And the other two are going to get married," said Nick. "Most respectable household this has been, really. Although I think poor old Perringer had his doubts about things at first. Play-actresses and all that, you know."

"Well," said Perringer, grinning, "after South America, you know, where young unmarried people are never allowed in each other's company alone for a single second—"

And he rolled his eyes and laughed.

"Yes, Nick?" said Sir Anthony.

"I thought you might like to launch 'em in the West End." said Nick. "Cost a bit—but you'd get your money back with a bit of luck. Finance 'em so as they hire their own theatre and buy a musical play and—"

"*Nick!* " screamed Betty.

"Well," Nick continued airily, "I believe Uncle Anthony can afford it, and I don't mind asking for things for other people. . . . They're not a bit of good really, of course, Uncle Anthony, but I the British public will put up with any old sort of leading artistes so long as there are plenty of legs in the show and some catchy tunes—"

"Don't listen to him, sir!" cried Basil explosively. "We wouldn't dream of letting you—"

"You're not going to dream of anything," Sir Anthony interrupted in the most casual tone. "It's going to be done. I shall keep in touch with Nick. You will let him know when you have found your play and your theatre and what it's all going to cost. I should like to come and see your play, but I may not be in England."

Nick's voice cut through the muffled explosions of inarticulate gratitude.

"What do you mean to be doing. Uncle Anthony?"

"My dear boy"—his uncle smiled—"I have set my hand to the plough and I do not mean—I never meant—to lay it aside for ever. There are other states in South America besides San Analdo. There is plenty yet for us to do—Perringer and I."

CHAPTER XXV
"YOU CAN GUESS HIS NAME"

Nick and his young wife were travelling abroad when *Stop It, Katie!* was produced in a theatre of adequate size in the West End of London, and it was thus past its fiftieth performance when Betty, glancing up at one of the boxes, saw two faces which caused her to emit a sudden sound like gargling. But as it was a comic song it did not matter. Indeed it heightened the effect. It was the show, I am afraid, that "made" Betty and Basil, rather than Betty and Basil who "made" the show. But the public—despite one or two of those nasty old newspaper critics— willingly and even joyfully accepted them as New Stars. And the Comedy Extravaganza seemed wound up to run for many months.

Better still, the young couple had leaped to a position from which only folly and misfortune— and a great deal of both—could dislodge them for a long while to come. And Betty, who held the purse—and boasted of having gone through Basil's pockets every night since their marriage—meant never to be poor again.

It was not surprising therefore that Nick and Milly should receive a note during the entr'acte, nor that it should contain a summons urgently demanding their presence "behind" immediately the show was over. But the note did not affect their plans. They intended going in any case. Betty embraced them both with some violence in her dressing-room, rather forgetting that she was still wearing a great deal of grease-paint which accentuated humour rather than sentiment. Basil, having shaken hands and failed to utter more than three words in face of the unfair competition of his wife, went mysteriously into a corner, whence the forcible extraction of a champagne cork was presently heard.

"Knew you'd be coming," he said, holding up a foaming bottle. "Keeping it for you."

"Darlings," Betty was jabbering, "It's money for jam. Two companies on the road already and two more going out. And everybody thinks we're set to run for at least a year. But if it does I shall be out of it a lot of the time."

"Why?" asked Nick.

"Oh, of course you *would* ask. Milly had much more delicacy. Well, we've beaten you, anyway. I hope it's a little Basilco. I don't want any hen-babies. Might take after their Mummy and become low comics."

"Congrats," began Nick.

"Oh," cried Milly, cutting into his speech as young wives—and certain older wives—are apt to do. "While you're still resting you must bring it down to see us and stay as long as you can. But you can't have the sealed room. That seal is still intact. Dear old Uncle Anthony is still officially dead and the will's still valid and—he's got other relatives, you know."

"I'll put up with the room we shared, darling, thank you. I wonder if Uncle Anthony—you don't mind me calling him Uncle Anthony—will be back by then? It would be fun if he happened to come down while I was there. Gee, he's a lad! I see he's been at it again."

"At what again?" Nick asked, suddenly wide-eyed.

Betty regarded him, her head on one side, her eyes full of mischief and insolence.

"Don't you read your papers, Honey-pie? Well, I don't blame you. Put such naughty things in them sometimes, don't they? Not fit for little boys."

"Have a heart," said Basil, laughing. "It was only in to-night. And it didn't give the name Cromer, of course. Still, we know it was your uncle, old boy. Stephen Corton was the name of the Englishman who stirred up the mud and caused a revolution in the jolly little state of Costa Mala. Another Purity Campaign, no doubt. Well, you look at a map of the East Coast and you'll see that there's a little village called Corton which is not a hundred miles from Cromer."

"And Stephen is my uncle's second name," Nick laughed.

"That almost proves it. But there's something much more conclusive. There was another Englishman mixed up in the how d'you do. When it was over they tried to make this Stephen Corton president, but he wouldn't take it on. So they offered the job to the other Englishman and he accepted it.

"You can guess his name, can't you? It was Perringer."

A.M. Burrage – The Life And Times.

Alfred McLelland Burrage, better known as simply AM Burrage, was born in Hillingdon, Middlesex on July 1st, 1889, to Alfred Sherrington Burrage and Mary E. Burrage. On his Father's side writing already ran in the family's blood as both he and an uncle, Edwin Harcourt Burrage, were writers of the then very popular boys' magazine fiction.

Life in late Victorian times was by no means easy and writing has always been a precarious career for most. For an insight into the young AM and his surroundings it is interesting to see how certain facts were captured in the 1891 census when he was aged one. The family is listed as living at Uxbridge Common in Hillingdon. His father is 40 and his mother 36. In the next census of 1901, and with it the end of the Victorian era, the family has moved to 1 Park Villa, Newbury. In that time his father has aged 17 years his mother 6 years and young AM has disappeared from the records. It's almost a precursor to one of his stories.

There is little documented about his growing up and education. What we can glean though is something about his environment. His neighbours were varied: a tailor's journeyman, a corn porter, a lodging-house keeper and a grocer's assistant. Nothing particularly illustrious, so times cannot have been as rosy as they should, especially in the light of his Father's hard work. Alfred Sherrington wrote for The Boy's World, Our Boys' Paper, The Boys of England, and various others. He also appears to have written under the pseudonym Philander Jackson and edited The Boys' Standard and that one of his more celebrated pieces was a retelling of the story of

Sweeney Todd entitled "The String of Peals; or, Passages from the Life of Sweeney Todd, the Demon Barber".

Sadly Alfred Sherrington Burrage died in 1906. There is a biographical note in Lloyd's Magazine, from 1921, which suggests that young Alfred McLelland was studying at St. Augustine's, the Catholic Foundation School in Ramsgate, and most probably away from home at the time.

A.M. Burrage was 16 years old when he had his first story published; the same year as his father's death, in the prestigious boys' paper, Chums. It was a great start to his professional career and whether doors had been opened by his father and family or not the young man's career now had to stand on its own. He was now primary provider for the household and this was the only way he could do it. His Mother, sister and aunt must be provided for.

Magazine fiction was his family's blood and business and for A. M. Burrage, business was good. He established himself as a competent and creative writer and was busy writing stories and articles on a weekly basis for publications such as Boys' Friend Weekly, Boys' Herald, Comic Life, Vanguard, Dreadnought, Triumph Library Cheer Boys Cheer, and Gem, under the pseudonym 'Cooee'.

However, unlike his father and uncle who had remained firmly and easily categorised as boys' writers, he had his sights set on the more well regarded, more lucrative, adult market. Burrage was aided in his early years as a professional writer by Isobel Thorne of the off-Fleet Street publishing firm Shurey's. Her publications have been characterised as "low in price, modest in payments, but whose readers were avid for romance, thrills, sensation, strong characterisation and neat plotting", and this estimation of her publications also fits nicely the description of Burrage's own writing at that time. For a young writer this sort of readership was vital, and the modest wages he received were bolstered by the exposure the publications brought him. Burrage was certainly helped by Thorne's use of young writers.

At the time Burrage was beginning to really establish himself as a writer, the entire magazine fiction scene was benefiting from what we would now see as disruptive influences: new printing techniques, a growing readership with more disposable income and leisure time and other media failing to provide – though obviously movies and such were only in their infancy at the time. The market was lively and commercial, and the readership interested, excitable and willing to pay. P. G. Wodehouse, of Jeeves fame, recalls these years:

We might get turned down by the Strand, but there was always the hope of landing with Nash's, the Story-teller, the London, the Royal, the Red, the Yellow, Cassell's, the New, the Novel, the Grand, the Pall Mall, and the Windsor, not to mention Blackwood's, Cornhill, Chambers's and probably about a dozen more I've forgotten.

With War clouds darkening the skies of Europe in 1914 Burrage was firmly established as a magazine writer, securing publication in London Magazine and The Storyteller, which were both highly prestigious publications. Alongside he had plenty printed in less illustrious publications such as Short Stories Illustrated.

By now Burrage, a young man of twenty-four-year-was eligible for the Armed Services. Under the 'Derby Scheme' he confirmed that he was available for service if called upon in December 1915. Conscription was to follow shortly though, by that time, Burrage had already voluntarily enrolled in the Artists Rifles.

The significance of Burrage's decision to join the Artists Rifles is made clear by the nature of the unit itself. They formed in the middle of the nineteenth century, a group of volunteer artists comprising musicians, writers, painters and engravers. Minerva and Mars were their patrons, one of wisdom, arts, and defence, the other of war. The unit boasted several significant figures as ex-servicemen, including Dante Gabriel Rossetti, Algernon Charles Swinburne and William Morris. It was a popular unit with students and recent postgraduates, and the training was considered and extensive.

In Burrage's vivid, celebrated account of World War I entitled War is War, he insists that he was a volunteer and not a conscript, though as has already been noted, it is quite possible that his decision to join such a respected territorial unit may have been more of an effort to secure himself a more congenial army posting; had he waited for conscription, he would have had little choice over those with whom he was posted. Unlike poets Wilfred Owen or Edward Thomas, Burrage did not achieve a commission, and he suggests in War is War that this may be a result of his extremely unmilitary personality and his shortcomings as a soldier.

Add to this the fact that as the breadwinner for the family he was putting himself in harm's way. If anything were to happen to him the result on the family would be devastating. With the death of
Edwin Harcourt Burrage in 1916 it came even more starkly into focus.

Even though he was now a soldier he was still a writer and writers had to write. It also helped that it was a distraction from the mindless carnage around him. He experimented with various genres, excelling in the one that was to prove most lucrative for him; the light romance, in which a male character invariably meets a female character, there is a problem or hurdle to their being together, they overcome it and they live happily ever after. Burrage's talent for this formula was such that he could work seemingly endless minor variations from the same basic storyline and so he was able to keep writing a steady body of easy work.

He gives a fascinating account of the practicalities of writing such fiction during wartime in War is War, in which he remarks on the difficulties of censorship: "the problem of censorship was an acute one to me. It was well enough to write a story, but the difficulty was to get it censored. Officers were shy of tackling five thousand words or so, written in indelible pencil..." After some time he managed to find a chaplain who was willing to undertake the censorship. However, in order to secure this chaplain's favour and thus his services he was obliged to appear to be holy. Though he did so in earnest while he was with the chaplain, his efforts were dashed when the chaplain found him, sprawled on top of a young girl, and realised Burrage's piety to be a fraudulent con. As Burrage had anticipated, the reality of his behaviour ensured that this particular opportunity was swiftly ended. Resourceful to the last, though, he writes of his solution: "there were 'green envelopes' which could be sent away sealed and were liable only to censorship at the base, but these were only sparingly issued... I met an A.S.C. lorry driver who had stolen enough green envelopes to last me for the rest of the war; and since he only wanted two francs for them I was free of the censorship from that day forward."

Although we know that Burrage had his family to support at home as an incentive to keep writing, at times in War is War he reveals a more intimate aspect of his relationship with his work.

"It was a great relief to me to write when it was at all possible – to sit down and lose myself in that pleasant old world I used to know and pretend to myself that there never had been a war. Some of my editors seemed of the opinion that we were not suffering from one now. One used to write to me saying "Couldn't you let me have one of your light, charming love stories of country house life by next Thursday." I would get these letters in the trenches during the usual 'morning hate' when my fingers were too numb to hold a pencil, when I was worn out with work and sleeplessness, and when I was extremely doubtful if there ever would be another Thursday".

Writing is a useful therapy and for Burrage it provided a means to escape if only for a short time to a world that he could control and move at will.   With the misery and harsh conditions of the War dragging on he was eventually invalided and so he returned to England.

One of the best insights we have as to the character which Burrage presented on his return from the war is to be found in Lloyd's's 1920 publication of Captain Dorry, one of Burrage's story series. In that publication there was included a brief sketch of Burrage, describing his personality.

A.M. BURRAGE is the type of young man who might very well walk out of one of his own stories. He commenced yarn-spinning as a boy of fifteen at St Augustine's, Ramsgate, writing stories of school life to provide himself with pocket-money. Since then he has won his spurs as one of the most popular of magazine writers. Everything he does has charm and reflects his own romantic spirit – for he is incurably romantic and hopelessly lazy. It is his misfortune, although he would not admit it, that his work finds a too ready market. Nevertheless, his friends hope that one day he will wake up and do justice to himself. Otherwise he may end up as a "best-seller", a fate which doubtless he contemplates with equanimity.

Despite the sketch's fairly accurate but negative summation of Burrage's literary output up to that point, some of his stories seem to exhibit a desire to write about more than just his usual romantic plots. The most immediate change of this nature is in his decision to bring some of his wartime experience into his work, despite being perfectly aware that such writing was not at all what his editors desired, for they feared it would upset and intimidate their readership.

An example of this can be found in "A Town of Memories", published in 1919 in Grand Magazine, in which he uses his well rehearsed romantic story with a slight shift of emphasis to explore his own return from the war and the general reception which soldiers received on their return. Following a young officer as he returns to the town in which he grew up, Burrage portrays an almost hostile environment into which he returns; he is unrecognised, and nobody pays any interest, respect or attention to him or his stories of the war, nor even to his reception of the Distinguished Service Order. Instead, the people of the town have their own interests and priorities with which to concern themselves. Though this contentious portrayal of post-war society certainly marks a slight shift in Burrage's writing, he returns to the romantic convention expected of him by reuniting the officer with a beautiful girl who had admired him throughout school. It would be harsh to not accept that market conditions expected one thing and to ignore them would mean turning his back on publications who still clamoured for his penmanship.

Another of Burrage's alternative directions is to be found in "The Recurring Tragedy", in which a General whose war tactics of attrition had been to the slaughtered cost of his soldiers, and he comes to re-imagine his own past as a Judas figure in a terrible vision. The Strange Career of Captain Dorry became a series for Lloyd's Magazine in 1920 about a gentleman crook and an ex-officer with a Military Cross who, idle in peacetime, meets a mysterious man called Fewgin whose business is in stolen goods and mind reading. Fewgin realises Dorry is a suitable candidate for recruitment into his gang of like-minded ex-military thieves, stealing only from "certain vampires who made money out of the war, and, by keeping up prices, are continuing to make money out of the peace". Again, in this motive, we see a glimpse of Burrage's own feelings on the war, as there is undoubtedly a bitterness towards those profiting from the suffering of others in such a manner. Fewgin justifies himself, saying:

"I help brave men who cannot help themselves. I give them a chance to get back a little of their own from the men who battened and fattened on them, who helped to starve their dependents while they were fighting, who smoked fat cigars in the haunts of their betters, and hoped the war might never end."

Burrage began to see slightly more success in the 1920s, achieving a couple of hard back publications entitled Some Ghost Stories and Poor Dear Esme. The latter, a comedy, concerns a boy who, for various reasons, is forced to disguise himself as a girl. Though these hard cover publications were a notable achievement, and one of which he was proud, the fact was that there was less money in it than in the magazines. In his history of the Strand Magazine, Reginald Pound portrays Burrage around this time, likening him to his equally prolific contemporary Herbert Shaw, considering them "two Bohemian temperaments that suffused and at times confused gifts from which more was expected than come forth. They had a precise knowledge of the popular short story as the product of calculated design. Both privately despised it, though it was their living."

The early 1920s, and with them a boom in prosperity, hope and happiness, now brought with them an increase in demand for war stories. Rather than preferring to ignore the atrocities of the war, which had seemed the general attitude in the immediate post-war years, society became more interested and concerned with the manner in which the war was fought, and the greed and political battles which had necessitated such bloodshed. Burrage answered this demand in 1930 with his own epochal piece, War Is War. He published under the pseudonym 'Ex-Private X', saying "were it otherwise I could not tell the truth about myself", though its publisher, Victor Gollancz, "who published the book and greatly admired it, had to point out that the critics would hardly take the book seriously if it became known that the author earned his living producing two or three slushy love stories a week".

In one of a series of letters he wrote to his contemporary and fellow writer Dorothy Sayers, Burrage bemoans how War is War "promised to be a great success, but was only a moderate one". The book itself was received with reviews on both sides of the spectrum. Cyril Fall's War Books, a survey of post-war writing published in 1930, gives a clear indication as to why the critics were so mixed in reception of the book. He writes:

This book is extremely uneven in quality. The account of the attack at Paschendaele and of conditions at Cambrai after the great German counter-attack are very good indeed; in fact among the best of their kind. But the rest is disfigured by an unreasoned and unpleasant attack on superiors and all troops other than those of the front line, which is all the more astonishing because the author is inclined to harp upon his social position as compared with that of many of the officers with whom he came in contact. He does not use as much bad language as many writers on the War, but his methods of abuse will leave on some of his readers at least a worse impression than the most highly-spiced language.

Dorothy Sayers was the editor at Victor Gollanz for anthologies of ghost and horror stories which included stories by Burrage. She says, in one of her letters of Burrage's story The Waxwork, a piece beyond the nerves of the editors, "what you say about "The Waxwork" sounds very exciting, just the sort of thing I want. Our nerves are stronger than those of the editors of periodicals, and we will publish anything, so long as it does not bring us into conflict with the Home Secretary". Though their correspondence began as strictly business, Burrage's acquaintance with Atherton Fleming, Sayers's husband, allowed their interactions to become less formal and friendlier. Burrage wrote of Fleming "I hope to encounter him soon in one of the Fleet Street tea-shops". 'Tea-shop' being a popular euphemism for the pub, where both Burrage and Fleming could frequently be found, though their alcohol consumption came to damage both their health and their professions, with Burrage coming off the worse.

Happily for Burrage, as a result of being featured in one of Sayers's anthologies, The Waxwork became one of his best-known stories and it would grab the attention of the film companies several times down the years even becoming an episode in the TV series 'Alfred Hitchcock Presents'.

The developing friendship between Burrage and Sayers enabled him to reveal more details of his personal life, admitting to her his "neuritis at both ends (legs and eyes)", and hinting at his troubles with alcohol: "Fleet Street is not a good place for a man who delights in succumbing to temptation, and whose doctor says that even small doses of alcohol are poison to him". Sayers sympathises, replying that Fleming "agrees with you entirely about the temptations of Fleet Street; he has, however, succeeded, through sheer strength of character, in being able to drink soda-water in the face of all his fellow journalists".

In another of Burrage's letters, he apologises for a delay in sending proofs of a story, with the words:

I have had a pretty thin time lately through illness and anxiety. And for days on end haven't had the energy in me to write a letter, and when I had the energy to send a complete set of proofs to you I found I hadn't the postage money (This is when you take out your handkerchief and start sobbing). I owed my late agent over £1000, so I got practically nothing out of War is War.

He stuck to it. Well, he is paid off now, and so are my arrears of income tax. All this took a toll of my very small earning capacity, and I have been sold up. This on top of something which promised to be a great success and was only a moderate one, was a bit too much for me. Still, in spite of sickness I am resilient and shall float again. "You can't keep a good man down," as the whale said about Jonah.

For a man who had so many stories in so many magazines, and was gaining pace in Sayers's anthologies as a talented writer of horror stories, his income will have been far higher than the then average wage, and yet as he says, he finds himself short of money.

Several questions are left unanswered about his personal life. It is unclear whether he was still supporting family, or whether he spent the majority of his money on alcohol, or whether he chose to conceal his true fortunes from those around him. Perhaps most incongruous is the apparent absence of a wife; though his death certificate indicates that he had one, listed as H.A. Burrage, he seems never to mention her to Sayers.

He was around forty-two when he wrote that apology letter to Sayers, though in tone and circumstance it seems to be from a man in a far later stage of his life.

Burrage continued writing until his death in 1956, and continued to be prolifically published. Indeed, the Evening News alone published some forty of his stories between 1950-56. His death is recorded at Edgware General Hospital on 18th December, and the causes of his death are recorded as congestive cardiac failure, arteriosclerosis and chronic bronchitis. He was sixty-seven years old, and his last address is listed as 105 Vaughan Road, Harrow.

Though his name is not often remembered in lists of prominent writers of his time, or even it's genres, his ghost stories are highly regarded by critics and fans alike, while his life story tells us much about the trials and stresses placed on authors during and after the war, and on soldiers returning from that war. His reluctant acceptance that the money was in the magazines while the esteem was in the poorly-paying hard covers, and his persistence as a writer, speak of a determined man, doomed to circumstance yet living as best he could.

In ending A.M Burrage wrote a few sentences which best sum up two things. Firstly his love for his son Simon (who sadly passed away in October 2013 and was a great and passionate advocate for his Father's works.) and secondly his succinct reasons for writing.

TO JULIAN SIMON FIELD BURRAGE
who at the moment of writing will
soon achieve the great age of four.
From somebody who loves him.

In War is War I admitted being a professional writer, or in other words one who depends for his bread and cheese and beer on writing, typing or dictating strings of sentences which his masters, the Public, are kind enough to buy and presumably to read.

The book brought me letters from a few old friends and a great many new ones. A large percentage of the new friends, who missed having seen that my identity was rather unkindly betrayed by the Press, wrote and asked (a) who I was and (b) what sort of stories did I write?

The answer to the second question will be found in the following pages. The answer to the first question is 'Nobody Much', worse luck.

Most of these stories were written with the intention of giving the reader a pleasant shudder, in the hope that he will take a lighted candle to bed with him—for candle-makers must be considered in these hard times. Some have already made their bow from the pages of the monthly magazines. The best have, quite naturally, been rejected.